THE TEXAS TATTLER

All the news that's barely fit to print!

Sinister Plot Stumps Feds
Divorce Scandal Takes the Spotlight

After a six-month no-stone-unturned search for missing "Midas" baby Bryan Fortune, the FBI closed their files on the case, declaring the debacle an unsolved mystery. The kidnappers remain on America's Most Wanted list, and Red Rock Sheriff Wyatt Grayhawk vows to solve the puzzle that has boggled the best criminal experts money and prestige can buy. As always, the ever-vigilant family holds out hope.

Top-secret sources close to the family report that cattle mogul Ryan Fortune has been on bended knee, pressuring lost love Lily Redgrove Cassidy to be his bride. Lovely Lily would be "Mrs." number three, by the way. Someone, please remind dear Ryan that a married man—even a Fortune—must get *divorced* before he can remarry.

Red Rock's tall, dark and eligible widower Dallas Fortune has been "rendezvousing" on the wrong side of the tracks! Numerous sources have spied the wickedly wealthy rancher in the *very* close company of single mom Maggie Perez Randall, daughter of the Fortunes' long-time housekeeper. Is it possible this solid gold cowboy has his very own Cinderella?

About the Author

JACKIE MERRITT

recently gave up a permanent home in favor of one
that can be moved—on a daily basis, if need be. She
and her husband are traveling in a large, comfortable
recreational vehicle, because, as Jackie says, "Ideas for
new stories don't come knocking on your door. You
have to go out and look for them. At least, I do."

Jackie plans to explore and soak up the atmosphere of
the Western states where she sets most of her books—
Wyoming, Montana, Idaho, Nevada and Washington.
Since many new story lines, names for heroes and
heroines, and just a lot of general information were
picked up by Jackie during previous trips to these
states, she has great hopes for the success of this latest
adventure.

But Jackie also laughs and says, "I have to be
honest and admit that I have no idea how long this
experiment will last. It might be a month or it might
be five years. Whatever the duration, hopefully it will
get my wheels turning and my fingers typing!"

Look for these upcoming books by Jackie Merritt:
HIRED BRIDE
August 2000
Fortunes of Texas

THE KINCAID BRIDE
May 2000
Silhouette Special Edition

A Willing Wife

JACKIE MERRITT

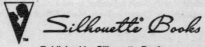

Published by Silhouette Books

America's Publisher of Contemporary Romance

Special thanks and acknowledgment are given
to Jackie Merritt for her contribution
to The Fortunes of Texas series.

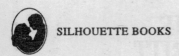 **SILHOUETTE BOOKS**

ISBN 0-373-65033-7

A WILLING WIFE

Copyright © 1999 by Harlequin Books S.A.

Visit us at www.romance.net

Printed in U.S.A.

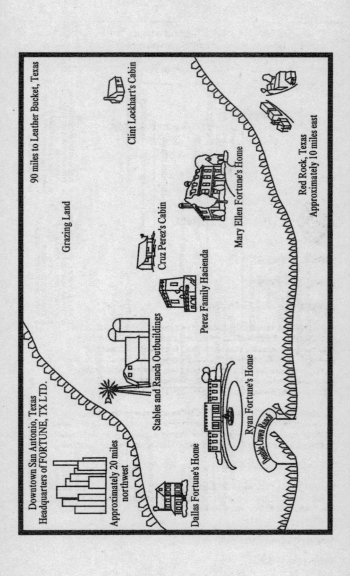

Downtown San Antonio, Texas
Headquarters of FORTUNE, TX LTD.

Approximately 20 miles northwest

Dallas Fortune's Home

Stables and Ranch Outbuildings

Grazing Land

90 miles to Leather Bucket, Texas

Clint Lockhart's Cabin

Cruz Perez's Cabin

Perez Family Hacienda

Mary Ellen Fortune's Home

Ryan Fortune's Home

Double Crown Ranch

Red Rock, Texas
Approximately 10 miles east

THE FORTUNES OF TEXAS

KINGSTON FORTUNE (d)

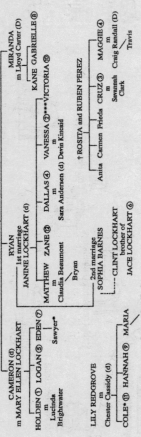

1st marriage
PATIENCE TALBOT (d)

Teddy §

2nd marriage
SELENA HOBBS (d)

RYAN

1st marriage
JANINE LOCKHART (d)

MATTHEW   ZANE ⑫   DALLAS ④   VANESSA ② ***VICTORIA ⑩
m   m   m
Claudia Beaumont   Sara Andersen (d)   Devin Kincaid

Bryan

2nd marriage
SOPHIA BARNES

- - - - CLINT LOCKHART
brother of
JACE LOCKHART ⑥

MIRANDA
m Lloyd Carter (D)

KANE GABRIELLE ⑧

† ROSITA and RUBEN PEREZ

Anita   Carmen   Frieda   CRUZ ③   MAGGIE ④
                           m   m
                    Savannah   Craig Randall (D)
                    Clark   Travis

CAMERON (d)
m MARY ELLEN LOCKHART

HOLDEN ①   LOGAN ⑤   EDEN ⑦
m
Lucinda   Sawyer*
Brightwater

LILY REDGROVE
m
Chester Cassidy (d)

COLE* ⑪   HANNAH ⑨   MARIA

James a.k.a. Taylor

TITLES:

1. MILLION DOLLAR MARRIAGE
2. THE BABY PURSUIT
3. EXPECTING...IN TEXAS
4. A WILLING WIFE
5. CORPORATE DADDY
6. SNOWBOUND CINDERELLA
7. THE SHEIKH'S SECRET SON
8. THE HEIRESS AND THE SHERIFF
9. LONE STAR WEDDING
10. IN THE ARMS OF A HERO
11. WEDLOCKED?!
12. HIRED BRIDE

---

*   Child of affair
d   Deceased
D   Divorced
m   Married
***   Twins
- - - -   Affair
†   Loyal ranch staff
§   Kidnapped by maternal grandfather

THE FORTUNES OF TEXAS™

 Meet the Fortunes of Texas

Dallas Fortune: The wealthy bachelor had no plans to become a father, but ever since he rescued an adorable four-year-old, he's found it impossible to resist the little boy and his delectable single mother. Is the marriage-shy rancher finally ready to say "I do"?

Maggie Perez Randall: She has no time for romance—raising her son is her number-one priority. But little Travis wants a daddy, and he's chosen their handsome neighbor as his perfect father....

Sophia Barnes Fortune: The scorned woman will stop at nothing to make Ryan Fortune pay for daring to love another. She'll even resort to kidnapping and harassment to claim her share of the Fortune wealth.

Logan Fortune: This dedicated businessman's life is thrown into a tailspin when he discovers he's the father of an adorable little girl. But what does this bachelor dad know about babies?

To all my friends in recreational vehicles
that we've run into during our travels.

One

Dallas Fortune left his pickup truck parked near his sprawling adobe house, located not far from the ranch's main house where his father lived, and walked the short distance to the barns and corrals. It was a sunny, clear day in late November, and the midday air was pleasantly warm. He'd been up since five and had already put in hours of work with the ranch hands.

More and more, Dallas was taking over duties that his father, Ryan, had once enjoyed doing, which was fine with Dallas for several reasons. First of all, he loved the Double Crown Ranch as none of his siblings did. Matthew was a doctor of medicine, Zane preferred working in the family's corporation, Fortune TX, Ltd., and the twins, Vanessa and Victoria, had chosen careers that had nothing at all to do with the ranch or the family.

A second reason for Dallas's dedication to the ranch's operation was his father. Ryan's plate was pretty full, considering the nasty divorce he was going through, the fact that Matthew and Claudia's baby son Bryan had been kidnapped right from under everyone's noses during a family get-together for the child's christening, and last but certainly not least, Ryan was crazy in love with Lily Redgrove Cassidy and couldn't marry her until his divorce was final.

But Dallas's third reason for putting in long hours and deliberately exhausting himself so he could sleep nights was deeply personal. His wife Sara had died two years ago while giving birth to their stillborn son. The double tragedy still haunted Dallas—and a third tragedy was that he didn't give a damn that it did. He'd become a loner, a man lost in his own past, and he often shunned social events and people, both friends and family, because some had the unmitigated gall to say right to his face that he had mourned long enough. Their attempts at matchmaking sickened Dallas. And the women who paraded themselves before him to get attention caused exactly the opposite reaction.

Dallas did have a few female friends, of course. His sister-in-law, Matthew's wife Claudia, had been a friend since college, and he had developed a more recent friendship with Savannah Clark Perez. Not once, though, since Sara's death had Dallas felt the slightest inclination toward anything *but* friendship with a woman.

He also did a bit of traveling now and again. In fact, he had just returned from Europe, a trip that had been mostly business, as almost everything was to him these days. Pleasure simply wasn't on his agenda anymore, and he apologized to no one for his attitude or life-style, either.

He wasn't thinking of those things as he hiked down to the barns and corrals today, however. His thoughts were on the herd of longhorns in one particular corral that had been sold and were scheduled to be picked up by a cattle truck at one o'clock. He had discussed the sale with his father, and Ryan had agreed with Dallas's decision to weed out some of the older longhorns. Dallas intended to be there when the truck arrived.

Approaching the corral, Dallas heard the longhorns milling around and bawling much more than he'd anticipated. Frowning, Dallas broke into a jog, and as he got closer to the penned animals he saw the reason for their disturbance. A small boy Dallas didn't recognize had climbed to the top rung of the corral fence!

Dallas's heart skipped a beat. One wrong move and that kid could fall into the corral. The longhorns were already nervous over his presence; the boy could be trampled to death.

Realizing that he had to be careful, and that the "wrong move" could be his own, Dallas circled the corral until he was behind the boy. Then, walking as silently as he could, he moved in on the child.

He grabbed him just as the boy lost his balance and fell forward. With a wildly beating pulse borne of dread and relief, Dallas lifted the youngster back over the fence and then set him on his own two feet on the ground.

Travis's small heart was beating a mile a minute. Holding back tears because he was really a very tough guy and didn't want to cry in front of the tall man who had rescued him, Travis stared up at him.

Dallas leaned down and looked directly into the boy's blue eyes. "And who might you be, young fellow?"

"Tra-Travis Randall."

"Well, Travis Randall, didn't anyone ever tell you that longhorns can be ornery critters, and that climbing the fence of their pen could be dangerous business?"

"I just wanted to see 'em better."

"Haven't you ever seen longhorns before?"

"Mama showed me some pictures."

"And what is Mama's name?"

"Uh, Maggie. Mama's name is Maggie."

Out of the corner of his right eye Dallas caught sight of someone running hell-bent for leather. He turned his head for a better view, and saw that the runner was a woman, a small woman with long, flowing dark hair and a figure any man would notice. She was wearing cut-off denim shorts and a white tank top that left little to the imagination.

"Could that lady heading this way at ninety miles per hour be your mama?" Dallas asked young Travis.

The boy took a look and visibly shrank. "She's mad."

"At you?"

Travis nodded and fell silent. Dallas rose and put his hand on the boy's shoulder, and both of them waited for Maggie to reach them.

Out of breath, she ran up, took one look at the pale face of her son, then knelt down and put her arms around him. "Something happened, didn't it? What was it?" Her gaze rose to Dallas's face.

Dallas cleared his throat. "Travis accidentally fell into the corral."

"And I suppose he 'accidentally' climbed the fence?" Maggie gave her son a small shake. "Didn't I tell you to stay in Grandma's yard?"

"Yes, Mama," Travis said meekly.

"He didn't *actually* fall, Maggie," Dallas said. "He'd just started to fall when I caught him."

"How do you know my name?"

"Travis told me. Are you Maggie Perez Randall?"

"Yes, that's my legal name—my married name. But I prefer Maggie Perez. And you're…?"

"Dallas Fortune."

He was a Fortune. She should have known. Good-looking, confident. Oh, yes, she should have guessed that he wasn't just another cowhand.

And maybe she should have remembered him from childhood. They'd known each other as children, after all. Obviously he was back from his trip. Where was it she'd heard he'd gone? Oh, yes, Scotland, to look over some special breed of cattle. Or was it France? Well, it didn't really matter. What did was that he was here now and he had saved Travis from a nasty fall.

Rising, Maggie offered her hand, which Dallas readily shook. "Thank you for being in the right place at the right moment. If Travis had fallen into that corral…" She couldn't even say it; just the thought of her precious son being trampled by cattle hooves was more than she could bear. But precious or not, Travis was going to get a good talking to, at the very least.

"Don't be too hard on him," Dallas said quietly, as though reading her mind. "Small boys are naturally curious creatures."

"He disobeyed me. From the day we arrived I told him that when he played outside he had to stay in the yard."

Dallas couldn't seem to stop looking into Maggie Perez's gorgeous dark eyes. She'd grown up to be a strikingly beautiful woman—naturally tawny skin, the kind of full rosy lips that a fashion model might envy, and a perfect body and legs. Her hands and feet were small, her wrists delicate, her fingernails beautifully shaped and shiny with colorless polish.

"Um, when *did* you arrive?" Dallas asked.

Maggie looked off into the distance and frowned slightly. It had seemed like such a good idea to return to Texas— to the ranch she'd grown up on and to her family—until she got her bearings again after being laid off from her job as a bank manager. But now she wasn't so sure. Unquestionably she wasn't accomplishing anything positive by living with her parents, even though Rosita, her mother, and Ruben, her father, were wonderful to her and Travis.

"I've…rather, Travis and I have been here for weeks and weeks," she murmured, unnerved by the swift passage of time. She really must get herself together and decide what she was going to do with her life. Her divorce was over a year old and hadn't bothered her nearly as much as had losing her job. But then she hadn't really been in love with her ex, nor had he loved her. Their marriage had been a result of her pregnancy, a foolish mistake for both her and Craig, and for a while she had hoped to make it work. Craig, too, had tried—for a while—but then it all started falling apart. Without love, relationships—even marriage— simply couldn't endure.

"Are you home for good?"

"No, of course not. Just until…well, I'm not really sure just how long we'll stay, but I know we're not here for good." Maggie was a trifle confused. Dallas seemed to be sincerely interested in talking to her, and why would he be? Heavens, he was attractive! At least six feet tall, and so lean and hard-muscled. And his eyes were a marvelous color, a light golden brown that reminded her of good whiskey. She liked the way he wore his sun-streaked brown hair, too, long enough to touch his shirt collar.

"Didn't I hear something about your living in Phoenix?" Dallas said, breaking into thoughts that Maggie knew full well she shouldn't be having.

"I *was* living in Phoenix, so you heard right," she said a bit brusquely. Admiring Dallas Fortune's good looks was just about the most foolish thing she could do while she was here, and if there was one thing she didn't plan on ever being again with a man, it was foolish. One stroll around *that* block was quite enough, thank you very much. "But I'm not going back to Arizona. I haven't actually done anything about it yet, but I've been thinking about looking for work in Houston," she found herself adding, in spite of all that common sense in her system telling her to take Travis by the hand and get the heck away from Dallas Fortune.

"What kind of work do you do?" Dallas asked.

"At my last job I was a bank manager."

Dallas nodded. "Banking is a good field." He wanted to ask about her husband in the worst way, but not in front of Travis. Something very unusual was happening to Dallas: he was attracted to a woman! Feeling her pull, inhaling her scent, realizing that his body was reacting exactly as it should to a beautiful, sexy lady—which it sure hadn't been doing with any other beautiful, sexy lady he knew. Obviously their chemistries blended in the unique and special way that brought a man and a woman together. Did she feel it as strongly as he did?

Travis was beginning to squirm. Maggie took his hand in hers. "We'd better be going. Thank you again, Dallas. I shudder to think what might have happened if you hadn't been here." She started walking away.

"Maggie, it was great seeing you again," Dallas called after her.

She turned around just long enough to say, "It was nice seeing you again. Goodbye," and then began walking so fast that Travis almost had to run to keep up.

"Mama, stop, you're going too fast," he finally complained.

"Don't you 'Mama' me, young man," she said sternly. "You could have been hurt very badly today. Do you understand what almost happened to you? If I catch you leaving the yard again without permission, I promise I will paddle your behind and you will sit on a chair in the house for a week. *Without* TV or toys. Do you understand?"

"Yes, Mama," Travis said with a tearful sniffle. He could cry now that he wasn't with Dallas, and actually a few tears might even soften his mother's heart.

They didn't. Maggie marched stoically on toward her parents' house with her son in tow, thanking God and Dallas Fortune that Travis hadn't been injured, or worse, today.

But she'd meant what she'd told her son, and his teary little face did not affect that decision in the least.

Maggie's homecoming—weeks and weeks before, as she'd told Dallas—had been everything she'd known it would be. She and Travis had arrived in the evening, surprising her parents to joyful tears. Rosita and Ruben had passed her back and forth, hugging and kissing her, and doing the same with Travis.

"Oh, he is such a handsome boy," Rosita had exclaimed

again and again. "And you are so beautiful, Maggie. Oh, my dear daughter, I've prayed so often that you would return to us. Now, let's get you settled in, then we'll have coffee and talk. We have a lot to catch up on."

Rosita rarely had the time to write long letters, and Ruben corresponded with no one. But over the years Rosita had often scribbled notes to her daughter, passing on what Rosita considered to be the most crucial information about everyone who currently lived or previously had lived, on the ranch. And, of course, there'd been the long-distance phone calls between mother and daughter.

Those notes and phone calls were the reason Maggie knew about Ryan Fortune's divorce problems, and about his new love, Lily Cassidy, which, in fact, wasn't a new love at all but an old love renewed. Then there was the bewildering event of baby Bryan's kidnapping.

Over coffee or tea at the kitchen table in the evening Maggie and Rosita did most of their talking. It began the first night Maggie returned to the ranch, and was what they were doing the evening of the day that Maggie and Dallas had met again because of Travis's disobedient behavior. With Travis tucked into bed and Ruben reading his paper in the living room, Rosita related the latest news. "Sheriff Wyatt Grayhawk is still investigating the identity of the mystery baby. Of course, as I told you before, FBI agent Devin Kincaid rescued a baby from the kidnappers who the family believed was baby Bryan. But when Claudia and Matthew saw him, they knew it wasn't their son. They've kept him and named him Taylor. More mysterious still is that the child turned out to be a Fortune—he has the crown-shaped birthmark and rare blood type. Yet no Fortune has claimed him."

Maggie sipped her coffee. "That is so odd, isn't it?"

"Very. He has to be the son of one of the Fortune men,

because if any of the Fortune women had given birth, someone would know about it.''

"But which man could it be? How will Wyatt find out?''

Rosita leaned forward. "I heard that he's mentioned a DNA screening on every one of the Fortune males.''

"But that's so...so personal!''

Rosita shrugged. "So is fathering a child and then pretending you know nothing about it.''

"Mama, most of the Fortune men have pretty fast reputations, but I can't imagine any of them knowingly denying their own flesh and blood.''

"I agree, but I have this feeling—''

Ruben shouted from the living room, "Rosita, stop with the feelings!''

"Oh, hush!'' she called back. "You know my premonitions are more often true than not.''

Maggie had heard the same exchange from her parents before, and she hastened to change the subject, grabbing at the first thing that entered her mind. "It's hard to believe that Cruz is married and settled down, isn't it? He always had so many girlfriends.''

"Ah, but things went very differently when he met Savannah. They had their ups and downs, of course. Only once in a while does true love run smoothly. But they are happy now.''

"And I'm happy for them.''

Rosita nodded. "Yes, we all are. And I'm so pleased about the child they are expecting.''

"I'm sure you are, Mama.'' Maggie smiled. "You will have another grandchild to love.'' Her smile faded slightly as she thought of her and Craig's shotgun wedding. Their marriage hadn't lasted. She hoped Cruz and Savannah's would endure forever.

"I'm so proud of him for striking out on his own,'' Maggie murmured, forcing her thoughts into a happier vein. "I can't believe he's finally going to have his own ranch. That piece of land he bought is breathtaking. He's going to make something of himself, Mama, and that's very exciting.''

''Yes, it is, but it wouldn't have been quite so easy to do if Dallas Fortune hadn't offered to invest in Cruz's dream.''

Maggie frowned. ''That's true, isn't it. Mama, for Cruz's sake I hope his ranch and horse operation doesn't end up being just another Fortune possession.''

''Dallas isn't like that, Maggie. I'm positive that his investment is in Cruz, not in the ranch itself.''

''Oh, I believe that Dallas's investment is in Cruz, too. But after Cruz works himself to death starting up the ranch and getting it in good shape and running smoothly, what is Dallas's attitude going to be then?''

Rosita looked shocked. ''Maggie, what are you thinking of? Dallas is not plotting to benefit from Cruz's hard work.''

Maggie sighed. ''I'm sorry, Mama.''

''Dallas is not going to take advantage of Cruz,'' Rosita repeated. ''He's not that kind of man.''

''What kind of man is he, Mama?''

Rosita thought a moment, then said with a saddened sigh, ''He's a lonely man, Maggie. He took the death of his wife and baby very hard.''

Maggie let that pass, for the moment, and the brief interval altered her mother's thoughts. Rosita began to beam. ''It's so good having you home, Maggie. Promise you will never leave again.''

Maggie replied gently, ''Mama, this is just a visit.'' She smiled. ''Granted, it's a long visit, but eventually Travis and I will have to live someplace else.''

''No!'' Rosita cried, then called to her husband, ''Ruben! Maggie said this is just a visit.''

Ruben appeared in the doorway still holding the newspaper. "Why do you say such a thing and break your mama's heart?" he asked Maggie.

"Papa, I can't live off you and Mama indefinitely," Maggie said weakly. She loved her father dearly, but he could be very daunting, and right now he wore an expression that made her feel like a child again.

"This is your home. You and Travis will stay," Ruben said with a finality that brooked no further debate. He returned to his chair in the living room.

Maggie looked down at her coffee cup. Her parents were united against her in this case. There was no point in arguing with either of them. When the time came, she and Travis would simply leave. Regardless of their generous, loving spirit, she could not live off her aging, hardworking mother and father. Rosita was head housekeeper in Ryan Fortune's huge mansion, and Ruben was a cowhand. They had already raised their family and should not have to raise Maggie's, too.

While it was good to be home for a visit, things weren't quite the same as they used to be. Or maybe they were *exactly* the same, Maggie thought, and she'd simply forgotten how deeply her mother had always involved herself in the Fortune family's troubles, and how quickly she had defended anything they'd ever done. Maggie now saw that involvement and defensiveness from a much different perspective. As strange as it seemed, Rosita loved the Fortunes, and she worried about them as she would a second family.

Maggie became introspective. Her mother might love the Fortunes, but *she* certainly didn't. Neither did she dislike them; they were simply there, rich beyond belief, and obviously bored with life, because one or more of them was forever getting into or causing trouble.

Well, she wanted no part of them. She'd come home to

see *her* family, and to get herself back on track, not to get involved with the Fortunes.

But today's event seemed to have worked against that philosophy, she realized, and though it would bring Dallas's name back into their conversation, she couldn't keep it from her mother.

Maggie related the incident as calmly as she could manage. "Travis could have been—" she couldn't force the word *killed* out of her mouth "—seriously injured."

"Well, thank God Dallas was there," Rosita exclaimed. "I'm so glad you met him again. He's a fine man, Maggie, but so alone. My heart goes out to him every time I see him."

"I'm sure he doesn't have to be alone, Mama."

"He's an honorable man who loved his wife," Rosita said with defensive pride in Dallas's lonely existence. "Mourning Sara's death the way he's done indicates respect for her memory. Too many people seem to forget a beloved spouse within months of their passing, which I will never understand. Do you think I could forget your father so soon if something should happen to him, God forbid? No indeed, Dallas is to be admired for holding his grief so close to his heart."

"Perhaps you're right," Maggie said quietly, recalling quite vividly the way Dallas had looked at her today. He hadn't been thinking of Sara then, Maggie thought. And she knew that he would have stayed and talked to her for longer, if she had encouraged further discussion.

But what did a Fortune and a Perez have to say to each other? Oh, they might do business together, as Dallas and Cruz were doing, but Dallas breathed the rarefied air of the very wealthy, and Maggie was the daughter of a housekeeper and a cowhand. Not that she was even a tiny bit ashamed of her parents' life-style or history. Rosita and

Ruben had raised their five children in this very house, and it had been a home brimming with love and good morals.

Still, the distance between the Fortunes and the Perezes was much farther than the walk from Ryan's southwest mansion to this cozy little house.

Strangely, knowing how far apart the two families really were didn't seem to keep Maggie from thinking about the unique color of Dallas's eyes or his wonderful smile. Sensible or not, she knew that he had stirred something within her today that had nothing at all to do with gratitude over his rescuing Travis.

She gave her head an almost angry shake to push Dallas from her mind. She was absolutely not going to get silly over Dallas Fortune.

"So, Mama," she said matter-of-factly, "how did your day go?"

Rosita frowned. "For me it went well, but it wasn't a good day for Ryan. His lawyer, Parker Malone, delivered some very bad news. Ryan's wife, Sophia, is demanding half of everything Ryan owns in the divorce settlement, which she certainly doesn't deserve. That woman is a disgrace," Rosita exclaimed disgustedly.

"She must be the same woman today that she was when Ryan married her, Mama," Maggie said gently.

"She was his first wife, Janine's, nurse, and I would bet anything that conniving Sophia set her cap for Ryan Fortune long before his wife and the mother of his children passed away! Oh, I remember so much about that sad time, Maggie. Ryan was devastated, and Sophia was there to console him. Console him, hah! Why did she stay on the ranch after her patient was dead and buried? I'll tell you why. It was to get her greedy hands on Ryan's money! She was never a nice woman, Maggie, never. Ryan was vulnerable, and Sophia took advantage of him. She's *still* trying to take advantage of him!"

Maggie couldn't help smiling. "Mama, do you eavesdrop on the Fortunes' conversations?" she asked teasingly.

Rosita looked hurt. "How could you say such a thing?"

Maggie reached for Rosita's hand. "Mama, I was only teasing you."

"Sometimes I hear things—how could I not? But I do not deliberately sneak around and spy on the Fortunes."

"Of course you don't."

"And sometimes they tell me things themselves. They know I care about them, Maggie."

"I'm sure they do."

Rosita became thoughtful for a few moments, then she smiled rather impishly. "You know, Maggie, Dallas is considered to be the area's most eligible bachelor. He's very good-looking, he's educated and he's a hard worker. Maybe you should be nice to him."

Maggie's eyes widened. "You just told me a few minutes ago how much you respected his long mourning period. And then we talked about Sophia, and you said that she took advantage of Ryan while he was in the same state after Janine's death. Surely you're not suggesting that I chase Dallas as Sophia chased Ryan!"

Rosita looked aghast. "Oh, my, I did sound as though I was, didn't I?"

"Yes, Mama, you did." Maggie studied her mother's stricken face. "But I know you didn't mean it. You were only teasing, too."

"Well...yes," Rosita said slowly, almost reluctantly, Maggie noticed just before her mother smiled again. "But you are not like Sophia. You are a good, honest, kind-hearted, decent woman, and Dallas would be lucky to have you for his wife."

"Mama, you're incorrigible!" Maggie got up. "I'm going to bed." Leaning over, she kissed Rosita's cheek. "Good night, Mama."

"Good night, Maggie."

Chuckling under her breath over her mother's brass, Maggie went into her room and shut the door. How could her mother possibly think that Dallas Fortune would ever marry a nobody? she thought while getting ready for bed. Especially when he was still in love with his deceased wife.

Maggie stopped buttoning her pajama top, as today's meeting with Dallas overwhelmed other thoughts. Unquestionably, he had looked at her as a man looked at a woman. She could get his attention, if she put out the effort. *But then what would happen?* she asked herself with a disdainful toss of her head. *A fling? A short-lived affair?* She wasn't here permanently, for one thing, and besides, her sexual experience was limited solely to the man she had married. She wouldn't even know how to have an affair. For that matter, she didn't even like the word *affair*.

Flirting with Dallas Fortune would undoubtedly end up in shame for herself and her family. She wanted no part of that sort of heartache, nor did she deserve it.

Settling down in bed, she told herself to forget Dallas's whiskey-colored eyes and great smile. Forget his long, lean body. Forget you even met him again!

"Good advice," she whispered, and took a vow to heed it.

TWO

Dallas put in a restless night. He kept picturing Maggie, and reliving the feelings he'd had while talking to her. Was he being disloyal to Sara because he found another woman desirable? He'd honestly believed it would never happen again, and the fact that it had was still surprising him, even at midnight.

How best to approach Maggie? he wondered, knowing he was driven to do it. Was she a lady who would like being treated delicately? Somehow that image didn't mesh with the blatant sensuality she exuded. Maybe she liked the he-man approach.

Truth was, Dallas finally had to admit, Maggie made him nervous. It had been a long time since he'd made advances toward a woman with anything in mind but a friendly chat. He was out of practice as far as flirting went—rusty as hell, actually. Maybe straightforward simple honesty was all he had to offer.

Punching his pillow because he was tired and his eyes wouldn't stay closed, Dallas tried again to steer his obstinate mind away from Maggie Perez. This time he thought about Travis and what a great little kid he was. Was he five years old? Six? He was a handsome boy, with his mother's dark skin and hair, and bright blue eyes that could only have been inherited from his father.

Where was Maggie's husband? Okay, Dallas thought disgustedly, obviously he was destined to torture himself all night with questions about Maggie. She hadn't said that she and her husband were moving back to Texas—she'd said that *she* was going to look for work in the Houston area. Did that mean that the man she'd married was no longer in the picture?

It occurred to Dallas at some point in the night that he was almost as drawn to Maggie's son as he was to her. Truth was, he realized, he would like to see them both again.

Something else occurred to him. He could ask Rosita, Ruben or Cruz about Maggie's husband. Rosita was the logical choice, because both Ruben and Cruz were rather closemouthed. But Rosita loved to talk; if Maggie was divorced, Rosita would tell him.

But, dammit, he'd rather ask Maggie herself! No, he would not take his questions to her mother, he'd take them directly to Maggie.

With that decision made and final, Dallas slept.

The following day Maggie was startled to look out the kitchen window—just to check on Travis's whereabouts— and see Dallas outside in the yard with her son. A pickup was parked near the front gate, obviously Dallas's. Maggie's stomach instantly tensed, and she chewed uneasily on her bottom lip. Why was he here?

In the next breath she couldn't help smiling. Dallas had taken off his western hat and placed it on Travis's head. Then he let himself be led around the yard while Travis showed him his toys. Maggie was amazed that a grown man would give some of his valuable time to a little boy he barely knew.

"How old are you?" Dallas asked the youngster.

"I'm five," Travis said with a big-boy swagger. "And I'm tough, Dallas."

Dallas swallowed his laughter and said solemnly, "Five is almost a man."

"Yep, and I'm gonna be a cowboy like Grandpa and Uncle Cruz. They're tough, too."

"Yes, they are," Dallas agreed. Ruben wasn't a tall man, but he was built like a bull and possessed astounding strength. Cruz had the height in the family, and everyone knew he was Rosita and Ruben's pride and joy. He wore his shiny dark hair long and sometimes tied back with a leather band, and it was common knowledge that Cruz had attracted women like flies to honey since he was twelve years old. Now, at twenty-nine, Cruz was settled down and happily married.

Dallas felt that their business arrangement was a good deal for both of them. Cruz had a special talent with horses, and Dallas was positive that Cruz would work hard and make his longtime dream of breeding and raising quality horses a huge success. Besides, Dallas personally like Cruz, who was two years older than himself.

"Trav," Dallas said, unconsciously shortening the boy's name, "is your mama in the house?"

"Yep! Want me to call her?"

"Thanks, but I think I'll knock on the door."

"Want me to come with you?"

"I'd really like to talk to her alone for a few minutes, if you don't mind, that is."

"No, that's okay."

Dallas ruffled the boy's hair. "See you later."

Maggie saw Dallas heading for the front door, and was instantly on edge. Did she look all right? She was wearing jeans and a pink blouse. Her wardrobe wasn't anything to boast about. Raising a child alone was an expensive endeavor and she'd had precious little money to spend on clothes.

But her hair was fixed and there was makeup on her face—not much because she didn't use a lot of makeup—Actually, she realized, she looked as good as she could—other than wearing glamorous, more expensive clothing, of course.

When Dallas knocked, Maggie held her breath for five counts, then opened the door. She hoped her smile was only pleasantly welcoming.

Before she could say hello, Dallas huskily said, "Maggie," in such an intimate way that she backed up a step. She swallowed hard and forced a "hello" out of her mouth.

Dallas suddenly believed he knew the best way to approach Maggie. She was so sexy-looking that she must prefer a man to act like a man. He figured he could carry it off.

"May I come in?" he asked.

"Uh, sure, yes, of course." Standing back, Maggie held the door open wider so he could enter. Her knees got weak when he passed by her at a snail's pace and even appeared to be inhaling the faint scent of the cologne she used so sparingly.

She couldn't think of one sensible thing to say to him. *Why are you here?* was just too blunt, although that particular question was definitely at the root of her confusion. Unnerved, she slammed the door shut a little too hard.

Dallas grinned. Obviously he was ruffling her feathers, which was a good sign that he was right about her preferring a man to *be* a man.

His smile broadened. "How are you today?"

"Fine," she said stiffly. "I'm fine. And you?"

"Right as rain," he quipped.

Maggie was beginning to remember her manners. "Would—would you like something cool to drink? There's fresh lemonade in the refrigerator."

"Thanks, I'd love a glass of lemonade."

Grateful that she had dusted and vacuumed the house that morning, Maggie said, "Go on into the living room. I'll get the drinks."

"Thanks." Dallas went one way, Maggie another.

When she walked into the living room a few minutes later with two glasses of lemonade, Dallas was standing at the one window in the room from which he could see Travis playing in the yard.

Dallas accepted a glass and said, "That's some boy you have, Maggie. You must be mighty proud of him."

"Yes, I am." She sat on the sofa. "Sit anywhere," she told him.

"Thanks." Dallas chose Ruben's favorite chair and took a big swallow of his lemonade. "This is good. Getting back to Travis, he sure seems focused on being tough—like his grandfather and uncle."

Maggie groaned. "He wants to be tough so badly, and I don't think he even knows the true meaning of the word."

"He's all boy, Maggie. Let me ask you something. Would you mind if I took him riding sometime?"

"He's never been on a horse, Dallas. Papa told him he would teach him to ride, but he hasn't had the time yet."

"I'd put him on our most gentle horse, Maggie, and guarantee his safety. For that matter, you could come with us and see for yourself that he's all right."

While she was trying to think of a response to that somewhat troubling invitation, Dallas's expression became caressing and intimate. "Know what I'd like to do right now?" he said softly. "Make love to you, Maggie. You're just about the only thing I've thought of since we talked yesterday."

She knew she should feel insulted: no man had ever spoken his mind so clearly to her before. But she was stunned because instead she felt overheated and achy in personal places.

"You—you don't mean what you just said," she whispered hoarsely. "We don't even know each other."

"We grew up together."

"Knowing each other as kids doesn't mean we know each other now."

"You're evading the issue. Will you go out with me tonight?"

Maggie felt as though a steel band around her chest was cutting off her air supply. "So we—we can make love? How dare you even suggest such a thing!"

"You're trying very hard to be angry, aren't you? Surely you don't prefer that a man hide his true feelings and seduce you when you're not looking." Dallas set his glass on the table next to his chair and then leaned forward. "Maggie, with you I think everything should be out in the open. I was struck dumb by you yesterday. You're one of the most beautiful women I've ever seen, but there's more to you than an incredible face and body. You hit me precisely where it counts for a man, and I thank you with all my heart for that."

"So I should sleep with you just because you—you feel grateful for something I didn't even know I did?"

"Not sleep, Maggie. I doubt that we'd be doing much sleeping. I need to know something. Where's your husband?"

"You don't even know I'm divorced—and you're asking me to go to bed with you? That does it!" Jumping to her feet, Maggie angrily advanced on the crudest man she'd ever known. "So you want to take Travis riding? You louse, you actually have the gall to use my son as an excuse to get to me! Well, read my lips, *Mr.* Fortune. I will never, let me repeat, *never,* have one personal moment with you! Is that clear enough?''

She'd made a tactical error. Dallas recognized it, Maggie didn't. In her fury she'd gotten close enough to Dallas that it was a simple matter for him to reach out, take her by the waist and pull her down on his lap. She didn't want to scream and risk scaring Travis outside, but she wiggled and fought and did her best to scratch out Dallas Fortune's whiskey-colored eyes!

''So you're a little wildcat,'' Dallas said with a satisfied laugh after catching her flailing hands in his. ''I figured you were. Come closer, little wildcat, and let me tame you.''

Maggie never did know how he managed to hold both her hands and press on the back of her head at the same time, but the next thing she *did* know was that his mouth was devouring hers. Fighting him did no good, so she did exactly the opposite. She sat statue-still until he stopped kissing her and looked at her with puzzled eyes.

''You didn't like being kissed like that?'' he asked.

''I don't like anything about you!'' she shrieked loudly enough to endanger his eardrums. Remembering Travis just outside, she lowered her voice. ''Take your hands off of me and get the hell out of this house, you…you *Fortune!*''

Dallas's heart sank clear to his toes. He'd completely misread Maggie Perez. She might look sexy as sin, but she obviously preferred a more gentlemanly approach from a man.

''Maggie, I—I'm sorry,'' he stammered, red-faced and embarrassed over the way he'd talked to her. ''Look, I can explain everything I did and said here today.''

''Are you going to let go of me?''

Dallas quickly released her hands and held up his own. ''Whatever you say.''

Maggie leaped off his lap, crossed to the other side of the room, then turned around and hit him with a murderous look. "I have never been treated so—so boorishly by a man in my entire life. You Fortunes think you can do anything you want, don't you? Well, your caveman tactics leave me cold, and I'd just as soon never set eyes on you again." She took a breath. "And to think my mother believes you're an honorable man!" she spat scornfully.

Dallas got up. "Maggie, I *am* an honorable man. If you'll let me explain—"

"Not today!" Maggie pointed at the door. "Get out!"

With a hangdog expression, Dallas walked to the door. But he couldn't leave without one more stab at making her understand. He looked at her pleadingly.

"I wasn't conning you about how I feel about Travis. He's a great little kid, and I really would like to be his friend."

"Go to hell! If I told my dad or brother what you tried, they'd...they'd—" She stopped herself. This man's family was her father's employer. Her mother's, too. And Dallas himself was her brother's business partner. Oh, God, she thought miserably.

"What did I try, Maggie? Was kissing you really that terrible?"

She didn't yell again, but the disdain in her voice was thick enough to slice. "You didn't just kiss me. You asked me to go to bed with you."

"Well, obviously I shouldn't have spoken so plainly, and I apologize. But I can't help wanting you," he said quietly. "You're the first woman who's made me feel like a man since my wife died. That was two years ago." Dallas took a deep breath. "Guess I'd better go. If you change your mind about anything—"

"Good Lord, I'm not going to change my mind! Just go!" Maggie threw up her hands.

"Okay. Don't get mad again. See ya, Maggie." Dallas went out the door.

"Not if I see you first," Maggie fumed under her breath, then dashed to the window to make sure he didn't do something else crazy when Travis was out in the yard alone.

Dallas walked up to the boy. "Trav, would you like to keep that hat?"

It was way too big for a child, but Travis beamed. "Could I? I've been wanting a hat like this one, Dallas."

"It's yours, son. I'll be going now."

"Will you come and see us again?"

Dallas glanced at the house and sighed. "I'd sure like to, Trav. I'd sure like to."

The second he'd driven away, Maggie ran outside. "Travis, why didn't Dallas take his hat?"

"He gave it to me, Mama. He said I could keep it."

"Oh." Maggie slowly turned and went back inside. Had she ever been more disappointed in a person than she was in Dallas Fortune? How could he have been so nice yesterday and so awful today? Oh, the things he'd said!

Maggie paced the house with her arms wrapped around herself. Something was wrong with her; she felt hot and cold at the same time.

Finally her emotions got the better of her. She collapsed on the sofa and cried her eyes out.

Cruz dropped in that afternoon, and Maggie threw herself at her brother to give him a big hug. He laughed and hugged her back.

"I wish you'd come around more often," Maggie scolded, thinking that if she was ever going to tell her family about Dallas's arrogant and insulting pass, this was her chance to do it. But, Lord, the stink it would cause! No, she couldn't tell anyone. She would handle Dallas Fortune by herself.

Cruz grinned. "Savannah and I have both been really busy. You're looking good, Maggie."

She felt better just because her brother was here. "Did you see Travis?"

"No, where is he?"

"In the yard." Maggie went to the kitchen window. "He's *not* in the yard! Oh, Cruz, he almost felt into a corral of longhorns yesterday, and I've threatened him with everything from a paddling to a week of sitting on a chair in the house if he left the yard again. What am I going to do with that boy?" She went outside and shouted, "Travis! Where are you? Travis, answer me!"

"I'll go and find him," Cruz offered. "He probably just wandered off again."

"Cruz, he's only five years old," Maggie wailed.

"But he's a Perez, Maggie."

"Which makes him immortal? I don't think so, Cruz. Come on, you go one way and I'll go another. I've got to find him before he pulls another naughty-little-boy trick and gets himself really hurt this time. He thinks he's tough, you know, and he doesn't have the strength of a flea."

Cruz laughed again as he walked off, conveying a boys-will-be-boys attitude. Ignoring it for the time being, Maggie headed for the corrals and barns, because that was where she'd found Travis yesterday. Cruz could laugh off her motherly concern, but her son's disobedience was no laughing matter for Maggie. This time he was definitely going to be punished, she promised herself.

Unless he's hurt! she thought with a burst of panic that caused her to start running. Travis wasn't anywhere near the corrals, and she started peering into outbuildings. Spotting the huge horse barn where the Fortunes had always stabled their best horses, Maggie's heart skipped a beat. With the hat that Dallas had given him, Travis might be playing cowboy, and she knew that often horses could be high-strung and skittish!

Maggie hurried to the barn and went in. It was well-lit and very clean. A wide aisle ran through the center of the building, with stalls on each side. She could hear horses snorting and moving around, and she wondered if her five-year-old son would actually have the nerve to go into a stall with a strange horse. Sometimes Travis's boasts about being tough were funny, but Maggie knew that he really did believe that telling people how tough he was made it true.

Scared to death, she began walking the aisle and looking into stalls. "Travis?" she called at each one.

About halfway through the barn, she heard her own name. "Maggie?" Dallas said as he stepped out of a stall. "What's wrong?"

Talking to Dallas again was the last thing Maggie wanted, but right now she had no choice. Still, her voice was cold as ice when she said, "Travis is missing again. I thought he might be in here."

Dallas set down the brush he'd been using on Jubilee, a valuable stallion, and began walking toward Maggie. Though concerned about young Travis, Dallas couldn't help looking at this incident as a heaven-sent opportunity to talk to Maggie again. "I haven't seen him, Maggie. Unless he's hiding somewhere, he's not in here. I'll help you look for him."

A frisson of alarm rippled through Maggie. Dallas might be offering to help her find Travis, but he was looking at her again with ill-concealed hunger in his eyes!

"Thanks," she said coldly, "but I don't need your help.

Cruz is helping.'' Spinning, she walked away, forcing herself to leave at a normal speed so Dallas wouldn't get any silly ideas about her being afraid of him. Not that he didn't affect her, dammit. Even though she was angrier with him than she'd ever been with anyone, she felt her tingling reaction to his good looks and maleness.

Dallas ignored her frostily stated declaration of independence and stayed right behind her. Just outside the barn he asked, ''Have you checked the equipment sheds?''

Maggie turned with blazing eyes, fully intending to give him yet another piece of her mind, when she heard Cruz shouting, ''Maggie, I've got him! He was playing in a haystack behind one of the barns. He's fine, and we're going back to the house.''

She heaved a relieved sigh. Forgetting how much she despised Dallas, she said, ''It looks as though keeping Travis on the ranch is a mistake. I have no idea why he started leaving the yard, but he keeps doing it, no matter how often I threaten, beg or cajole him.''

''Have you tried explaining the dangers he could run into on a ranch?'' Dallas asked quietly, then quickly switched gears. ''Maggie, you have to let me explain what happened earlier today.''

She was instantly angry again. ''Have you forgotten I was there? What possible explanation could there be for your treating me like a tramp?''

Dallas groaned. ''My God, I don't think of you as a tramp.''

''Well, you certainly fooled me,'' she snapped, and turned to leave.

Dallas rushed to keep stride with her. ''Maggie, don't go off like this. Talk to me, please. Everyone deserves a second chance, even a man who made a horse's ass of himself.''

"We're single-minded on that, at least," she said with heavy sarcasm. She kept walking, and it irritated her that Dallas kept pace beside her. "Will you please stop following me? I'm not the least bit interested in anything you might have to say, and if I said what I've been thinking, your ears would get scorched black!"

"A red face and black ears," Dallas said. "Paints a pretty picture, don't you think?"

"Stop trying to be funny," she snapped.

"Sorry," he mumbled. "Maggie, just stop and talk to me for a minute. Please."

"I will stop, just long enough to ask you why you even *want* to talk to me."

He wiped his hands on the legs of his jeans. "I'm not sure I can explain it. What is it that happens when a man meets a woman and immediately knows that she's special? It's not something that a person chooses to happen—it just does."

Maggie's lip curled. "Yeah, I'm so special that it's a wonder you didn't offer me money for sex!"

"Oh, my God! Maggie, how can I make you understand that it wasn't like that? For some stupid reason I thought you would, uh, appreciate honesty. I wanted you to like me so much that I...I..." Dallas wished the earth would just open up and swallow him whole. He had never in his life talked to a woman as he had to Maggie, but in defense of his apparently unforgivable faux pas, he had said nothing that wasn't in his heart.

He looked so miserable that Maggie suddenly felt sorry for him. Wearily she said, "Just forget it happened, okay?"

"Can *you* forget it happened?" Dallas asked hopefully.

She walked away from him with one final comment. "The only answer I have for that question is, I'll think about it."

Three

Maggie greeted her mother when Rosita got home from work that evening, then watched Rosita suppress laughter over the huge hat on her small grandson's head.

"Come here, you rascal, and talk to me," Rosita said, sitting on a kitchen chair and pulling the boy onto her lap. "Now, tell your grandmother where you got that, uh, wonderful hat."

"Dallas gave it to me, Grandma. Didn't he, Mama?" Travis looked to his mother for confirmation. Rosita also looked at Maggie, only her eyes contained a suspect twinkle that made Maggie feel like squirming. She hastened to relate the only explanation that wouldn't cause trouble between the Perezes and the Fortunes.

"He came by to see Travis," she told her mother.

"And maybe to see you, too?" Rosita said with unabashed relish.

Travis slid from his grandmother's lap. "I'm goin' outside, Mama."

Maggie instantly became all mother. "No, you are *not* going outside. I told you before that you will play inside the house until I can trust you not to leave the yard. Go and wash up for supper."

"Aw, heck," Travis groused as he left the kitchen dragging his feet.

"What was that all about?" Rosita asked.

"He left the yard again today. Cruz came by, and we

both went looking for Travis. Cruz found him playing in a haystack behind one of the barns. Mama, I just don't know what to do with my son. He will not obey me.''

"He obeys you most of the time, Maggie. He's just so fascinated with the ranch. Try to see it through his eyes. He's always lived in a city, and out here there are so many exciting things for a boy to explore.''

"There are also many dangers for a young child.''

"That's true, but he has to learn, Maggie. Do you think I didn't worry about you and Cruz and your sisters when you were growing up?''

"We were different, Mama. We were always ranch kids.''

Ruben came in and, as was his habit each evening, he kissed his wife's cheek. To Maggie he said, "Something smells good in here.''

"It's beef stew, Papa.''

Getting to her feet, Rosita said, "It's so good of you to make supper, Maggie. And the house is so clean, and you even did the laundry. I don't have to do a thing when I come home. You're spoiling me.''

Maggie smiled but had pensive thoughts. Her mother was sixty years old and was still working as hard as a young woman. True, it didn't seem to bother Rosita, Maggie had to admit. Other than one lovely white streak, Rosita's hair was as black as it had always been, and her skin glowed from good health. She'd grown a bit plump over the years, true, but the beauty she had possessed in her youth was still visible, especially when she smiled.

"Wash up, Papa,'' Maggie said. "Supper will be on the table in five minutes.''

"Bossy, just like your mama,'' Ruben said, but he smiled at his daughter and went to do as she'd asked.

Rosita eyed her daughter. "So, Dallas Fortune came by today."

Maggie winced. She should have realized what that over-size hat on her son's head would do to Rosita's curiosity. "We'll talk after supper, Mama. Everyone's hungry now."

While the Perezes enjoyed their fine meal, Dallas heated a frozen dinner in the microwave. He could go to the main house and eat at his father's table anytime he wished. He could also eat with the ranch hands, which he often did.

But tonight he felt that he wasn't fit company for anyone. He'd made a fool of himself today with Maggie, and he couldn't stop wondering what the devil had come over him. Scowling and brooding over it while he ate his chicken dinner, he tried to recapture the misguided logic that had made him think Maggie would respond to such a blunt overture.

Pushing his chair away from the table, he rubbed the back of his neck in almost painful agitation. His behavior was inexcusable, and so uncharacteristic of the man he really was that he wondered if he hadn't temporarily lost the good sense he'd been born with.

Was there anything he could do to make amends? Since he'd already apologized more than once, another apology wasn't apt to change her opinion of him.

But there had to be a way to prove his worth to her, he thought with a panicky sensation in his gut. If he could only make her understand how empty his life had been before meeting her again, and how hard she had hit him. If she would really listen to him just once without that derisive look in her eyes, then he might get through to her.

As hopeless as it all looked, Dallas remained certain of one thing. He was not going to give up on Maggie. He couldn't.

* * *

In the comfortable dining room of the ranch's main residence, Ryan Fortune and Lily Cassidy occupied one end of the long dining table. Tonight they were eating alone, a rare pleasure in the usually active household.

They were a handsome couple, so much in love that even if their hands weren't touching, their gazes were. They were the same age, fifty-three, and each looked much younger. Ryan was a tall, muscular man with dark brown hair and eyes. His mother, Selena, had been an exquisitely beautiful woman of Mexican descent, and Ryan looked a great deal like her.

Lily's ancestry was Apache and Spanish, and her exotic beauty only became more pronounced with time. She and Ryan had "dressed" for dinner, and her silky sea-green gown was both fashionable and becoming to her voluptuous figure.

"You're very beautiful in that dress," Ryan said.

Lily smiled indulgently. "You say the same thing when I'm wearing jeans and an old shirt."

"Only because it's true. My love, please let me make our engagement official with a public announcement."

Lily's beautiful smile faded. "We've discussed this many times. You're still a married man. Please, let's not cause gossip by putting the cart before the horse. When your divorce is final, then we'll make our announcement. Please don't be impatient, darling."

Ryan sighed. "I'm tired of it all, Lily, and so must you be. Parker's a good lawyer, and I'm confident he's doing all he can. But Sophia is a dirty fighter, and I doubt if Parker ever came up against anyone like her before."

"I know, my darling, I know...."

Maggie was tucking Travis in bed for the night, when he said, "I like Dallas, Mama. He's nice."

The hat Dallas had given the boy was on the nightstand next to the bed. Travis hadn't even wanted to take it off for his bath and had insisted it go to bed with him. The only reason it wasn't in bed with Travis was Maggie's patient explanation that the hat could get crunched in the night.

Maggie sat on the bed to lean over and kiss her son goodnight. "He likes me too, Mama. I can tell."

An uneasiness crept into Maggie's system. Even though Craig had rarely been around, and hadn't been much of a father when he had shown up, Maggie wondered if Travis missed him. He'd been, after all, the only man in Travis's life since the boy's birth. Was Travis transferring his need for a father from Craig to Dallas?

That idea was so disturbing that Maggie found it difficult to behave normally. She couldn't possibly have foreseen something like that happening on the ranch, but self-reassurance on that point offered little solace. Just how did a single mother turn a child off a man who had been nothing but kind to him?

Pulling herself together, Maggie quietly led her son through his prayers, then kissed his smooth, soft, little-boy cheek. "Good night, son. I love you very much."

"Good night, Mama. I love you very much."

It was their normal bedtime ritual, but when Maggie left Travis's bedroom tonight she felt as though her heart had just been broken. *Damn you, Craig, why couldn't you have been the kind of father Travis deserves to have?*

On her way to the kitchen, Maggie saw her mother coming out of her bedroom, wearing nightgown, robe and slippers. Rosita's long hair had been released from the bun she trussed it into every morning, and she was carrying a hairbrush.

"Let's sit in the living room," Rosita whispered.

Nodding silently, Maggie followed her mother. Once there she spoke out loud. "Did Papa already go to bed?"

"He's tired tonight."

"You look tired, too, Mama. You don't have to stay up on my account."

"I'm not quite ready for bed." Rosita smiled mischievously. "I want to hear all about Dallas's visit today."

Knowing there was no way to avoid this conversation, Maggie gave in gracefully. "Why don't you sit in this chair so I can brush your hair the way I did when I was a little girl?"

"Oh, that would be nice." Rosita sat on the straight-backed chair and handed the brush to her daughter. She murmured when Maggie began gently running the brush through her hair, "Hmm, that feels wonderful. Now, tell me about Dallas Fortune's visit."

Maggie knew she had to make this story simple. Rosita's sharp mind would pick up on the slightest hint that something other than seeing Travis again had brought Dallas to this house today.

"He wasn't here very long," Maggie began in a deliberately neutral voice, as though Dallas just showing up unannounced was a common occurrence and meant nothing for her. "I heard his truck and looked out the window. He had already gotten out and was talking to Travis."

"And that's it? You and he didn't talk?"

Lies had always gotten stuck in Maggie's throat. Besides, there really was nothing wrong with her and Dallas saying a few words to each other. If only that was all that had happened!

"Well, yes, we did talk. After Travis hauled him around the yard to show off his toys, Dallas knocked on the door."

Rosita became excited. "What did he say?"

"I believe it was something like, 'Hello, Maggie.'"

Rosita twisted around to look at her daughter. "Are you being fresh with me?"

Maggie couldn't help laughing. "No, Mama, I'm not being fresh. But that's what he said."

"That's *all* he said?"

"He also asked how I was, and then he talked about what a great little kid Travis is."

"This all took place on the porch? Didn't it occur to you to invite him in?"

"It occurred to me," Maggie admitted quietly. "I asked him in and offered lemonade. He drank a glass and left."

"Well, you must have talked about something while he was drinking his lemonade!"

"I believe that was when he referred to Travis as a great little kid. I agreed, of course."

"Hmm," Rosita murmured thoughtfully. "He was probably thinking of the baby he lost. It's so sad to lose a child. And poor Dallas lost his wife at the same time." Rosita wiped away a tear and recovered her composure. "Did he say anything nice to you?"

"Like what, Mama?"

"Maggie, for heaven's sake. Did he say you were pretty, or hint that he would like to see you again?"

"Mama, he came to see Travis," Maggie hedged, glad that Rosita's back was turned so she couldn't see Maggie's guilty face.

"That's what he wanted you to believe," Rosita said, and folded her arms across her bosom in a gesture that appeared smugly satisfied. "Now I know what is happening," Rosita declared. "Dallas likes you. He'll be back."

"Mama! Don't you dare play matchmaker with Dallas and me! I'm not the least bit interested in him!"

"Oh, hush," Rosita said. "You couldn't find a better man than Dallas Fortune, and don't try to convince me that you wouldn't like to marry again. It's not natural for a young woman to live without a man. The same goes for Dallas, living all alone in that big house of his. You're perfect for him, and I have a feeling that he knows it.''

Maggie groaned. ''Now you've got us married? I don't believe this.''

''Maybe you should believe it,'' Rosita said serenely. ''At the very least, you should give it some serious thought.'' Rosita got up from the chair and took the brush from her daughter's hand. ''I think I'll go to bed now. Good night, dear.''

Maggie had to forcibly beat back an impulse to blurt out the truth about Dallas's visit today, just to see the shocked expression on her mother's face. She paced the floor long after Rosita had retired, recalling with anger and humiliation Dallas's insulting propositions one minute, and picturing the resulting ruckus should she ever relate the incident to her family the next.

Dallas might have her mother snowed, but Maggie knew what kind of man he really was, the big phoney! Walking around making everyone think he was still mourning his wife, and then coming on to Maggie with downright scandalous suggestions. Oh, yes, she was definitely on to Dallas Fortune.

It was later, after Maggie had gone to bed, that a feeling of melancholy settled upon her. She could have liked Dallas so much. Why had he ruined any chance they might have had of becoming more than acquaintances?

''Men!'' Maggie muttered disgustedly. Rosita was right; Maggie *would* like to marry again. But was there one single man on earth who wasn't a cad, a cheat or a liar? One man who truly liked and respected women?

She doubted it. If it weren't for her parents' long and happy marriage, she would also doubt that it was even possible for a man and woman to live together in harmony for any length of time.

Around ten the next morning Rosita phoned from the main house. "Maggie, Cruz and Savannah are coming to dinner tonight."

"Oh, good," Maggie exclaimed. "What should I fix for dinner? I'd like it to be something special."

"Well, Cruz adores barbecued ribs. There are ribs in the freezer, and maybe you could make a nice potato salad."

"Great. I'll plan the meal around that."

"Thank you, sweetie. See you this evening."

"'Bye, Mama. Don't work too hard."

As she hung up the phone, Maggie moved the kitchen curtain aside to check on Travis. She had relented on yesterday's decision about confining him to the house, because his sad little face under that huge hat had been more than she could bear. "But," she'd told him firmly, "this is your last chance, son. If you leave the yard today without permission, you will remain in the house for at least a week."

"I won't be a bad boy, Mama, I promise."

Maggie had hugged him. "You're not a bad boy, sweetheart," she'd said with a catch in her voice. "I just don't want you to get hurt." Then she had watched him joyously run for the door.

Holding the edge of the curtain in her hand, Maggie became so stunned that she nearly pulled it from the rod. Dallas was in the yard talking to Travis again! She wondered why she hadn't heard a car pull up, and then she noticed a handsome black horse tethered to a post.

Groaning out loud, Maggie let the curtain fall back into place. What was wrong with that man? She'd done everything but physically attack him, and he still had the gall to drop in. What could she say that might penetrate his ego-tistical stubbornness?

Maggie angrily narrowed her eyes. Travis already liked Dallas and believed that Dallas liked him. There were more ways than one for her trusting little son to get hurt on the Fortune's Double Crown Ranch. Dallas's insincere atten-tions could cause more damage to Travis than any fall the boy might take. She had to put a stop to this before it got completely out of hand.

Detouring to the freezer just long enough to take out two packages of ribs to thaw for dinner, Maggie then hurried to the front door. Yanking it open, she found herself no more than a foot away from Dallas. His hand was up, and she knew that he'd been all set to knock on the door.

"Good morning," he said as calmly as you please, as though people *always* opened doors before he knocked on them.

Maggie couldn't be nice. "What do you want?" she asked in a cold, unfriendly voice.

Dallas's heart sank, but he vowed again not to give up on Maggie. How could he, when she affected him so strongly? Even angry, she was so darned pretty that he wanted to stand there and stare at her.

Pretending that he hadn't picked up on her foul mood, he smiled. "I'd like to take Travis for a ride."

"And I suppose you told him the same thing and got him all excited about it," Maggie said with scathing sar-casm.

"I wouldn't do that, Maggie. I asked him to stay in the side yard while I talked to you. Since he's never been on a horse before, I thought it might be best to get him used to being so far off the ground by having him first ride with me."

Maggie almost shouted, "No!" but a sudden burst of

very disturbing knowledge stopped her. She could be as protective of Travis as she wanted, but the damage—as far as Dallas went—had already been done, and could very well be irreversible. Was there any point now in stopping Travis from learning to ride a horse, just because Dallas would be his instructor?

A great weakness overtook Maggie. She loved riding herself, and it was only natural for a boy with Travis's lively curiosity and imagination to be drawn to horses. She'd brought this on herself by bringing Travis to the ranch, even though she couldn't possibly have predicted a relationship between her five-year-old son and one of the Fortune men.

"Well?" Dallas said quietly, awaiting her verdict.

Maggie didn't want to say yes. She didn't want Dallas to further encourage her son's affection when she knew in her soul that Dallas was using Travis as an excuse to see her. Obviously Dallas hoped to wear down her objections to having an affair with him—she could see it in his eyes—and it wasn't going to happen.

"I want you to understand something," she said bluntly. "Your phoney friendship with my son is not going to undermine—"

"Phoney!" Dallas exclaimed heatedly, interrupting her. "Maggie, there is nothing phoney about my feelings for Travis!" Dallas looked off for a moment, then brought harder eyes back to her. "You've got me all wrong, Maggie. I caused it myself and I wish to hell it were possible to take back everything I said to you the first time I came here. Isn't there some way we could start over?"

"Nothing leaps to mind," Maggie drawled. "I really wish—" The hurt look in Dallas's eyes didn't halt her little speech, but the sight of Travis peeking around the corner of the house did. Had he been eavesdropping all along? she wondered uneasily. He should be scolded for listening to a grown-up conversation, but she'd laid down so many new rules since they'd come to the ranch that his little head was probably spinning from them. Eavesdropping was something that had never come up for discussion in Phoenix—there'd been no reason—but there was no question that their acute change in life-style at the ranch had demanded a great many new rules.

Regardless, Maggie suddenly felt sorry for her adorable little son. And guilty for denying him the pleasure of a ride on a horse, even if it was with Dallas. After all, she and Travis weren't going to be here much longer, and once they left Travis would forget all about Dallas.

"All right," she said in a much calmer voice. "You may take Travis for a ride."

Dallas wondered what had changed her mind, but he wasn't about to open that can of worms. "Thanks," he said evenly. "And don't worry about him. I'll watch him like a hawk."

"Please do."

Dallas started to leave the porch, then stopped on the stairs to turn and look at her. "By the way, Rosita invited me to supper tonight. She said Cruz and Savannah would be here, and that you were making ribs. I'm looking forward to it."

How could her mother do that to her? But even while the nerve-racking question formed in her mind, so did the answer. Rosita would like nothing better than to see her daughter married again, and it would never occur to Rosita that a Perez wasn't good enough for a Fortune. If she knew what was really brewing in Dallas's mind, she wouldn't be so quick to play matchmaker, thought Maggie.

Silently, Maggie watched Dallas lift Travis up to the saddle on his horse's back. Below his big hat, Travis's little face was flushed and excited. Dallas mounted and nudged the horse into a walk.

"'Bye, Mama!'' Travis yelled.

"Goodbye, sweetheart. You hang on tight!''

"I will, Mama.''

Feeling totally defeated, Maggie went inside. Dallas's plans to eat with them tonight changed everything. Dinner was *not* going to be an enjoyable family affair.

Four

All afternoon, while cooking and preparing extra-special dishes because His Highness, Dallas Fortune would be eating at the Perez table that evening, Maggie fumed to herself. There was no way she could be anything but nice to Dallas in front of her family. She would have to smile at him, talk to him and generally act as though she was as pleased as Ruben and Rosita were to have him as a dinner guest.

Of course, any and all visitors to the Perez home were treated well, but Dallas being a Fortune raised him far above the ordinary-guest category, and perhaps that was what galled Maggie most. Other than the fact that Rosita would probably not have been so quick to hand out an invitation if she wasn't positive that Dallas and Maggie would make a perfect couple.

Oh, yes, Maggie thought with a sardonic twist of her lips. Her mother's matchmaking was precisely the reason that Dallas was coming to dinner, and the reason that instead of a delightful evening of visiting with Savannah and Cruz, Maggie was going to have a perfectly miserable time.

To add insult to injury, ever since Dallas had returned Travis to the house after their horseback ride, the boy had been on cloud nine. Several times Maggie had had to bite her tongue to stop herself from snapping at her son simply because he'd talked incessantly about Dallas. *He let me*

*hold the reins, Mama. Dallas's horse is named Vic, Mama.
Dallas said the next time I could ride by myself, Mama.*

So, Maggie thought venomously, no matter which way
she turned, there was Dallas. Her mother adored him, her
son adored him. Undoubtedly her father liked Dallas. And
if Cruz *didn't* like him, he certainly would not have let
Dallas finance his pending business venture. She was in the
middle of all that hero worship, and not one member of her
family knew or even suspected that their hero wasn't all he
was cracked up to be.

And if she told them what kind of man he really was...?
Maggie pursed her lips. They would probably say she'd
misunderstood Dallas's intentions. They'd probably be
thrilled that he would even look at Maggie twice!

It was too late to tell them anything about that day. How
would she explain not having said something about it before this? To keep the peace sounded like a pretty lame
excuse, especially since she'd allowed Dallas to take Travis
riding, and to give him that big hat. If she'd been truly
insulted, why hadn't she snubbed Dallas's every advance,
even those he'd made toward Travis?

Maggie stopped grating carrots for a salad and frowned
over that question. Good heavens, she thought uneasily.
Surely there wasn't some part of her that had *liked* Dallas's
crude approach!

No, she would never believe that. But for some reason
she was able to separate the Dallas of that day from the
man he had been around her on other occasions.

"Damn," she mumbled, and resumed the grating at a
furious pace. To find herself suddenly ambiguous about
Dallas was a disturbing jolt. She tried not to think about
him at all, but she couldn't stop herself from recalling his
ardent apology and plea for them to start over.

"No," she said out loud. All Dallas wanted from her

was a one-night stand. How could she forget that for even
a moment? He wasn't two men, he was one. And just because he could alter his personality—apparently on an
hourly basis—didn't mean she should remember the good
and forget the bad. Her life was up in the air as it was; she
certainly didn't need a man muddying the waters. Even if
he was the most attractive man she'd ever known.

Her own thoughts made Maggie gasp in outright shock.
Obviously some portion of her was out of control. How
else could she admit an attraction for a man that she
shouldn't even notice?

"Hello, Maggie," Savannah said.

Maggie hugged a beaming Cruz, then her sister-in-law.
Maggie truly liked Savannah, and thought the woman beautiful with her long blond hair and big blue eyes. But considering how popular Cruz had always been with women,
Maggie wasn't at all surprised that his bride was so pretty.

Rosita came in from the kitchen and hugged her son and
daughter-in-law. "Welcome. Papa should be home soon.
Wait until you see the feast Maggie prepared for our dinner."

"I didn't know you could cook, Maggie," Cruz teased.

Just then Travis bolted into the room full tilt and excited.
"Aunt Savannah! Uncle Cruz!"

Savannah smiled and picked up the little boy. "Hello,
sweetheart. How have you been?"

"Great! Hey, Uncle Cruz, you wanna play catch?"

"Sure. Go get your ball."

"Yeah!" Travis exclaimed, and ran for his bedroom.

"Thank you, Cruz," Maggie said with a delighted smile.
She looked at Savannah. "Would you like to join Mama
and me in the kitchen?"

"Yes, of course," Savannah replied.

Travis ran in with his ball, and he and Cruz went outside. Rosita, Maggie and Savannah walked into the kitchen, and Savannah said, "My goodness, it smells wonderful in here."

"Maggie's been cooking all day," Rosita said proudly. "We are going to have a fine dinner."

"Well, I had nothing better to do," Maggie said, even though she was very pleased with her mother's praise. "Savannah, sit anywhere. There are only a few things left to do before everything will be ready."

"I'd be glad to help," Savannah said.

"Maggie has almost everything ready. You just sit down and relax," Rosita said firmly.

Maggie heard the sound of approaching vehicles, and winced. One was her father's truck and the other could only be Dallas's. Her nerves began jumping around, and it took effort to look unconcerned.

She hadn't said a word to her mother about inviting Dallas to a family get-together, even though her stomach had not stopped churning with nervous anticipation all day. This was, after all, her parents' home, and they could invite whomever they wished to dinner, whenever they wished.

But neither had Rosita mentioned it, and Maggie suspected that her mother knew full well that her daughter wasn't thrilled with having to deal with Dallas Fortune tonight. Maggie looked at the whole thing as interference, plain and simple, but she suspected that her mother was tickled pink over her own inventiveness.

Ruben came into the house, then the kitchen. He greeted Maggie and Savannah and kissed his wife's cheek, then headed for the bathroom for his usual after-work shower. Wondering about Dallas, Maggie glanced out the window and saw that he had joined Cruz and Travis in their game of catch.

A dozen things flashed through her mind: He was tall and handsome. He was manly and sexy. He moved gracefully, catching and tossing the ball with enviable ease. He smiled a lot. He seemed to be enjoying himself.

Her throat suddenly dry, Maggie moved away from the window. Travis was reveling in both Cruz's and Dallas's attention, and everyone would think she had totally lost her senses if she ran outside, grabbed her son and hid him in his bedroom. But that was what she wanted to do. Not because of Cruz—Cruz was family—but because Dallas just kept burrowing his way deeper into her son's affections. And nothing could ever come of it, other than heartache that Travis was not old enough to comprehend.

If only she could take Travis and leave the ranch, Maggie thought with a sudden passionate wish to be away from Dallas's influence. She'd considered sending her résumé to Houston banks, and maybe it was time she did that. It would be great if she had the money to move to Houston even without a job, but it just wasn't possible now. Yes, she would mail out résumés tomorrow.

"Maggie, this salad looks delicious," Rosita said.

"What? Oh, thank you, Mama." Maggie came back to earth with genuine hope in her heart. Surely one of Houston's many banks would hire her.

"Well, everything's ready," Rosita declared. "Where's Ruben?" She left the kitchen, calling, "Ruben, dinner is ready! What's taking you so long?"

Savannah got up. "Shall I tell the others?"

"Yes, please do," Maggie replied. Alone in the kitchen, she took long, deep breaths. Somehow she had to appear calm and nonplussed during dinner. She could not let Dallas or her family know how she felt about Dallas's presence at the Perez table.

She had to make the best of things. She really had no choice.

Frustrated because she could not fall asleep, Maggie glanced at the lighted face of the bed stand clock: 11:20 p.m. The house was silent. Everyone else was sound asleep. Obviously she was still keyed up over the evening, too tense to relax. Annoyed with herself, Maggie threw back the covers and got up; she had rolled and tossed long enough. Maybe a breath of fresh air would settle her nerves.

She slipped out of her nightgown and, simply because they were handy, pulled on the same skirt and blouse she'd worn for dinner. Finger-combing her hair back from her face, Maggie tiptoed through the house and took a jacket from the foyer closet. Opening the front door as quietly as she could, she stepped out onto the porch. The cool night air was wonderful on her face, and she breathed deeply.

Cautiously pulling the door closed behind her, she saw the huge full moon that seemed to be hanging directly over the Double Crown Ranch. It brightened the earth, almost turning night into day. This was one of those incredibly beautiful Texas nights that she remembered from her youth.

Her mood changed instantly. Smiling to herself, Maggie tiptoed across the porch to the stairs. On the ground, she walked normally, and decided a stroll in the moonlight was exactly what she needed. She left the Perez yard and then stopped to think about direction. She knew the ranch's lay-out almost as well as she did the arrangement of the house she'd grown up in.

Recognizing an unusual sense of daring within herself, she decided that the open fields held little appeal. She would hike around the buildings and maybe take a moonlit look at Ryan Fortune's imposing home.

The hike itself was exhilarating. Everything was so still

and quiet, just lovely in the bright moonlight. And Maggie felt quite alone and free to wander wherever she wished. During the day she would not be this bold because there was always someone around—ranch hands doing their jobs, in particular. And, of course, there was always the chance of running into one of the Fortunes. Not that she'd ever been on bad terms with the family. In fact, as a child she had sometimes played with the twins, Vanessa and Victoria, who were only a year younger than herself. Dallas, she recalled, was a year older than she was and had occasionally showed up during play times to tease her and his sisters. Typical kid stuff, Maggie thought with a rather nostalgic sigh. Truth was, growing up on this ranch had been pretty darn great. It certainly beat the way Travis had been raised thus far.

And would she be able to do any better in the future? Houston and Phoenix were both large cities. Travis would have to go to school and have after-school care while she worked in Houston. The one advantage she would have in Texas is that she would be able to bring Travis to the ranch on weekends and holidays to see his grandparents.

It was one thing she'd thought of before leaving Phoenix and coming home. But now, with Dallas hovering over her son the way he'd been doing, she probably should rethink that idea. But, dammit, why should she have to alter her plans because of Dallas Fortune? Why didn't that man mind his own business and leave her and Travis alone?

Maggie heaved a sigh. She couldn't say that Dallas in any way had impeded the Perez family's enjoyment of her excellent dinner and of being together. He'd laughed when everyone else had about some silly comment or joke, and he'd appeared relaxed and at ease throughout the evening. Oh, she'd caught him looking at her with those eyes of his more than once, but he'd said nothing offensive or even suggestive to her, certainly nothing that should rile her.

And yet he *had* riled her, just by being there. If the man had one ounce of common decency, he would have refused her mother's dinner invitation. He had to have known that his presence would annoy Maggie. He had to have known he was a thorn in her side—he wasn't stupid!

"Oh, well," she said with another sigh.

She suddenly slowed her steps. Just ahead of her was a house—Dallas's house, the one he'd had constructed after his marriage. Until now she'd had no interest in this home. For the most part Dallas had been away and there'd been no reason to even go near his house.

Maggie eyed it for a few moments, making out its low-slung style, noting its dark windows. Unlike his father's home, Dallas's place had no yard lights. Of course there could be dozens of outside fixtures and Dallas simply hadn't turned them on, Maggie realized. It struck her then that his house looked lonely, even a bit ghostly in the moonlight. Was he a lonely man? Did her mother's opinion regarding Dallas's long mourning period have some validity?

But if that really was the case, why had he come on to her so strongly? Maggie wondered uneasily. *You're the first woman that has made me feel like a man in a very long time.* Wasn't that one of the things Dallas had said to her?

It just wasn't possible for her to understand that man! Maggie stood still for another minute or so, wondering why she would even want to understand Dallas. And yet there was a curiosity that she couldn't seem to stem.

She began walking again, this time slowly and cautiously, thinking that she would curl up and die if anyone spotted her snooping around Dallas's house in the middle of the night. Not that she would allow herself to get so close to the house that a potential onlooker could misconstrue her midnight stroll as snooping.

But *she* knew she was snooping, and it made her nervous. Not so nervous that she turned around and left, however.

When she spotted the gazebo, a beautiful little structure to the right of the house, she sighed longingly. Her own dream house, which she had very little hope of ever attaining, included a gazebo. She had to take a closer look at this one. This was probably the only chance she would ever have to do so. Gearing up her courage by telling herself that there wasn't a soul awake on the entire ranch, and that even the yard dogs that wandered at will were either sleeping or off exploring one field or another, Maggie stealthily began tiptoeing toward the gazebo.

Sitting in the gazebo, nursing a drink of scotch and a splash of water, Dallas suddenly became alert. Someone was out there, moving very quietly but unquestionably coming closer. Who on earth would be wandering at this time of night? Twisting around, he peered through the slats of the latticed wall behind him—and nearly choked. *Maggie!* He could hardly believe his own eyes, but yes, the night-wanderer was definitely Maggie Perez.

Dallas narrowed his eyes to see her better. She was heading straight for the gazebo. A small smile toyed with his lips. Since she couldn't possibly know that the gazebo was a favorite spot of his when he suffered from insomnia, it stood to reason that she also had no idea that he might be in there. This could turn out to be very interesting.

Soundlessly he set his glass of scotch on a small table, and waited.

Maggie approached the short set of stairs leading up to the floor of the gazebo, then came to a sudden halt. The interior of the structure looked black as pitch; obviously the moon, bright as it was, was not a strong enough light to insinuate itself through the narrow openings of what she could now see were latticed walls. She stood there thinking about what she was doing. Hiking around the ranch at that time of night was one thing; entering a building that was strictly private property was quite another.

But if she took just one quick look and left immediately after, who would ever know? Dallas wouldn't. His house was completely dark; he was undoubtedly fast asleep.

So there really was no one to worry about, Maggie decided. Before she could talk herself out of trespassing on Dallas's personal property, she tiptoed up the wood stairs and then took one step into the gazebo. It wasn't nearly as dark inside as she'd thought when she'd been outside, but the first thing she really saw was the shadowy figure of a man getting to his feet.

"Hello, Maggie," Dallas said quietly.

She let out a shriek of pure terror and turned to run. She shrieked again when Dallas caught her by the arm and stopped her.

"Hey, it's just me! Calm down and stop screeching," Dallas said. "You'll wake up everyone on the ranch."

It finally registered on Maggie's shattered nervous system that the man gripping her arm so tightly was Dallas.

"Oh, God," she groaned. She'd been caught in the act— and by Dallas himself. Humiliation and embarrassment nearly destroyed her. Her knees got so weak that it was a wonder her legs held her upright. "I—I'm sorry," she whispered tremulously.

"Maggie," Dallas said gently, "you can come to this gazebo anytime you wish. Don't be sorry."

"B-but I trespassed on...on your home!"

"That's the silliest thing I've ever heard," Dallas scoffed. "Come over here and sit down."

Maggie didn't have the strength to resist, and she let him lead her to a padded bench along one of the walls. He sat next to her and then pressed a glass into her hand.

"Take a swallow of this. It'll calm you down," he said.

"What is it?"

"Scotch and water. Go ahead, take a swallow."

She couldn't deny that she needed something to quiet the persistent racing of her pulse, and she lifted the glass to her lips and took a big swallow. She choked and coughed on the hard liquor going down her throat.

"This is a lot more scotch than it is water," she gasped.

"Guess it is, but it will make you feel better. I didn't mean to scare you to death, you know. Have another swallow."

The first swallow was warming her insides, Maggie realized. Not that she felt totally calm, by any means. She'd have thought that Dallas would be at least a little put out over her nervy invasion of his home, and it was rather amazing to Maggie that he wasn't. In fact, he was trying to make her feel as though she'd done nothing wrong! Could he really be the nice guy her mother proclaimed him to be? But if he was, why had he propositioned her in such an insulting way?

Confused by it all, Maggie lifted the glass for another swallow. This time she didn't choke on the scotch, and, in fact, decided it definitely contained medicinal properties. She never had been much of a drinker, especially of hard liquor. A glass of wine now and then was pretty much the extent of her experience with alcoholic beverages. Not that she intended rushing to Red Rock and buying herself a bottle of scotch at the first opportunity; it certainly wasn't *that* tasty.

In fact, two swallows of it were enough. She handed the glass back to Dallas with a quietly stated, "Thank you."

"You're welcome. You can finish it all, if you'd like."

"No, I've had enough." She peered at him in the semi-darkness of the gazebo. "Why are you out here at this time of night?"

"Probably for the same reason you are. I couldn't sleep."

"Is—is insomnia a common occurrence for you?"

Dallas sighed. "To tell you the truth, I run in spells. Sometimes I sleep just fine, sometimes I don't. How about you?"

"I guess it depends on what's on my mind when I go to bed."

"So, what was bothering you tonight? My having dinner with your family?"

Maggie hesitated while the truth and a lie vied for prominence. But why should she make herself look foolish by lying about something that was perfectly obvious? Dallas's question indicated that he already knew the truth, so there really was no point to her denying it.

"Yes," she said evenly. "That's what kept me awake."

"Hmm," Dallas murmured. "It's kind of interesting that I bother you enough to keep you awake." After a silent few moments, he asked, "Don't you think so?"

Maggie felt uneasy. He seemed to be working up to saying something that she would undoubtedly be better off not hearing.

She started to get up. "You've been very nice about my trespassing, but I really must apologize again. I'm sorry and it won't happen again."

"Maggie, I told you that you can visit my gazebo anytime you'd like." He found her hand and, with a gentle tug on it, urged her to sit down again. "Please, don't go," he said softly.

His hand around hers—the most innocent of all possible

caresses between a man and a woman—caused a catch in Maggie's throat. She knew she should break free and run for home as fast as her legs could carry her. And yet she stood there and let him hold her hand, and when he tugged on it a second time, she let herself be guided back to the bench.

"Oh, Maggie, if you only knew," Dallas whispered, and cautiously put his arms around her.

Her face was against his shirt, and she could hear his rapid heartbeat. She closed her eyes. It had been so long since a man had held her like this, and it was such a wonderful sensation to feel strong arms around her... Both her will and common sense began deserting her.

She felt his lips on her hair—another glorious sensation—and then he took her chin and tipped up her face. Though she couldn't clearly see his eyes, she felt their impact with startling clarity. Her breathing became choppy.

"Dallas," she whispered in a feeble attempt to stop what she knew in her soul was going to happen next. "W-we can't..."

He said nothing, for a debate about whether they could or couldn't was the last thing he wanted right now. It seemed like a small miracle that she hadn't immediately resisted his embrace, and there was only one way he could look at it: she wanted exactly what he did.

He began feathering kisses on her face and felt an emotional dam break within himself. "Maggie, oh, Maggie," he whispered hoarsely, and pressed his lips to hers in a kiss that gave her his heart and soul. When her mouth opened for his tongue, the desire he'd been feeling for Maggie from the moment they'd met again went off the scale.

Maggie's head was spinning from the most passionate, caring kiss of her life. Dear God, she thought in the back of her dazed mind. I could fall in love with this man! But falling in love with a man she could never have—except for a brief love affair—was a terrifying thought, and she quickly turned her head and tore her mouth from his.

"Maggie," Dallas pleaded while trying to kiss her again.

Breathing hard, she pushed against his chest and gasped, "We can't do this! Let go of me, Dallas." Her common sense was returning quickly, and she could hardly believe what she'd just allowed to happen. "I have to go home," she said rather frantically. "I never should have come here in the first place."

Dallas knew it was over. For tonight, anyway. Slowly he released his hold on her. "You're still judging me by how stupidly I behaved that first day," he said sadly.

Maggie jumped up from the bench. "No—no, I'm really not. Good night."

She was almost home by the time she realized that her parting words were true. She was no longer judging Dallas for any reason; she was worried about herself now!

Five

The next day Maggie was a wreck. Exhausted from a sleepless night and hours of soul-searching, she had to force herself to do the smallest chore. Fixing Travis's breakfast seemed like a monumental task. Helping him get dressed, then making his bed and hers further drained her pathetically small bank of energy. Preparing and mailing her résumé would have to wait, she decided. She simply didn't have the strength to do it today.

By the time noon rolled around and she made lunch for her son, she was yawning and just barely able to keep her eyes open.

"Son," she said after Travis had finished his bowl of soup and sandwich, "I'm very sleepy. If I take a short nap, will you promise to stay in the yard while I'm resting?"

"Yes, Mama," the small boy replied. "How come you're sleepy?"

"Because I didn't sleep very well last night."

"Okay," Travis said, completely accepting the simple explanation. "And I'll be very, very quiet so I don't wake you up."

Maggie kissed his cheek and hugged him. "You're my little sweetheart, aren't you?"

"I'm a big boy, Mama." Travis squirmed out of Maggie's arms and ran for the front door.

"Remember your promise to stay in the yard!" she

called after him, then headed straight for the sofa, where she collapsed and shut her eyes. She was asleep in seconds.

Maggie's eyes opened slowly. It took a minute to get her bearings and to figure out why she was sleeping on the sofa instead of her bed. Then she glanced at the mantel clock and let out a yelp. She'd slept more than two hours! What had Travis been doing for so long? Where was he now?

Jumping up, she ran to the door, stepped out on the porch and shouted, "Travis?"

"What, Mama?" The boy appeared from behind the house.

Maggie felt limp with relief. He'd stayed in the yard, as he'd promised, but she still shuddered to think of the things he could have done with no one keeping an eye on him. Then she noticed the rope in his hands, and, frowning, she left the porch and walked to the back of the house.

"Where did you get the rope, sweetheart?"

"It's a lasso, Mama. Dallas gave it to me. Watch me throw it." Travis swung the rope over his head several times, then tossed the looped end at a fence post. It fell short and he said, "Aw, heck."

Maggie had gone stiff at hearing Dallas's name, but she managed to speak normally to her eager little son. "That was a good try, Travis. When did Dallas give you the rope?"

"Mama," Travis said patiently. "I told you, it's a lasso." He began winding the rope into a coil for another try at the post.

"Yes, of course it's a lasso, but when did Dallas give it to you? Travis, was he here while I was napping?"

Travis nodded. "I told him you were sleeping."

"He—he wanted to talk to me?"

The boy shrugged. "Guess so. Watch me, Mama."

Maggie watched as her son threw the lasso again and again, and when he finally looped the post, she applauded his success by clapping her hands.

"That's wonderful, son," she exclaimed.

Travis was strutting around, proud as a little peacock. "Dallas said if I practiced a lot, I could get as good as him. Mama, he *never* misses the post!"

"He showed you how to use the ro—I mean, the lasso?" Maggie asked weakly. "Was he here for very long?" Travis was wearing the big hat Dallas had given him. He looked adorable—five years old and no bigger than a peanut, and acting so tough because he had a genuine cowboy hat and could rope a fence post. Maggie loved him so much at that moment that she was flooded with emotion.

Travis looked perplexed, then said, "I think he was here for five or eight hours."

Maggie had to swallow hard to keep from laughing. Like many children his age, Travis did not yet possess an accurate sense of time passing. She had taught him how to tell time from a clock, but that had been an easy accomplishment because he was smart as a whip about learning anything that had to do with numbers. Maggie was positive that her son was mathematically inclined, and hoped to expand his talent with good schools. Would she find a good school in Houston? The kind of school that encouraged its students' special aptitudes and rapidly advanced them in whatever field they shone in?

Well, that was another issue, she told herself. Meanwhile, why had Dallas come by again today? *Because of last night, you nitwit! Remember that you kissed him back. He's bound to have all sorts of crazy ideas because of that. How could you have been so stupid as to even go near his house? And then to actually walk into his gazebo! Why wouldn't he have taken advantage of the situation?*

Maggie heaved a distressed sigh. "I'm going in now, son."

"Okay." Travis was intent on swinging the lasso again, and Maggie could tell how determined he was to do it the way Dallas did.

Walking away with her head down, Maggie suffered a feeling of defeat. As things stood now, it was not in her power to halt Dallas and Travis's friendship. Plus, her opinion about Dallas using Travis to get to her was not nearly as forceful as it had been. She suspected that if she left her son with her parents and went to Houston by herself, Dallas would still come by to see him. Not that she would even consider leaving without Travis. He was the one unquestionable joy in her life; she would be miserably unhappy without him.

Maggie sat on the porch swing and stared dully at the miles of open fields beyond the Perez home. Her life had no direction. She was living off her folks, and they were unanimous in their belief that she should be living under their roof. To their way of thinking, she and Travis should have come home to the ranch immediately after her divorce. Truth was, Maggie realized unhappily, if Dallas hadn't insinuated himself into the picture, she wouldn't be so upset about her drifting existence and the fact that she was eating food that her parents had worked hard to buy.

And then there was that kiss last night. She hated the fact that she got warm all over every time she thought about it, but how could she ignore such blatant proof of the chemistry between her and Dallas? That was what scared her most—that blasted chemistry. It sure hadn't done anything but cause her trouble in the past.

Maggie thought about her failed marriage, which, in all honesty, had been a failure from the start, even though she had tried very hard to make it work because of Travis. The whole thing was a darn good argument against premarital sex. Craig, too, had made her warm all over, Maggie recalled cynically. That had lasted for about a month after their shotgun wedding. Then he'd gone on to greener pastures, and the truly sad thing was that she hadn't cared what he'd done. She'd probably still be married to the jerk if he hadn't wanted to marry another woman.

Well, that was in the past and best left there. Her worry now was the present, and she felt so helpless, about herself, about her son and about Dallas. It was a lot to deal with and there really seemed to be only one solution: get herself off this ranch. Those résumés were going out in tomorrow's mail, come hell or high water!

Rosita came home that evening all atwitter over events at the Fortune mansion. "Lily's birthday is coming up, and Ryan talked to me about throwing a big surprise party for her and inviting everyone they each know. Since he asked for my opinion, I told him that I didn't think Lily would appreciate being surprised like that when there are so many other things going on in the family. Terribly disturbing things, Maggie, like baby Bryan still being missing, and Ryan's divorce battle getting worse by the day. No, indeed, I couldn't then and still can't imagine Lily being thrilled over a houseful of guests with so much else going on, and I told Ryan exactly that."

"Did he agree with you?" Maggie asked, only because her mother wanted to talk about it. Maggie herself couldn't drum up any real interest in what the Fortunes were doing. The kidnapping was awful, of course, and Maggie felt genuine sympathy for the parents, Matthew and Claudia. Ryan, too, must be suffering over that. Probably the whole family was. But if they were all suffering over the loss of baby Bryan, how could any one of them plan a party?

"Oh, yes, he agreed," Rosita said emphatically. "He decided to take Lily and her children out to dinner for her birthday celebration."

"Much more sensible," Maggie murmured. "Have you met Lily's children?"

"Indeed I have. Cole and Hannah are wonderful, but Maria, Lily's youngest, is a very strange young woman. I get very peculiar feelings when she's around."

"Peculiar? In what way, Mama?"

Rosita thought a moment, then shrugged. "I haven't been able to tie these feelings to something specific, but they are strong and persistent, so I don't believe they're going to go away. Sooner or later we'll all know what Maria is up to or involved in. That's the one thing I'm very certain of."

Travis was the star of the dinner table, full of excited chatter about the lasso Dallas had given him.

Maggie felt her mother's eyes on her, and finally she looked back. One of Rosita's eyebrows went up as she said, "So, Dallas was here again today?"

"I didn't see him," Maggie said quickly.

"Mama was taking a nap," Travis volunteered.

Rosita's expression transformed into motherly concern. "Weren't you feeling well today?"

Maggie sighed. "I was just tired, Mama. Please don't start thinking that I'm wasting away from some awful disease just because I took a nap."

"Don't be sassy to your mama," Ruben said. "Travis, tell us some more about your new lasso. Have you roped anything yet?"

"The fence post," Travis said proudly.

"Maybe you'll show me what you can do after supper?" Ruben said.

Travis glowed. "Yes, Grandpa! *Right* after supper!"

* * *

As had become their nightly routine, Maggie and Rosita stayed up and talked after Travis and Ruben went to bed. Again Maggie brushed her mother's hair.

"Mama, tell me how you and Papa met," Maggie said.

"You've heard that story a dozen times."

"Not for years. Please tell it again."

"Well, I started working for the Fortunes at fourteen years of age. Goodness, that was a long time ago." Rosita became nostalgic and murmured, "I've spent most of my life on this ranch."

"Which is the reason you know the Fortunes so well."

"Yes, I've gone through the best and the worst with them." Rosita sighed. "Anyhow, I was a good girl and paid little attention to the young men working as ranch hands. Until the day I saw your father. He was so handsome, Maggie, so strong and full of life. My heart nearly stopped at first sight of him, and I knew at once that he was the man I would marry."

Maggie stopped brushing and became very still. "Exactly how did you know it, Mama? Did you suddenly, mysteriously see your own future? Did you actually say to yourself 'Ruben Perez is going to be my husband'? And how did he react to seeing you that first time? Was it love at first sight for both of you? Did Papa immediately declare his feelings?"

Rosita laughed. "Oh, my, no. Your father was shy around girls, and he could barely look me in the eye. But I could tell he liked me, and since I knew in my soul we were meant for each other, I did everything I could to draw his attention. You know that *I've* never been shy, and I have to admit that I deliberately devised situations where we would run into each other."

Maggie smiled. "You chased him until he caught you. Mama, you never told me that before."

"Well, you were probably too young to hear such things. Anyway, when we finally got better acquainted, Ruben was much less shy—and we fell in love. We were married a year after we met."

"But you were in love all along. Did you ever worry that Papa might not fall in love with you?"

"Not for a moment," Rosita said serenely.

"How wonderful to be so positive," Maggie said softly.

"Well, you must have been positive about Craig."

"Never, Mama," Maggie murmured. "I've never been in love the way you were with Papa."

Rosita turned on her chair to see her daughter's face. "Maggie," she said sadly. "You've been so cheated."

Maggie took a breath. "I did it to myself. You know I was pregnant when Craig and I got married. I tried very hard to convince myself that I was in love with Craig, but I wasn't, no more than he was in love with me. When we stopped kidding ourselves, the end came very quickly."

"Such a sad story," Rosita said with a big sigh. The next moment her countenance brightened. "But you are still very young, Maggie, and I'm sure you will experience the same kind of love that I have with your papa. One day a fine man will come along and—" Rosita smiled "—maybe he already has."

Maggie's heart fluttered. "You're thinking of Dallas."

"And why wouldn't I, when he can't seem to stay away from this house? Maggie, do you think he dropped in all the time before *you* came home?"

"He's a Fortune, Mama," Maggie said quietly.

"For goodness' sake, what difference does that make? If you love someone—" Rosita suddenly stopped talking and frowned. "I did something very bad one time."

Maggie stared. "I doubt that you've ever done anything bad."

"What I did was very wrong. It happened a long time ago. I was about twenty-four, or so, and I had recently added Lily to the household staff."

"The same Lily that Ryan Fortune intends to marry after his divorce from Sophia?" This was a story Maggie had not heard before, and she couldn't help being curious about it.

"One and the same. Ryan and his brother Cameron were about eighteen and nineteen, and Lily was breathtakingly beautiful. I think both of the boys wanted Lily, and one day I walked into the kitchen—Lily had been scrubbing the floor—and I saw the boys shoving each other around, working themselves up to a fist fight.

"Believe me, I wasn't kind about tossing them out of the kitchen. Then I turned to Lily and told her to stay away from the Fortune boys. I recall saying something like, 'They'll gobble you up like a sweet peach, then spit out the pit. Especially that Cameron, who's no better than a heartless coyote.' You see, Lily was such an innocent young girl, and I felt she needed looking after. Later I realized that she'd taken my warning in a much different way than I'd intended. She started believing that she wasn't good enough for a Fortune, and it was my fault that she felt so inadequate."

Rosita looked her daughter in the eye. "Regardless of what caused it, Lily felt the same way you do, Maggie. And look how things turned out. Ryan and she have always loved each other, and now they're finally going to be married."

"Mama, you didn't say anything so terrible. You were concerned about Lily and all you were doing was trying to protect her."

"Protect her from what? Love? If I had kept my mouth shut that day, Lily and Ryan might have been married to each other these many years." Rosita paused. "And now you are faced with a similar situation. You think you're not good enough for a Fortune, and you are, Maggie—you are good enough for anyone. You're beautiful and smart, and in my heart I know that Dallas feels something for you. Don't throw it away, Maggie. Give him a chance."

Maggie gave up on any more hair-brushing tonight and made her way over to a chair, where she sat down heavily.

After a few moments she spoke. "I made a terrible mistake with Craig, Mama," she said quietly, "and I no longer trust my judgment where men are concerned. I could not bear another bad marriage, and this time I also have Travis to consider."

"Dallas has great affection for Travis."

"He appears to, yes, but..." Maggie slowly inhaled. "I don't know what to think about that. It worries me, because Travis needs a father, just like every other child does, and what if he gives too much of himself to Dallas and then nothing comes of it? I don't want my son hurt, Mama, and it could happen." After a moment Maggie repeated quietly, almost to herself, "It could happen."

Rosita studied the forlorn expression on her daughter's face. "Maggie, you're going to have the same concern with any man you meet," she said softly.

"I know, Mama," Maggie said with a heavy sigh.

"Dallas is kind to Travis," Rosita reminded.

"So far, yes."

"I don't think he's pretending or putting on a big show for your benefit. I believe he really likes Travis."

"Maybe you're right, Mama. But even if that's true, how do I get past my own lack of confidence around men? And regardless of your success story about Lily and Ryan, I can't forget that Dallas is a Fortune and I—I'm just a very ordinary person.''

"Maggie, you have to stop thinking that way!''

"I wish I could, Mama.''

Dallas knew it was a million-to-one shot that Maggie would come to the gazebo again tonight, but still he hoped. With a scotch and water that he barely sipped—his usual routine with hard liquor—he watched the moon and let his brooding thoughts wander.

He had always loved the Texas hill country. From the time he'd been a little shaver, people had said that he was more like his father than his other siblings were, and Dallas couldn't doubt it. His heart and soul were truly intertwined with the ranch. He'd never had cravings to be anything but the rancher he was, and he felt very fortunate to have been born into his career.

He'd experienced the same passion he possessed for the ranch only one other time—when he'd met and fallen in love with Sara Anderson. He'd still been in his teens, and at his father's insistence, he and Sara had waited to marry until Dallas had finished college. He was twenty-two when they married, and they had been single-minded on immediately starting their family.

When Sara had finally gotten pregnant after years of trying to conceive, they had been overjoyed. But things hadn't been right with her pregnancy from the start. Her doctors had strongly advised Sara to stay in bed, which her nature had not permitted her to do. She'd always been an extremely active person, and nine months of inactivity was too much to ask of her.

Dallas remembered discussions between them about it. He'd tried to convince Sara that she should listen to her physicians, but Sara had laughed and called the doctors old-maid worrywarts. "Goodness, Dallas, women have babies every day. I doubt very much that every mother-to-be doesn't have some sort of problem. I'll be fine. Stop worrying about me."

And after a while he'd given up trying to keep Sara in bed. After her death while giving birth to their stillborn son, he'd nearly gone crazy blaming himself. He should have *forced* Sara to take better care of herself. Dammit, he should have tied her to their bed!

Two years later Dallas still felt a great deal of responsibility for the senseless loss of his wife and child, but at least he could think about Sara now without the horrific pain he'd suffered immediately following her death. He'd obviously gone into shock, because he honestly could not recall the details of her funeral. He remembered hordes of people milling around him, but not who they were, nor what they had said to him.

Dallas pushed what he *could* remember of that sad and morbid event from his mind, and thought of the Sara with whom he'd fallen so deeply in love, the Sara who had laughed so easily and had loved to tease him into laughing, as well. She'd been a beautiful person, both inside and out, and she'd been sweet and kind and generous with everyone.

Sighing heavily, Dallas took a sip of his drink. The moon wasn't full tonight. It looked as though someone had pared a small sliver from its right side.

His next thought startled him: Sara would not have wanted him to live alone for the rest of his life. He had mourned long enough. It was time that he got on with life—

Maggie's image was suddenly in his mind. He wanted her physically; denying that would be a lie. But Maggie was so very different from Sara. Maggie had a volatile personality and a short temper; he'd never seen Sara as anything but calm and collected, very sure of herself, very confident of her place in the world. Maggie seemed to be living on the edge—and maybe she always would.

Dallas suddenly realized that he was comparing Maggie and Sara, which wasn't fair to either woman. It seemed especially unfair when he admitted that Maggie excited him in a way that Sara never had. Their love life had been good, very good, but there was something about Maggie that made him want to rip off her clothes and make love to her until they were both exhausted. In short, he hadn't been as consumed by sex with Sara, and it was practically all he'd thought about since meeting Maggie again. If she hadn't stopped him last night, he would have taken them both to heaven.

That fantasy was too real for Dallas's comfort. In the first place, given Maggie's attitude toward him, it was probably never going to happen. And why wouldn't she give him attitude, considering the way he'd talked to her that first day?

Disgusted with himself, Dallas got to his feet. He'd wrangled with past and present enough for tonight. As he left the gazebo he poured the remaining liquid in his glass on the grass, and then walked to his house.

Maggie wasn't coming back to the gazebo. Why in hell couldn't he just face facts and forget Maggie Perez? Forget that she was even living on the ranch, forget how strongly she affected him, forget everything about her, from her full, ripe lips to her full, ripe body.

Cursing under his breath, Dallas went into his dark, empty house and slammed the door behind him.

Six

Rosita came home around noon, surprising Maggie. "I have the afternoon off," Rosita declared with a big smile.

"That's wonderful, Mama! Why don't you put on your house slippers and get comfortable in the living room?"

"What do you think I am, an old lady?" Rosita said with a derisive snort. "I'm going visiting. I haven't seen my friend Emma Field in a while, and I phoned her from the big house. She was thrilled with the idea of a get-together. Maggie, Emma also has one of her grandsons staying with her—he's six, Emma said—so I told her I would bring Travis with me. The boys can play, and Emma and I can catch up. You can come along, too, if you'd like. I know Emma would be delighted to see you."

Maggie remembered Emma Field very well. Rosita and Emma had been close friends even when Maggie had been a child, and one of Maggie's memories of the woman was of her pinching Maggie's cheeks until they hurt, and gushing over Rosita's darling little daughter. Emma was also as nosy as a person could be. Rosita might like her, and that was just fine, but Maggie had no desire to answer a bunch of questions that were none of Emma Field's business.

"Would you mind if I didn't go with you?" Maggie asked her mother. "I'm in the middle of baking a cake, and it would hold you up for at least an hour."

"Oh, dear, Emma's expecting me before then."

"Then you go along and have a good visit," Maggie said, immensely thankful that she'd started mixing the cake.

"Is it all right if I take Travis with me?" Rosita asked.

"Of course it is. He probably needs his face and hands washed. I'll go get him. He's in the backyard with his lasso." Maggie dashed outside for her son.

"Grandma wants to take you visiting with her. You'll get to play with a boy around your age. Won't that be fun?"

Travis looked doubtful, though Maggie could see in his eyes that the prospect of playing with a boy his age had his wheels turning. "Can I take my hat and lasso?"

"I don't see why not. Come inside, son. We need to wash your face and—" Maggie eyed her son's T-shirt, which wasn't nearly as clean as when he'd put it on that morning "—change your shirt."

Ten minutes later Maggie waved goodbye to her mother and son, then returned to the kitchen to finish the cake. Being entirely alone—a rare occurrence for Maggie—was a pleasant feeling. She didn't have to check on Travis every five or ten minutes, and, in all honesty, she felt an unusual and quite lovely sense of freedom. Humming to herself, she slid the cake in the oven. While it was baking she stirred up a bowl of icing.

When the cake was done, Maggie placed it on a trivet to cool, then tidied the kitchen. An idea kept running through her mind while she worked: with Travis under his grandmother's wing, she could take a horseback ride. Her father owned a small remuda, and Maggie knew he wouldn't mind if she took one of the horses out for a ride.

She changed into jeans, a long-sleeved shirt and boots, stuck one of her dad's old hats on her head, then hurriedly frosted the cake. Becoming more excited by the minute, she left the house, took a saddle and the other things she would need from her father's storage shed, and then headed for the small fenced pasture where Ruben kept his horses separated from the Fortune's fine stock.

It took about ten minutes for Maggie to sweet-talk one of the horses into permitting her to get close enough to lead her out of the enclosure. Then she swung the heavy saddle up and onto the mare's back. Once Maggie was mounted, the mare pranced around nervously for a minute or so, then calmed down and accepted her unfamiliar rider.

Maggie leaned forward and stroked and patted the mare's neck. "You're a fine horse, yes, you are," she crooned until the mare became even more docile. Finally feeling in control, Maggie headed the horse into the rolling hills of open country.

This is fantastic, she thought with a song in her heart. Out there by herself and on a horse she felt young and carefree. It was a wonderful sensation that had eluded her for a very long time, and she savored it to the fullest.

That marvelous feeling lasted until she started thinking again of her current situation. Marrying the wrong man could really mess up a woman's life. The only good thing that had come out of her ill-fated marriage was her son. Now, here she was, living off her parents and hoarding her very small cache of money for the day when she could finally make the move to Houston. She had mailed her résumé to a dozen banks this morning, and now it was a waiting game. She could only hope that someone in authority at one of the banks would recognize her potential.

Disturbed by circumstances she could do nothing about, Maggie forced her thoughts back to the pleasure of being on horseback. She really should see to it that Travis learned to ride on his own. There was no reason why she couldn't teach him herself.

She was miles from the main ranch, determined to recapture the sensation of freedom and youth she'd felt before, when a cloud passed over the sun. Glancing up, Maggie frowned. It wasn't just a lazily moving, fluffy white cloud blocking the sun; it was a huge black cloud that seemed to be speeding across the sky. And the wind—it had been a lovely little breeze only moments ago—was suddenly tearing at her clothes.

The very first show of lightning was an ear-splitting, jagged streak from cloud to earth, followed almost instantly by a deafening roll of thunder. "Oh, no," Maggie whispered. Electrical storms could be killers in this part of Texas. Everyone knew it, and anyone with a lick of sense got themselves under cover at the onset of such a storm.

But for her there was no cover; she was out in the open and miles from the house. Lightning was suddenly striking all around her—Maggie could even smell it. And her horse was getting spooked! Maggie tried to maintain control of the mare, but she feared she was fighting a losing battle. The horse kept pulling against the bit in its mouth and wildly rolling its eyes. Lightning struck too close for comfort—and the frightened animal reared violently.

Maggie felt herself falling, and she kicked her right foot free of the stirrup so she wouldn't be hung up when the mare bolted. In the next fearful beat of her own heart, Maggie found herself on the ground with the wind knocked out of her. Trying to catch her breath, Maggie sat up and watched the mare gallop around and around in a wide circle. Obviously the animal was too disoriented by fear to even know which direction to run.

Maggie's own fear had her heart pounding like a jackhammer. But there was no one to help her, and if she was going to live to see tonight, she had to catch that mare and make tracks for home.

She really didn't want to stand up. There were no trees

in the immediate vicinity, and she would be the tallest object on the landscape—a sure target for lightning that just kept getting more fierce.

On her hands and knees, Maggie started crawling toward the mare's circular path, praying the animal would maintain its same panicked pattern. The wind howled around her, throwing dirt and dry grass into her face. She had seen storms as bad as this one before, but she'd never been caught outside when one struck, and she was sick-to-her-stomach afraid. Her only hope was to catch the mare and try to calm her enough to let Maggie get on her back again.

Maggie knew that the second phase of the storm would be a drenching rainfall. She'd seen rainfalls so dense one couldn't see through them, and if she didn't catch the mare before it started raining, she never would.

Driven by utter terror, Maggie reached the path the mare had been running and prepared herself to stand up and grab some portion of the horse when it came galloping by again. If she could get hold of the bridle or the flying reins, she would at least have a chance of stopping the mare.

The mare's frantic hoof beats grew louder, and Maggie launched herself to her feet just as the animal flew by. All sense of reason suddenly fled Maggie's mind, and she ran after the mare, yelling, "Wait! Stop!"

Dallas and his horse, Vic, were heading for one of the line shacks that dotted the huge ranch. They were on a ridge, and Dallas suddenly caught sight of the strangest thing going on in the valley below. It looked as though someone was chasing a horse! In a circle, no less.

He was too far away to recognize the horse or the person, but whoever it was running insanely after that horse stood a damn good chance of getting himself struck by lightning. If he'd been thrown, he should be lying flat on the ground. Which one of his men didn't know that?

"They all know it," Dallas muttered under his breath, and turned Vic's head toward the valley. "But whoever is down there isn't thinking clearly. Probably got spooked when his horse did."

Dallas knew that he was risking getting struck by the almost constant bolts of lightning, but he couldn't just ride off to the line shack and ignore the man running in circles in the valley, trying to catch a horse that was obviously scared out of its wits. Dallas recognized blind panic when he saw it.

Once down the ridge, Dallas urged Vic into a full gallop. The big horse ate up the ground, and it was only minutes before Dallas saw the man's hat go flying in the fierce wind. It was then that he realized who was chasing that horse: Maggie! Freed of the hat, her long dark hair was being tossed around like a paper boat on white-water rapids. What in hell was she doing out here alone in this kind of storm? And where was Travis? *God, please don't let that boy be on another horse somewhere in this melee!*

Dallas shouted as loudly as he could, "Maggie! Maggie, get down on the ground!"

But the storm's violence was all that she heard, and she kept running after the mare. Suddenly, as though born of the storm itself, there was another horse, and its rider leaned over and plucked her off the ground.

She shrieked as though the devil himself had grabbed her, and Dallas shouted, "Calm down and get yourself settled behind me! We've got to get the hell out of here!"

An improbable rescue coming out of nowhere destroyed the last of Maggie's strength. Tears ran unchecked down her dirty cheeks, and she weakly laid her head against Dallas's back and held on to his shirt. Vic ran like the wind, and Maggie paid no attention to direction.

"Where's Travis?" Dallas shouted.

"He's with Mama."

"Thank God," Dallas muttered.

Within minutes the deluge started, and it was as though someone or something had punched a hole in the massive cloud and spilled its contents. The dirt on Maggie's face and in her hair ran into the dirt on her clothes, and the whole muddy mess kept running until it hit the ground. She was saturated in seconds, and so was Dallas. Along with the rain came a drastic drop in temperature, and she shivered and nestled closer to the natural warmth of Dallas's body.

When Vic stopped abruptly, Maggie became more alert. Dallas was off his horse in one fluid movement and reaching up for her. She let him take her down to the ground, and then tried to make sense of surroundings she could just barely make out through the blinding rain.

"Where are we?" she asked.

"At a line shack. Come on, I'll lead you in, then come back and see to Vic." Dallas took her hand, and she stumbled over unfamiliar ground to the door of a small cabin. Dallas merely opened the door for her to go in and then left again.

An enormous bolt of lightning and an explosive roll of thunder shook the earth. Shivering, Maggie sank onto a chair and wrapped her arms around herself. She was still sitting there when Dallas came in.

"You're white as a sheet. You've got to get out of those wet clothes," he said gruffly, and walked over to the bed and pulled off its top blanket. "Use this as a cover-up. That door over there opens onto a wood shed. You can change in there. As soon as I do the same in here, I'll build a fire in that stove and make us some coffee."

Holding the blanket, she got up, felt her knees buckle

and fell back to the chair. "I—I can't seem to get my bearings," she stammered.

Dallas studied her pale face and wildly dilated pupils. He'd seen people in shock before, and that was what Maggie looked like—dazed and barely aware of what was going on around her.

He gentled his voice. "Will you let me help you undress? You have to get warm and dry, Maggie."

Even through the numbness gripping her brain, Maggie felt embarrassment. "I—I'm sure I can manage...if I stay sitting down."

Dallas hesitated, then nodded. "All right, if you're sure. I'll use the wood shed and you change in here." Plucking another blanket from the bed, he went through the door to the wood shed.

Maggie picked at the buttons on her shirt. Her fingers seemed to be no more cooperative than her legs, and she worried that Dallas might come back with her half in and half out of the blanket. Impatiently she gave up on the buttons and tore her shirt open, strewing buttons right and left. Taking off her soaked boots was a terribly time-consuming chore, but finally she was down to her wet jeans and bra. Pulling the blanket over her shoulders, she managed to inch the drenched jeans down her legs. Her panties and bra felt like ice on her skin, and, throwing caution to the wind, she got rid of her underwear, too.

Completely encased in the blanket, she began to warm up. It felt wonderful. The storm was still raging outside, but the interior of the little cabin was dry and cozy. She was just starting to take note of what it contained when Dallas called through the door, "Is it all right if I come in now?"

"Yes," she called back.

Dallas walked in, and Maggie's eyes widened. He had

wrapped the blanket around his waist and secured it with his belt! His upper body was completely nude, and the unexpected sight of so much male brawn nearly undid Maggie. She quickly looked away and clutched her own blanket even more tightly around herself to make sure that no part of *her* was on display.

"Are you feeling better now?" Dallas asked as he started building a fire in the iron stove.

"Much better," Maggie replied. She suddenly remembered Dallas asking her where Travis was, and her heart softened considerably. Not only had Dallas rescued her from God only knew what fate, but he'd been concerned that Travis might be out in that storm with her.

She could no longer tell herself that Dallas Fortune was using her son to get to her; Dallas truly cared about the boy. It was an eye-opening moment for Maggie, even though it had disturbing aspects. Her son had a real friend in this man, and how could she deny Travis the emotional benefits of friendship with an adult male who had only been kind to the boy?

The other side of that coin, of course, was how affected Travis would be over leaving that sort of relationship behind when they finally moved to Houston. Maggie's hands clenched nervously under her blanket as she pictured herself explaining the facts of their lives to her five-year-old son. *We have to leave the ranch, sweetheart. Mama has to work to support us.*

But I don't want to leave Dallas, Mama. He's my friend.

She groaned silently and took a peek at Dallas, who had the fire going nicely and was now preparing a pot of coffee. It seemed she was in a frame of mind to torture herself, because she started thinking of that kiss in Dallas's gazebo. To rid herself of that memory she tried to concentrate on his crude behavior the first time he'd come to the house.

But that, too, was a form of self-torture, she soon realized, because Dallas had made it so plain that he wanted to make love to her. Did he still feel that way? They were so alone out here in this little cabin. If he had another pass in mind, wouldn't this be the perfect opportunity? And since she had responded so heatedly to him in the gazebo—for a few moments, at least—would she react in the same impassioned way if he kissed her again?

She swallowed hard and with a shake of her head drove the sexual cobwebs from her brain.

"How did you happen to come along at exactly the right moment?" she asked quietly.

Dallas looked at her and shrugged. "Fate, I guess." Then he smiled at her. "Obviously you were not destined to be struck down by lightning today."

His mentioning fate made Maggie uneasy. If fate had conjured up a person to snatch her from death's door today, why not her father or brother? Why not one of the dozens of ranch hands on the place? Why had fate sent Dallas Fortune?

Dallas's observation was not one with which Maggie could agree, but she didn't say so. Instead she said, "Well, I thank you for saving my life. And I also thank you for asking about Travis."

Dallas placed the coffeepot on the stove to brew. "You said he's with your mother?"

"Yes, Mama had the afternoon off and she took Travis with her to see a friend." Maggie glanced out a window and saw how fierce the storm still was. "I hope they're all right."

"I'm sure they are. Rosita has weathered many storms of this velocity. She knows the drill."

The aroma of perking coffee filled the cabin. "That smells good," Maggie commented.

"Sure does," Dallas agreed as he got two mugs from a cupboard.

"Are all the line shacks so well-equipped?" She'd always known about the line shacks, but she'd never been in one before. "A person could actually live in this cabin."

"That's the idea, although they're really designed for roundup. And for emergency situations like today's storm, of course," he added. "I'm sure some of the other line shacks, too, are being used as cover until the storm passes, same as we're doing." Dallas's gaze fell on Maggie's pile of wet clothes. "I hung my things over a line in the wood shed. I'd better do the same with yours, or you'll have to put them on again still soaked." Dallas grinned. "Unless you don't mind going home wrapped in a blanket, that is."

"I shudder to think of the raised eyebrows that would cause," Maggie said dryly.

"Yeah, if anyone saw us riding in wrapped in blankets, they might think you and I had been up to something." Dallas calmly walked over to pick up her wet clothes, but then, when he was close enough to touch her, he sent her another grin. "Your face is red, Maggie."

"It is not!" she denied sharply, but she knew he was right. She could feel the heat of a full-blown blush even on her ears.

Chuckling, Dallas walked away with her clothes and went into the wood shed.

"Damn conceited man," Maggie sputtered. With Dallas in the next room, she chanced exposure by moving her hands from under the blanket and finger-combing her wet hair back from her face. I must look a fright, she thought, and then asked herself why she would *care* how she looked.

It was probably because Dallas looked utterly gorgeous in that stupid blanket. His wet hair looked appealingly sexy, while hers was undoubtedly hanging in stringy strips. It was totally unjust that getting drenched didn't damage a man's looks one iota. It completely destroyed a woman's—certainly the makeup she'd put on that morning had to be gone.

God, she was stark naked under this blanket! Naked and plain as dishwater with stringy hair and no makeup. Since there wasn't a man alive who would find anything attractive about a woman in her condition, she should stop thinking silly thoughts about Dallas making another pass. Disgusted over her own wild imagination, Maggie heaved a sigh.

When Dallas returned, she was staring out the window.

"Is it slowing down any?" he asked.

"What? Oh, the storm. No, it doesn't appear to be. It shouldn't last this long, should it?"

"Never can tell," he said. "The coffee's done. Ready for a cup?"

"Very ready." The problem with that idea was that when he brought a mug of steaming coffee to her, she had to slip a hand from under the blanket and take it.

Dallas laughed at how cautiously she maneuvered the blanket and herself to stay covered from her throat to her feet.

His laughter irritated her. "I'm glad you find this whole thing so amusing," she snapped, while taking the mug of coffee from his hand.

"The whole thing isn't amusing—but you are. What do you think I'm going to do, jump your bones if I catch a glimpse of bare skin? Aw, heck, now your face is red again."

"Are you deliberately trying to make me angry?"

"Why would I do that? I'd much rather that you and I became good friends." Dallas's eyes darkened perceptibly as his amusement vanished. "In fact, I think you know that I'd like us to be a lot more than just friends."

For heaven's sake, don't blush again! "That is a subject I'd rather not talk about!" Maggie brought the mug to her lips, and realized that her hand wasn't as steady as it should be. Dammit, he was getting to her with innuendo alone! *Stay cool, stay calm, or at least act as though you are!*

"Hmm, good coffee," she said in the most casual way possible.

"Glad you like it, but be careful, it's hot enough to melt the iciest resistance."

She couldn't stop herself from flaring. "Are you saying that I'm a cold person?"

"You are with me."

"What do you expect me to do—throw off this blanket and parade around naked?"

A slow-burning grin formed on Dallas's face. "That is the most incredible idea I've ever heard. Beats any fantasy I could think up."

"Yeah, I'd just bet," Maggie scoffed. "Well, don't hold your breath." She suddenly felt something hot and burning on her thigh. She had inadvertently let the mug in her hand tip to spill some of the scalding hot coffee on the blanket! She panicked, yelped and jumped off the chair at the same moment. The blanket fell away and the mug slipped completely from her hand, crashing on the floor and splashing hot coffee on her feet.

"Maggie!" Dallas shouted in dread, and set his own mug down to free his hands. He saw the tears in her eyes and took her by the shoulders. "Are you burned?"

"My—my right thigh...and my feet," she whispered tremulously. Her nudity was so humiliating that she couldn't look him in the eye. How could she have been so careless with hot coffee?

"I'm going to take a look," Dallas said firmly. "And don't be embarrassed, for God's sake. If you're burned badly, you need attention.'' He got down on the floor and checked her feet. Pink blotches had appeared wherever the coffee had landed, but there were no blisters. Her feet might hurt a little, but they would be fine.

''You said your right thigh?'' he asked, and got on his knees, which put his face only inches from the triangle of dark hair at the base of her belly. His heart raced as blood rushed to his groin, and he almost forgot the reason he was on his knees in the first place, especially when he thought of what he'd really like to do at this particular moment.

He gruffly cleared his throat and got his mind back on track. There was a pink blotch on her thigh, but again there was no blistering.

He spoke hoarsely. ''I think the burns are minor. You're going to be just fine.''

''They—they're not hurting as much as they were,'' Maggie volunteered in a voice that matched Dallas's for huskiness. Standing naked before a man on his knees was a startlingly new experience, and it was turning her inside out. The pit of her stomach burned much hotter than the blotches on her feet and thigh, and the acute urgency she felt could not be construed as anything but what it was: sexual desire, so strong and powerful that she felt weak from it. Did she have the willpower to stop this before it really got started?

''Good...I'm glad,'' Dallas whispered, and put his hands on the back of her thighs and laid his head on that tormenting triangle of hair.

Maggie sucked in a breath, but she didn't back away from him or tell him to get up. Even though she knew exactly what this kind of intimacy led to, she stood there and basked in Dallas's adoration of her body.

Seven

"Maggie, you're so beautiful," Dallas said raggedly.

She didn't dispute his flattery, because she *felt* beautiful. Forgotten were the thoughts she'd had only minutes ago about looking a fright. Her mind seemed to be encased in a lovely pink haze, and there wasn't a single wish anywhere within her to break free of its delicious influence. In fact, not only did she feel beautiful, she felt more womanly, more female, than at any other time in her life. She suffered no questions about who or what was causing such a re-markable change in herself, because the answer was still on his knees, caressing her with his mouth and hands in a way she'd never before experienced.

Dallas's caresses were loving, she realized vaguely—not merely needful, but loving. It was as though he were hold-ing and touching a priceless treasure instead of a flesh-and-blood woman. How strange.

All thought stopped completely for Maggie when Dallas began kissing his way up her body. Then he was standing and seeking her mouth with his own. She parted her lips just before he kissed them, and she moaned softly when his tongue slipped into her mouth. Her hands crept up his chest to encircle his neck, and his went around her waist, bring-ing her so close to him that she could feel the rapid beating of his heart against her breasts.

Between kisses that kept getting hotter, Dallas breath-lessly whispered, "Oh, Maggie...Maggie."

And the only thing she could do in response was to whimper, "Dallas...Dallas."

When kisses were no longer enough, he picked her up and carried her to the bed. He laid her on it and followed her down, so that he was on top of her. Then he took her face between his hands and looked deeply into her eyes. For a long time that was all he did, simply look into her eyes, and she found herself probing the depths of his with heart-wrenching curiosity.

He appeared on the verge of saying something. But then, in the next heartbeat, he kissed her again, and her curiosity about what he'd been thinking vanished in a maelstrom of powerful emotions. In a passionate state of utter surrender, she closed her eyes and rubbed his back and shoulders while he lavished kisses to her breasts. Again the pink haze enveloped her, and she was barely aware of Dallas getting rid of his belt and blanket.

The sensation of his nude body covering hers nearly destroyed her ability to breathe, and she started taking in air in short gasps. Dallas, too, was breathing laboriously. Somewhere in the back of Maggie's dazed brain was the knowledge that she had never before become so passionately involved with a man. Never had she wanted to make love so badly that every cell of her body cried out for fulfillment.

She spread her legs without direction from Dallas, and she writhed restlessly beneath him, seeking what she was driven to have. With a sensual groan, he heeded her silent call and slid into her. At first they were both a little crazy, thrusting wildly, demandingly. But then they settled into a rhythm of movement that permitted eye contact.

Putting most of his weight on his forearms, Dallas watched her eyes as he moved within her. "It's perfect," he whispered hoarsely. "You're perfect."

She dampened her lips with the tip of her tongue and whispered, "So are you."

"We're perfect together."

"Yes...yes," she gasped.

"I knew it would be like this for us the minute I saw you again."

She didn't want to talk anymore. Conversation was diluting her mood. "Don't talk," she said unsteadily. "Not now." Pulling down his head, she mated their mouths in a kiss that said it all. *I want you...I have to have you...but please don't talk.*

Dallas felt a discordant note, but ignored it and let desire overwhelm him. Breathing hard, he concentrated on the pleasure of making love for the first time in years. *Maggie...Maggie.* Her name was a litany in his mind. She was incredible, beautiful, sensuous, and he wanted to sing her praises. But later, he told himself. If she didn't want to talk now, he could wait until she did.

Maggie was in a fever of longing, and she wrapped her legs around his hips to draw him deeper inside her. The wildness began again, and went on until they each cried out with the force of a simultaneous release. They were both sweating. Totally drained, Dallas collapsed upon her.

With her eyes closed, Maggie slowly regained her senses. When she could think again, her first thought was that they had made love without protection.

"Let me get up," she said frantically.

"What?" Dallas lifted his head and looked at her.

"We didn't use anything. I have to get up."

The facts of life were a cold intrusion on Dallas's mellow mood, but he moved to the bed and said, "The privy is just beyond the wood shed." He watched Maggie leap off the bed and grab the blanket he'd dropped on the floor, then added, "It's still raining. You're going to get wet again."

"So what?" she snapped, startling him. She ran for the door.

Frowning, Dallas crawled beneath the sheet on the bed, then put his hands behind his head and stared uneasily at the ceiling. She'd sounded angry, and anger was the last thing he'd expected from Maggie in the aftermath of their truly spectacular lovemaking. This should be a time of shared thoughts and ideas, a time of soft kisses and maybe some laughter. Yes, he would love to laugh with Maggie. He would love to see her relaxed and happy, even a little giddy because they had found something rare and beautiful in each other.

Outside in the privy, Maggie was tending to business with tears dripping down her cheeks. She'd reduced herself to another notch on a Fortune bedpost. What in heaven's name had come over her? Pink haze, indeed. She was the worst kind of woman there was, an easy mark. Dallas was probably smug and laughing over how easy she'd been. Well, he'd gotten what he'd so crudely said he wanted from her—and right at the moment she didn't know which of them she loathed more, him or herself.

On the way back into the cabin, she grabbed her clothes from the line. They were no longer dripping rainwater, but neither were they dry. She didn't care. She was going to get dressed and get out of this—this bordello disguised as a cabin! It would be a long walk home, but she'd make it. It was still raining, but the thunder and lightning had stopped, thank heaven.

When she walked in and saw Dallas still in bed, obviously awaiting her return for a rerun, her anger built.

"Turn your back," she demanded.

Dallas pushed himself up on an elbow. "What's going on?"

"I'm getting out of here, that's what's going on!"

"Maggie, why?" He looked confused, but Maggie saw his bewildered expression as a big act.

"I don't think I have to explain myself," she said coldly. "Fine, if you won't turn your back, I'll use the wood shed!" The little addition to the cabin had been chilly when she'd passed through it, and pulling on damp clothes would be much easier to do without a bout of shivers. But apparently it was her only choice. She started out again.

Cursing violently, Dallas threw back the sheet and followed her. She tried to slam the door in his face, but he held it open.

"You *do* need to explain yourself," he said harshly. "What in hell happened in the five minutes you were gone to cause this? You're mad as hell at me, and I have a right to know why!"

"You have a *right?* You have no rights at all where I'm concerned!"

"Maggie, I didn't force you into anything. Are you thinking I did?"

"Maybe you didn't use physical force, but you definitely took advantage of me!"

"So you bear no blame at all for making love with me? Maggie, that's a damn lie, and you know it."

"I—I was in shock," she stammered, albeit with a defiant tilt to her chin. Her voice rose. "Would you please put something on? I'm tired of seeing you naked."

Grimly, Dallas stared at her for a long moment, then let go of the door. Muttering under his breath, he went over to the blanket she'd dropped near the chair and wrapped it around himself. Then he poured out the cold coffee in his mug and refilled it from the pot on the stove. He was glad it was still raining hard. No one with a lick of sense would leave a dry cabin and set out walking in this kind of drenching rainfall, and he sure as hell wasn't going to offer to take her home on Vic, at least not until she did some talking.

Leaning against the woodwork framing a window, Dallas stared broodingly at the falling rain and thought of Sara. She had not been an on-again, off-again person. Never would she have treated him the way Maggie was doing. How could he be so wild for a woman who was so opposite to Sara?

Maggie walked in and stood near the stove to soak up some warmth. Her damp clothes were miserably uncomfortable, and she was chilled to the bone. She felt Dallas's gaze boring into her, and she finally looked back, letting the disgust she felt for herself—and for him—show on her face.

Her expression was so intense that Dallas felt as though he'd been slammed by something tangible. It angered him that she could be so loving one minute and so cruel the next.

"Just what is your problem?" he asked in a none-too-kind tone.

"My problem? Well, yes, I suppose it is 'my' problem," she said with searing sarcasm. "Fortunes don't make mistakes, do they?"

"Do you really see what happened between us as a mistake?" Dallas was dumbfounded. It wasn't as though he'd had to coax her into bed, after all. "And what does my last name have to do with anything?"

"Oh, don't play the innocent," she retorted. "I've known all my life that you Fortunes always get what you want."

"Good Lord, don't tell me that my being a Fortune is what's been causing all the friction between us! Maggie, surely you're not that petty."

She flushed, but held her ground. "Don't try to convince

me that you're not aware of who you are every minute of every day!''

"Now you're being ridiculous." Dallas drained his mug in one big swallow and set it on the windowsill. His eyes were hard as marbles when he looked at her. "In fact," he said coldly, "you're ridiculing my family name, trying to make me feel ashamed of who I am. It won't work, Maggie. I'm no more ashamed of being a Fortune than you are of being a Perez, and the simple truth is that there's no reason for either of us to regret who we are. You're weighing our value as people by net worth, and that's completely unfair. And, I might add, the worst kind of snobbery there is. I know for a fact that no one else in your family feels inferior because they have less money than the Fortunes."

"Inferior!" she cried. "Do you actually have the gall to suggest that I feel inferior to you?"

"Well, you sure as hell aren't treating me as an equal!" Dallas narrowed his eyes. "Maybe you feel *superior*. Is that it, Maggie?"

"Now who's being ridiculous?"

Dallas sighed. "Maybe we both are, but if feelings of inferiority or superiority aren't causing this ludicrous disagreement, what is?" He paused a moment, then said thoughtfully, "From what you've said so far—especially that crack about Fortunes always getting what they want—it appears to me that you're angry because you made love with a Fortune. Should I deduce that if I were anyone else—if my last name was Smith or Jones—you wouldn't be angry?"

Maggie knew she'd given herself away, and she wasn't proud of being petty and snobbish, as Dallas had said. An uncomfortable new idea crept into her mind: Was she also envious of the Fortunes' wealth? Since marrying Craig, her life had been continual financial drudgery. The divorce hadn't changed much of anything, except that when she got a paycheck now she knew she could keep it and pay the bills. When Craig had been in and out, he had often helped himself to whatever cash was in her purse, which had caused stressful, bitter arguments. At least she was freed of that particular oppression.

Dallas could see how hard Maggie was thinking. Had something he'd said gotten through to her? Was she reevaluating their relationship? God, he hoped so. He wished that she would suddenly smile and tell him that she didn't care what his name was. If she would just once admit they had something special going for them, everything would be okay. He was sure of it.

Another question had occurred to Maggie, this one even more disturbing: Had she been falling in love with Dallas all along? Why else would she have responded to him with such uncontrollable fervor?

Oh, no, she thought frantically. She wasn't perfect, far from it, and maybe, just maybe, she *was* petty, snobbish and even envious. But her disastrous marriage to Craig was proof of one unquestionable flaw in her character: she was a bad judge of men, and she should definitely look long and hard before leaping into another serious relationship. If she *had* been falling in love with Dallas, it had to come to a screeching halt, here and now.

At the very least, she had to slow things down with Dallas enough to give herself time to consider from every angle all that had happened between them. And that decision had nothing at all to do with who Dallas was; it had to do solely with who she was. It was time she figured that out. Other than Travis's mother and a member of the Perez family, who was she?

A knot the size of a fist suddenly appeared in Maggie's stomach. Why in heaven's name had she meekly accepted everything that life had thrown at her without once asking herself if she was the cause of her own misery?

Dallas could remain silent for only so long. "Maggie," he said quietly, "why don't you share your thoughts with me?"

She blinked, as though coming out of a trance. "I—I'm sorry for all the mean things I said," she said in a thin, shaky voice. "What happened here today was no more your fault than mine."

Dallas could hardly believe his own ears, but he contained his sudden elation behind a solemn expression, and walked over to her.

"Thank you for that," he said softly, and raised his hand to touch her hair.

She backed away. "No, please don't do that," she said dully.

He was startled to see tears spilling from her eyes. "Maggie, why are you crying?" Rushing forward, he put his arms around her. She tried to pull back from him, but he held on to her and cradled her head against his chest. "It breaks my heart to see you so unhappy. Honey, talk to me, please talk to me."

She knew her tears were wetting his chest, but she couldn't seem to stop crying. Even so, she had to make him understand what she was going through.

"Dallas," she said with a sob, "you have to leave me alone. I—I need time to...to think." She felt the muscles of his arms stiffen and knew he didn't understand at all. "I'm...all mixed up," she whispered. "I realized how mixed up I really am only a few moments ago. I need the time and space to—to understand myself. I'm asking you to give me those things. If you can't..."

He waited for her to finish the sentence, and when she didn't, he said sadly, "Are you saying that if I don't give you some time and space, we don't stand a chance?" He separated their bodies and took her by the shoulders so he could see her face. "Maggie, I care about you. I care about Travis. How can I stay away from the two of you? You're asking too much."

She wiped away tears from under her eyes with her fingertips. "You may visit Travis whenever you wish. He'd be heartbroken if you suddenly stopped dropping by to see him. What I'm asking is that you give *me* some room. I can't explain myself beyond that. Not today, anyway."

Dallas felt crushed. He'd believed that something beautiful and important had begun today in this little cabin, and to hear in plain language that it had only upset Maggie was a blow. He tried to bolster his flagging spirits by reminding himself that she hadn't said they stood no chance at all, that she had merely asked for time and space to sort out her feelings. But the attempt really didn't eliminate the dull ache in his chest.

Still, arguing with her about it seemed counterproductive. At least she was speaking to him now without anger. In fact, if her eyes weren't still teary, he would think she was completely emotionless.

He suddenly heard the silence. It had stopped raining; the storm was over.

"I'll get dressed," he said tonelessly. "We can leave now." He started to go to the door leading to the wood shed, but stopped before he reached it. "Take all the time you need," he said without looking at her. "I've lived through worse. I can wait."

Maggie started crying again. Yes, he'd lived through worse—*much* worse. He'd lost his wife and infant son.

"Damn, damn, damn," she said out loud, sobbing. Why was life so cruel?

* * *

Maggie rode home behind Dallas. Evidence of the raging storm was everywhere she looked. Huge puddles in low spots, broken limbs of trees lying in treeless areas—obviously blown by the fierce wind—and grass flattened to the ground as if ironed down.

But though she kept an eye peeled for her father's horse all during the ride, she never saw the mare. It worried her enough to ask Dallas, "Do you think my horse made it back without injury?"

"I hope so. Ruben prizes his horses."

"Yes, he does," Maggie agreed uneasily as a dreadful thought dwarfed her concern for the mare. If it *had* returned without her, the whole place would be in an uproar. A missing rider was no trivial matter on a ranch. Her family would be searching for her, and so would anyone else that her father could round up.

About a quarter-mile from the ranch, Dallas said, "There's your father, Maggie. And Cruz and a bunch of the men."

Maggie peered around him. "They're on foot. What are they doing?"

"I think they found your horse."

Maggie's heart nearly stopped when she saw the mare on the ground. "Oh, no," she moaned. "She's hurt."

"I think so," Dallas said quietly.

When Ruben caught sight of Dallas and his daughter, he shouted, "Maggie! You're all right!"

"She's fine, Ruben!" Dallas called.

"Thank God!" Ruben ran out to meet them.

Maggie slid from the horse's back and into her father's arms. "Papa...the mare," she said fearfully.

"You're safe and that's what matters," Ruben said gruffly.

"But is the mare hurt?"

Ruben's eyes were sad. "She has to be put down, Maggie. Her neck is broken. There's nothing we can do. It would be cruel to let her suffer any longer."

"No!" Maggie cried. Her father held her back, while Cruz fired one shot from his rifle. Totally devastated, Maggie buried her face in Ruben's shirt and wept violently. "It's my fault. I shouldn't have taken her out of the corral."

Ruben patted Maggie's back. "It was no one's fault. The storm caught us all by surprise. Come, I'll take you to the house. Cruz will handle things here." He led Maggie to his own horse and helped her mount.

She sent Dallas a teary look, and, soberly, he lifted his hand in a small wave of farewell. She tried hard to smile at him, but couldn't. Weeping into the back of her father's shirt, she said again and again during the ride to the house, "I'm so sorry, Papa."

It was a day she knew she would never forget for as long as she lived.

That night Maggie went to bed immediately after tucking Travis in. She desperately needed to be alone, and her facade of strength collapsed the second she closed her bedroom door. She'd told the story of Dallas's rescue at least three times, always stopping short of what had happened between them in the cabin, of course.

But that was the part of the day she couldn't stop thinking about. During supper, her father had been happy she was safe, but sad about the mare. Her mother had chattered practically nonstop about how she, Emma and their grandsons had weathered the storm, but Maggie had known that Rosita was talking so much because she had wanted to take her husband's mind off the lost horse. Travis's eyes had been as big as saucers throughout the meal.

"Dallas just picked you up while he was on Vic, Mama?" the boy had asked repeatedly, as though he couldn't even imagine such a remarkable feat.

"Yes, son," Maggie had answered every time.

But then Travis had altered his focus. "Grandpa, could you do that?"

Maggie had quickly intervened. "Of course Grandpa could do that. He's even stronger than Dallas is."

"He is? Are you, Grandpa? Are you stronger than Dallas?"

"That's enough questions, son. Eat your supper."

And so, when Maggie finally shut herself in her bedroom for the night, she completely gave in to the pressures and stress of the day and fell across the bed fully clothed. She was physically and mentally exhausted. She closed her eyes telling herself that she would rest but a minute and then get up and put on her nightgown.

She awoke shortly after midnight and immediately began worrying about having made love without protection. That worry went around and around with another one: Just how did a woman go about discovering who she really was? Was she hoping to find something within herself that would strengthen her self-confidence? Some redeeming quality that had so far eluded her?

Maybe there's nothing, she thought with a feeling of melancholy. Nothing but what I've known about myself all my life.

Then the sex-without-protection worry hit her again. She was making the same mistakes with Dallas that she'd made with Craig! My Lord, what if she had conceived today? Quickly she calculated dates and time, and her heart sank when she realized that she could be in her fertile period.

Another shotgun wedding would destroy her. She groaned out loud as that idea really sank in: What on earth made her think that Dallas would step up to the altar as easily as Craig had?

I care about you, Maggie. And I care about Travis.

Was it true? Dare she believe it was true? But what, exactly, did the word *care* mean to Dallas? She'd been worrying about falling in love with him, and he had talked about "caring" for her. There was a world of difference between the two terms. Certainly one person could care about another without love being anywhere in the picture.

"Oh, hell," she muttered. Switching on the bed stand lamp, she got up to find a nightgown.

Dallas, too, was trying to sort out the day's events. Wide awake and annoyed because of it, he tried to figure Maggie out. Again. Seemed to him that was just about all he did lately, he thought wryly. But how dare Maggie belittle the Fortune name, or act as though he was a womanizer just because some of the Fortune men were a little too quick to open their zippers.

If Maggie resented his wealth, they were lost. If she couldn't deal with him being a Fortune, they were lost.

But if she resented him for anything at all, why had she made such passionate love with him? She sure hadn't been resentful when she'd been under him on that bed in the cabin! When he'd been inside her and making her cry out for more....

Dallas groaned. His own thoughts were arousing him, and if Maggie were in his bed right this minute he'd prove the chemistry between them again in very short order. Why couldn't she just admit and accept their overwhelming attraction to each other? Why did she keep looking for reasons to keep them apart?

Now she needed time and space to understand herself? Bull! She was scared of commitment because her marriage to Travis's father had failed. It was as simple as that.

Why could he see that so plainly and she couldn't?

Eight

"I hate this damn place!" Clint Lockhart angrily kicked an overstuffed chair with stained upholstery and a sagging cushion. "Why can't we meet in your suite at the Austin Arms instead of a dump like this?"

Sophia Fortune impatiently rolled her big blue eyes heavenward. "Would you please stop behaving like a child? You know as well as I do that we can't be seen together. I don't like this sleazy motel, either, but it's off the beaten path and none of *my* friends would even come near a place like this." She couldn't resist giving Clint a dig. "Of course I can't speak for *your* friends," she said haughtily.

"Save that lady-of-the-manor act for someone who doesn't know you," Clint snarled. "It's wasted on me."

"My, aren't we testy tonight," Sophia drawled. It was 11:00 p.m. She had given Clint instructions to rent the motel room at 10:30, and to make sure the ice bucket was filled. She had left her car in a dark corner of the motel's parking lot, cautiously waited a few minutes until she was certain that no one had followed her, then, carrying a bottle of whiskey, she had scurried across the lot to room 10. Because she didn't trust Clint not to go through her purse, she had slid it under the seat and locked the car.

"There's not a reason in the world why you and I should be at each other's throats," she said, and slowly removed her long black coat. The black lace bra spilling her voluptuous bosom, the minuscule bikini panties, black garter belt and black hose definitely got his attention, she realized smugly, just as she'd planned. The anger remained in Clint's blue eyes—a permanent condition that she'd come to accept—but now there was also a simmering appreciation of her perfect body. She let him take a good long look, then turned to the dresser where he had placed the bucket of ice and she had set the bottle of whiskey.

Clint started walking toward her, and she laughed. "Before we get all hot and bothered, darling, let's have a drink and do some talking." She was already filling two of the disgusting plastic glasses provided by the motel with ice and whiskey. She handed him a glass and held up her own. "Cheers," she said brightly.

"Cheers, my hind leg," Clint muttered, but he took a swallow of whiskey. Looking her straight in the eye, he said flatly, "I need some money."

"Well, darling, so do I! Why else would I be suing the pants off Ryan?"

"You have money. You couldn't be living at the Austin Arms if you didn't."

Sophia sighed, looked in the mirror and pushed a curl of her strawberry blond hair back in place. "Credit cards, darling," she murmured. "I'm living on credit cards."

"You can get cash with credit cards."

"Yes, but how much cash? Three hundred? Five? Good Lord, Clint, what's a few hundred bucks? I tip my hairdresser that much every week." Sophia's face and eyes suddenly became hard as granite. "If our plan to kidnap baby Bryan had worked, we would be sharing fifty-million right now. *That's* the kind of cash I want, Clint, and by hook or by crook I'm going to get it."

"Yes, but am I?"

Sophia's hard expression changed to one of incredulity. It was a deliberate ploy; she was extremely proud of her acting ability. "Surely you haven't been thinking that I would cheat you out of your share of whatever I get in the divorce! I thought you trusted me!"

"Trust you? There's nothing I would put past you, Sophia, not one damn thing." Clint kept his gaze trained on her while taking another swallow of whiskey. "And let me tell you something that you really should pay attention to. The day you try cheating me out of anything will be the sorriest day of your life."

"Now you're threatening me?" She spoke boldly, challengingly, but a chill went up her spine, nonetheless. One of the reasons she'd gotten involved with Clint in the first place was his aura of danger. It had turned her on, along with his good looks and the fact that he hated the Fortunes far more than she did, even though he worked at their ranch. More than once she had realized that Clint Lockhart would happily throttle the Fortunes one by one with his bare hands if he thought he could get away with it.

The truth about Clint, Sophia had come to understand during their affair, was that he had despised the entire Fortune clan since early childhood, when serious financial problems had befallen his own father, and Kingston Fortune—Ryan's father—had been the highest bidder on the Lockhart's 100,000-acre ranch. Clint's grudge against the Fortunes had become an obsession by the time he turned twelve, and then to add insult to injury, both of his sisters had married Fortune men. Janine, Ryan's deceased first wife and Sophia's predecessor, had been the sister that had gotten Clint a job on the ranch, and Sophia knew now that Clint had waited years and years to exact some kind of vengeance on the Fortunes for stealing the ranch he should have inherited.

Sophia could still charm Clint into bed, and he was definitely a secret ally in her battle with Ryan over the enor-

mous divorce settlement she felt she deserved, but that was
the extent of their relationship. Truly, the subject of *trust*
was laughable when applied to the two of them. She didn't
trust Clint as far as she could throw him, but she needed
him—for the time being, at least.

But threats aside, she couldn't really believe that he
would do *her* any physical harm. After all, they were co-
horts, partners, and without her he would never get rich.
Not that she intended to make Clint rich, but she had to
keep him convinced of it until she actually got her hands
on half of Ryan's immense fortune. Clint was her pipeline
to events at the ranch, her spy, and until the divorce proceedings finally shifted in her favor, she needed him.

"Let's not threaten each other, darling," she purred.
"I'm not without contacts, as you well know, and if I believed you truly meant to harm me, you might have to start
watching your own back." She coyly flipped the collar on
Clint's shirt. "Now, let's forget all that nonsense and do
some serious talking. Tell me what's going on at the
ranch." Sophia perched herself on the end of the bed, striking a pose in her costly, sexy underwear that any man
would be hard-pressed to ignore.

Clint never tried to tell himself that Sophia wasn't the
best lay he'd ever had, because she was. Trusting her was
another matter, and more and more of late he found himself
disliking her. Even though he wanted her right now, he
didn't like her. She was a snooty bitch and thought she
ranked far above him, and no one was better than he was—
no one! Someday Sophia just might find that out the hard
way.

Still, she was the road to riches beyond his wildest
dreams, and the means to get back at the Fortunes, even if
they never did learn of the behind-the-scenes role he had
played in Sophia's demands for half of Ryan's wealth in

their divorce. It would be enough that *he* knew it, Clint had decided when this thing with Sophia first started.

Of course, that was before baby Bryan's kidnapping—that Sophia and he had engineered together—and then the botched demand for ransom, which was strictly Sophia's fault because she was the one who had hired the idiots who'd messed up the whole thing, and Clint resented her for it. In fact, he had a few things to tell her tonight about the baby that had been recovered in San Antonio, which was going to give him great pleasure.

He sank to a chair and spoke sardonically. "Everything seems to be just hunky-dory at the ranch. Ryan wants to announce his and Lily's engagement, and Lily's daughter, Hannah, is champing at the bit to get their wedding plans off the ground. From the bits and pieces of gossip I've heard, Lily is the one who's doing the procrastinating."

Sophia turned red with rage; she forgot all about her seductive pose on the bed and jumped up to pace the worn carpet. "God, how I hate them! Aren't any of them still unstrung over the kidnapping?"

"There was a lot of confusion when they discovered the baby they got back wasn't Matthew's kid." Clint smiled maliciously over the news he had to impart next. He enjoyed making Sophia squirm and this bit of information should accomplish that quite nicely. "He's a Fortune, though, 'cause he's got the birthmark."

Sophia whirled. "The strange baby has the birthmark? Are you sure?"

"It's no secret. Everybody's talking about it."

"Well, they're damn good at talking," Sophia fumed. "But are they *doing* anything?"

"For one thing, they've got Sheriff Wyatt Grayhawk investigating the identity of the mystery baby."

"They do?" Sophia's eyes narrowed thoughtfully.

"Clint, we have to be especially careful. We probably shouldn't meet at all for a while."

"Forget that notion!" Clint exclaimed heatedly. "You're not getting rid of me that easily."

"Oh, for heaven's sake, would you stop being so damn paranoid? If we play our cards right, we're each going to have more money than we could possibly spend in one lifetime." She could see the rage building in Clint, and decided it was time to change tactics. "Do you have anything else to tell me about Ryan and his precious Lily?"

"No, that's all I know."

Sophia put on a sexy smile and crooked her finger. "Then come over here and show me again what a big man you are. Wait!" she cried when another idea struck her. "What if we caused a little trouble for precious Lily?"

"What kind of trouble?"

"Oh, phone calls to Ryan's private line in the middle of the night. Hanging up if Ryan answers instead of Lily, that sort of thing. I'm sure they're sleeping together in Ryan's suite. The right kind of harassment just might make Ryan think that his precious Lily isn't a hundred percent on the up-and-up with him." Sophia laughed snidely. "I'd love to see his face when that possibility occurs to him."

Clint thought it over. "How would harassing Lily make Ryan agree to the financial settlement you've asked for? Sophia, it appears to me that you're looking for revenge because he finally kicked you out. Now, I really don't care if you want to play a few silly games with your husband, but bear in mind that the only part of Ryan Fortune I want is his money."

"That's all you ever think about—money, money, money!" she snapped.

Clint got to his feet. "And I suppose you don't?" he said icily.

Sophia saw him advancing on her, and from the flinty look in his eyes she wasn't sure if he intended to kiss her or kill her. Laughing nervously, she quickly lay down on the bed and held up her arms.

"Come on, lover, let's forget everything else and have some fun," she cooed.

"I think the evening went well, don't you?" Ryan said as he handed Lily a tulip glass of champagne. They were in Ryan's bedroom suite, having a private little celebration of Lily's birthday after the dinner party in Red Rock with her children.

Lily looked down at her glass. "For the most part, yes," she said quietly.

She'd been unusually withdrawn during their drive back to the ranch, and now she seemed to be implying that all had *not* gone well tonight. Whatever it was that was still disturbing her had gone over Ryan's head. He himself had enjoyed seeing Lily's family; the food had been good; Cole, Hannah and Maria had presented birthday gifts to their mother; and Ryan had truly thought the evening had been a success. Apparently not.

He sat next to her on the settee and took her free hand in his. "You're worried about something. What is it, Lily?"

She sighed. "I-It's difficult to talk about."

Ryan pressed on. Lily worrying about anything unnerved him, and he was determined to get to the bottom of her concern. "You hadn't seen Cole in some time. Did he alarm you in some way with a comment that I missed hearing?"

"No, it's not Cole." Whenever Cole's name came up while talking to Ryan, Lily felt as though a big hand was squeezing her heart. Ryan believed that all three of her children had the same father, Chester Cassidy, and it wasn't true. Lily knew that she had to tell Ryan everything, but so far she had not been able to reveal the secret she had guarded for more than thirty-five years: Cameron, Ryan's deceased brother, was Cole's father. Oh, how would she ever explain what had happened with Cameron to Ryan without destroying him? And what if he stopped loving her because of it?

Though guilt and fear had once again started eating her alive, Lily forced herself to go on with the conversation. "He's doing very well with his law career in Denver. He looks wonderful, doesn't he, so tall and handsome? I'm very proud of Cole. And I'm equally proud of Hannah. It—it's Maria. Ryan, did you notice how she eluded every direct question that anyone asked her? Cole said he would like to visit her at her home while he was here, and she gave him a dozen different excuses why he couldn't. I wonder if she's ashamed of where she lives," Lily mused, then added quickly, "I'm sure there is nothing wrong with the trailer she's renting, but perhaps she thinks there is."

"Lily, I've told you several times that she's welcome to move to the ranch. If she's unhappy living in an out-of-the-way trailer park near Leather Bucket, then she should come and live with us." Ryan adoringly twined a tendril of Lily's glorious hair around his forefinger. "Lily, I would do as much for your children as I would for my own. You have to know that."

"I do, darling," she said softly. "But I doubt if Maria would ever live in this house. Ryan, when I followed her to the ladies' room tonight, she told me again that you would never marry me."

"After all that's happened, she still believes that? How can she, Lily?"

"She—she's a strange girl, Ryan. She said she would only believe it when she saw it with her own eyes." Lily sighed again. "How can she be so different from Cole and Hannah? I wonder how many mothers wonder that same thing about one of their children."

Lily went on. "Looking back, Maria was always different." It flashed through Lily's mind that she was again having secret thoughts about one of her children. Not that Maria's irrational behavior and accusations through the years were anywhere near the monumental secret that Cole's birth father was. Actually, Maria's resentment of the Fortunes stemmed from her belief that one of the Fortune men had used her mother for sex, then had cast her aside when she'd become pregnant with Cole. Maria had come up with that scenario because Cole bore the Fortune birthmark, and when she had questioned her mother pointblank about it, Lily had eluded a direct answer. Her youthful past was, after all, Lily believed, none of Maria's business.

Sighing quietly, Lily went on, speaking of Maria. "She hated school and wouldn't go to college. She was forever being rude to Cole and Hannah, and to me, of course. But even knowing her as I do—or did... Ryan, I realized tonight that I hardly know her at all anymore, but there was something unusual..." Lily paused to think a moment. "I don't quite know how to describe the feelings I had tonight about Maria, but I sensed that something was terribly wrong. Ryan, I—I fear that she's in some kind of trouble. Serious trouble."

"Did you suggest such a thing when you were talking to her in the ladies' room?"

"No, she was so busy lambasting me because I'm stupid enough to believe in you that I hardly got to say a word."

"She treated me respectfully," Ryan reminded.

"To your face, yes. She knows I would not sit still if she ever did anything else. I don't believe that she wants a complete break with her family. She would not have come to dinner with us if that was her goal. But she's so...so secretive. Yes, that's the right word. She seems to be guarding a secret.''

''Well, maybe she has a right, Lily. It's possible that she's met a man that she isn't yet ready to present to the family. It could be something as simple as that making her seem secretive. Perhaps you're overly concerned about something that doesn't amount to a hill of beans.''

''Perhaps,'' Lily murmured. ''I truly hope that's all there is to it.''

Ryan smiled. ''We've been serious long enough. It's time I gave you *my* birthday present.''

''Darling, your dinner party was present enough!'' Lily exclaimed in protest.

But Ryan merely smiled again, got up, walked to a dresser and returned to the settee with a small, beautifully wrapped package. Seated again, he placed the package on Lily's lap. ''Open it, my love. I've looked forward to this moment all evening.''

When the gift was unwrapped, Lily gasped. ''Oh, Ryan, you shouldn't have!''

Ryan took the emerald-and-diamond necklace from the jeweler's box and put it around her neck. Then he sat back and looked at her. ''It's perfect on you. I knew it would be.''

Lily touched the stones in the necklace. ''It's the most beautiful thing I've ever seen, but it must have cost a king's ransom. Ryan, where and when would I wear a necklace like this?''

He drew her into his arms and lovingly kissed her forehead. ''How about on our wedding day?''

Tears crept into the corners of Lily's eyes. With all the trouble that Sophia was causing, would there really be a wedding day for Ryan and her? Lily hid her face in his shirt so he wouldn't see her teary eyes, and whispered, because she knew it was what he wanted to hear, "Yes, my darling. I'll wear it on our wedding day."

After a moment she added, "But I'd like you to keep it in your safe until then."

There was a lot of cleanup to be done in the wake of the storm, and Dallas rode his horse from one group of men to another, overseeing the work being done. The ranch's running creeks were the most serious problem, because the heavy rainfall had washed debris into them from higher elevations.

Coming up on a group of men shoveling and forking tree limbs out of one creek, Dallas saw Ruben. Dismounting, Dallas motioned Ruben over. "I just wanted to say again how sorry I am about your mare, Ruben," Dallas said.

"We both know these things happen, Dallas."

"Yes, we do, but knowing just how tough ranching can be at times doesn't make a man feel any better about putting down an animal he values. Uh, Ruben, how is Maggie doing? She took losing that mare pretty hard."

"She's still blaming herself. I told her it wasn't her fault, but it's like she isn't hearing me." Ruben took off his hat and wiped his perspiring forehead with his handkerchief. "Maybe if she heard it from someone else. Maybe if *you* talked to her," Ruben said. "Would you mind?"

Dallas looked off at the other men. Maggie had asked him to leave her be. More than asked—*begged!* He'd been steering clear of the Perez home to give her all the space she'd said she needed, even though he thought her request was a lot of damn foolishness. Maybe he didn't always handle problems in the best way himself, but he knew one thing for sure: ignoring a problem never made it go away.

The trouble with that particular axiom, of course, was

that he really didn't know with any degree of certainty what Maggie's problem was. Obviously it had to do with him, but was that because he was a Fortune or simply because he was a man she hadn't been able to resist? That very question had been part of their argument in the cabin, but Dallas still didn't know what to believe.

"Forget it, Dallas," Ruben said gruffly. "You're a busy man, and I shouldn't be laying a Perez family problem on your shoulders."

It was interesting to Dallas that he'd been thinking the word *problem* at almost the same moment Ruben was saying it.

"I'll talk to her, Ruben. I'll do it as soon as I get back to the ranch."

"Well...I appreciate your concern, Dallas, but I shouldn't be imposing on your time."

"It's no imposition at all," Dallas said, and changed the subject. "Looks like the crew is making good headway with this creek."

"It was almost dammed up tight," Ruben said. "A couple of the others are just about as bad. It was one helluva storm, Dallas."

"Yes, it sure was. I'll see you later, Ruben." Dallas climbed on his horse and rode away.

Maggie couldn't shake the effects of that stormy day. She couldn't remember ever feeling so down in the dumps before, not even on the day she'd lost her job in Phoenix, which had been one very tough nut to swallow. But she recalled herself snapping to and facing her dilemma without the awful despondency she felt now. It was when she'd decided to come home to her parents for a while, just until she got her bearings again.

Of course, she thought with no small amount of bitterness, she hadn't been worried about being pregnant then, had she? How could she have been such a fool that stormy day? Who knew better than she that making love without protection was as stupid as playing Russian roulette with a loaded pistol? Hadn't she learned her lesson with Craig? Her parents and siblings had accepted one shotgun wedding without censuring her, but a second?

Of course, she could find out for sure by borrowing her mother's car and driving to Red Rock for a visit to a drugstore to buy a home pregnancy test. And maybe she would do that, she thought, heaving a disconsolate sigh. Knowing for certain, even if the test turned out positive, would be better than what she was going through now.

Oh, Lord, what if the test *did* come out positive? She could never go to Dallas if it turned out that she had conceived! she thought, panicked by the mere thought. She would face the music on her own, even if it meant a break with her family so they would never know what had really taken place in that line shack during the storm.

A break with my family? Oh, could I really do that? Terribly disheartened, Maggie watched through a window as her son tossed his beloved lasso at the post. In the back of her troubled mind she realized that he was getting better at it, looping the post at least as often as he missed it. *Why is it that practice makes perfect in everything but human relations?*

Sighing heavily, she started to turn away from the window, but froze instead when she spotted a horse and rider coming toward the Perez house. In two seconds she recognized Dallas and Vic, and her first frantic impulse was to run. Leaving the window she dashed through the house, as though seeking a hiding place.

When her ridiculous reaction caught up with her, she was in her bedroom, breathing as hard and fearfully as a trapped animal. Then, for some reason, her mind cleared a bit. She had to get hold of herself before Dallas knocked on the door. She might feel like a trapped animal, but she certainly shouldn't let herself look like one.

Hurrying to the bathroom, she brushed her hair and put on some lipstick. Not to impress Dallas, God forbid, but just so she wouldn't give her true state of mind away by looking like she'd been moping around. Which was exactly what she'd been doing—but she certainly didn't want Dallas knowing it.

Then she waited. From outside came voices, Dallas's and Travis's, but she couldn't make out their words. And she waited some more. As the minutes ticked by, her emotions whirled within her. One second she felt hot, the next cold. If it were anyone else outside with her son, she would go out herself and get this over with, whatever "this" was.

And then she remembered telling Dallas that he could visit Travis anytime he wished, and she suddenly felt very foolish. He hadn't come to see her, he'd come to see Travis!

Collapsing on a chair in the living room, she finally admitted that her misery wasn't all caused by worry about a pregnancy that, in all probability, didn't exist. She was unhappy and restless and down in the dumps because of Dallas. Because she had memories that were almost too hot to handle. Because no matter how hard she tried not to think of him naked and on top of her on that bed in the line shack, she couldn't *stop* thinking about it.

Groaning, she covered her face with her hands. If he touched her now, she would do it again. She would open her mouth for his tongue, and open her legs for his body. Her frazzled nerves were caused by desire, not by resentment.

At long last she heard a knock on the door. Dragging

herself to her feet, she crossed the room and opened it. Dallas was standing on the porch with a sober expression on his face and his hat in his hands.

"Hello, Maggie."

"Hello."

"Could I come in for a minute? Ruben asked me to talk to you about something."

She certainly doubted the truth of that opening. Her father didn't ask other people to talk to his children. Ruben Perez was a proud man, and he would never go to his boss with a problem. If the "something" Dallas had mentioned *was* a problem, of course.

It just seemed like a trumped-up reason to talk to her, and Maggie couldn't help saying so. "My father does not ask people to talk to his children," she said coolly.

"Well, today he did. Are you going to let me come in or not? If you say no, then I'll just tell Ruben that I tried and failed. It's really no big deal, either way."

Maggie suddenly wasn't so certain. Maybe she didn't know her father as well as she thought. "Did it seem like a big deal to him?"

"It's not a matter of life and death, if that's what you're getting at. But I do believe he's worried about it."

"Papa doesn't worry," Maggie said thoughtfully. "Not that I know of. What is he worried about?"

"You."

"Me!" Oh, no, did her father suspect—or *know*—what she and Dallas had done at the line shack? Why else would he involve Dallas in a family problem? "Come inside," she said in an unsteady voice, and then stood back so he could enter. She gestured at the living room sofa. "Sit down." Her trembling legs carried her back to the chair she'd just been using.

"Does—does he know?" she asked anxiously.

Dallas frowned. "Does he know what?"

"That you and I...that we..." Maggie's face turned crimson.

Dallas finally caught on. He could easily put Maggie's fears to rest on that subject, but he decided to let her fret for a while. As uptight as she was about him and their romantic interlude in the line shack, fretting a bit just might do her some good. Actually, even though he'd never laid a hand on a woman in anger, he felt like shaking some sense into Maggie.

"Did you tell him?" he asked, frowning to add tension to his question.

"My God, no! Do you think I'm crazy? It had to have come from you. Who did you tell? Papa must have heard it from someone else." She got up to pace and wring her hands.

Dallas liked the skirt she had on. It was blue with red and yellow flowers, and it flared enticingly around her legs as she moved.

"I didn't tell anyone," he said calmly.

She whirled to a stop. "You must have! If Papa heard about it this soon, it's probably all over the ranch," she moaned.

"Well, no one heard it from me. If Ruben knows about it, then you must have let the cat out of the bag yourself."

"I most certainly did not!" Maggie frowned. "Wait a minute. You said *if* Ruben knows about it. Isn't that why he's worried about me?"

"No, he's worried about you blaming yourself because he had to put down the mare."

Maggie stared at him with her mouth open. "You deliberately led me to believe—"

Dallas got up. "Sorry, but you did that to yourself. I'll tell you something, Maggie. If everyone on the ranch knew how we'd spent our time in the line shack, I would not give a damn.'' He walked to the door, then turned around and looked at her before opening it. ''If you *are* blaming yourself for the mare's death, you shouldn't be. I can at least tell Ruben we talked about it. But I know now what you're really blaming yourself for—it's for being human and making love with a man. I know something else now, too. It wouldn't have mattered who the man was. For some damn reason you don't *want* to be human.''

Dallas looked pensive for a moment. ''What I can't figure out is, if you don't want to be human, what do you want out of life? Maybe you should try figuring that out. See you later.'' He paused one more time before leaving. ''Incidentally, you look great in that skirt. I always did like a woman to dress like one.''

Nine

Maggie tried to be as enthusiastic as her mother was about Ruben's upcoming birthday. But when she looked at the calendar during the weekend prior to the big day, all she really saw was the rapid passage of time. It worried her. Would she still be here for Christmas, still hoping to receive a job offer from a Houston bank, still on edge over Dallas, still living off her folks?

Being laid off from her job in Phoenix had been the catalyst that had brought her back to Texas and her parents' home, and only another job would give her the means to leave again. It really had been silly—and probably childish—of her to think that all her problems would disappear if she was with her family, but she had definitely left Phoenix with very high hopes.

She'd been doing pretty well, too, until Dallas entered the picture. *He* certainly wasn't her path to happiness. He hadn't even been nice the day he'd come by to talk to her about the mare. He had deliberately let her think that her father had somehow found out what she and Dallas had done the day of the storm, and then he'd had the nerve to tell her she didn't even want to be human. Maggie hated him for that, and realized for the first time in her life that it was possible to hate and love a man at the same time.

Not that the feeling she recognized as love would be cherished by any sensible, sane woman. There were no soft, sweet emotions connected to the sensation; instead she suffered a red-hot ache in the pit of her stomach that nearly drove her crazy.

She could only conclude that what she felt for Dallas wasn't the sort of love that inspired poets. What she felt was almost pornographic. Dare she even call it love?

"And so no one will be here for the weekend," Ryan Fortune explained to Rosita after telling her that he and Lily were flying to Bermuda the following day. "Since there's no reason to either cook or clean while we're away, I'm giving the entire household staff a four-day break from routine." Ryan smiled. "You, especially, deserve a nice long weekend with your family, Rosita. And with Ruben's birthday coming up, I'm sure you'll have plenty to do at home."

"Thank you, Ryan. Ruben will be pleased." Rosita frowned then. "What about Matthew and Claudia? They'll still be here, won't they?"

"Matthew and Claudia feel that they need to get away for a few days, and have made reservations at a nice resort on the Gulf. They will, of course, take Taylor with them. And they're using the Fortune airplane so they can return immediately if there is any word on Bryan. There's no reason for my other children or Lily's to visit the ranch while she and I are away, so the house is going to be quite empty. I'd like to simply close it up while we're all gone."

"Dallas will be on the ranch alone," Rosita murmured.

"Yes, but Dallas has his own home and seems to prefer being alone, Rosita. He hasn't even been much for family get-togethers since Sara died," Ryan said quietly.

"Ryan, Dallas has mourned long enough," Rosita said sadly.

"I know he has, but what I don't know is what I can do

about it, Rosita. He has to find his own way back, just as everyone does who loses a loved one.''

"That is true," Rosita murmured. "He's just so alone in that beautiful house of his. I worry about him.''

"I think we all do, Rosita.''

"Maybe he would come to my house for Ruben's birthday dinner," she mused.

"I'd be surprised if he said yes, Rosita.''

"Oh, no, Ryan, Dallas ate supper with us not too long ago.''

"He did? That's great, Rosita. How'd you get him to agree?''

Rosita smiled with motherly pride. "I'm sure he came because of Maggie.''

A slow smile appeared on Ryan's face. "Well, now, isn't that interesting?''

"It might turn out to be interesting, Ryan. It just might.''

Seated at the kitchen table and making a list of groceries needed for the birthday celebration, Rosita said casually, "Dallas will be eating dinner with us, Maggie, so there will be seven of us.''

Maggie choked on the water she was about to swallow. After coughing a few times, she asked in a thin, breathless voice, "You invited him to Papa's birthday dinner?''

"Are you all right?" Rosita asked.

"I'm fine. Mama, why did you invite Dallas?''

Rosita smiled serenely. "Because his entire family is leaving the ranch for four days, and he's going to be the only Fortune on the place. Inviting him to dinner just seemed like the right thing to do. Anyway, I had your papa ask Dallas to come, and he said yes.''

An overwhelming feeling of nature's forces working against her came upon Maggie. Obviously she could tell herself a thousand times that she would never speak to Dallas again, and nothing would come of her determination.

"For a supposed loner, he sure does show himself a lot," she said flatly.

"Now, Maggie, Dallas saved your life during that horrible storm. I can't believe you would begrudge him a fine meal."

"I don't begrudge him a fine meal, for Pete's sake! I just don't want him eating it with us!"

"Why are you so angry?"

"Because—because..." Maggie sputtered, then closed her mouth. Any anger she felt toward Dallas had to be contained. *Anything* she felt for or about Dallas had to be contained. It would not do at all for her mother to get an inkling of how far things had gone between her daughter and Dallas.

In the next heartbeat, Maggie realized that she herself was going to give it away by coming down hard on Dallas without a reason that Rosita would see as logical or deserved. She forced a smile and an apology. "I'm sorry, Mama. You have every right to invite anyone you please to Papa's birthday dinner. I'll take Travis, drive to Red Rock tomorrow and do the shopping for you."

"That would be very helpful, sweetie," Rosita said. She checked her grocery list and murmured, "Let me see now. Have I forgotten anything?"

"Travis, *please* leave that hat at home," Maggie pleaded after a simple request had merely made her small son look stubborn. "Tell you what, why don't I buy you a new one today in Red Rock. Wouldn't that be fun? Wouldn't you just love to pick out a brand-new hat?"

"I don't want a new hat. I like this one. But if you want

to buy me something, Mama, I would like some chaps, like Uncle Cruz wears.''

''Would you also like them in an extra-large size, as your hat is?'' Maggie asked dryly.

''Sure,'' Travis said cheerfully. ''Just so they're like Uncle Cruz's.''

''Wonderful,'' Maggie mumbled under her breath, realizing that the word *size* meant very little, if anything, to a five-year-old child. ''Come on, son, let's go. We have a lot of shopping to do.''

One of the items Maggie planned to buy was not on her mother's list—a home pregnancy test. Fear of a positive result made Maggie jittery, but she had to find out for sure.

It was a traumatic experience to lock herself in the bathroom and read the directions on the test box that evening, and Maggie's hands were shaking. She lowered the seat of the commode and sat on it to ponder how she would deal with a positive result. She'd previously decided that she would never go to Dallas, but looking into the face of reality, as she was doing at the moment, wasn't that a rather ridiculous decision? After all, if she was pregnant, she hadn't gotten that way by herself.

And yet, the thought of approaching Dallas with that sort of news gave her cold chills. The thought of approaching *any* man with news of that nature gave her cold chills. She'd gone through it once—with Craig—and she honestly didn't think she could do it again. Recalling Craig's initial reaction—his curled lip and sardonically raised eyebrow, as though she'd deliberately gotten pregnant to entrap him— Maggie thought of the same awful expression on Dallas's face. Oh, she would die, she thought with tears in her eyes. She would just die if she ever caused a man to display such disgust for her again. And, stupidly she'd married Craig anyway, when she and Travis would have been much better off if she'd told Craig to stuff his halfhearted, "Well, guess I'll have to marry you," up his nose and raised her son on her own.

So, no, she would not go to Dallas if the test was positive. That decision hadn't been ridiculous at all, and she would stick by it. Wiping the tears from her eyes, she took a breath to calm her distraught soul, and started the test.

A short time later she had her answer: She was *not* pregnant.

What took her totally by surprise was that she didn't feel elated. A little relieved, yes, but not at all thrilled or exhilarated. In fact, she felt rather down and strangely empty.

She simply did not understand herself, she thought, frowning intently while she got ready for bed. She didn't understand herself at all.

When Maggie got up the day of Ruben's birthday celebration, she told herself that she could deal with Dallas for one more meal, and, for heaven's sake, to relax and just let things happen. Anything else would alert Rosita, and the last thing Maggie felt she needed right now was her mother catching on to what had really taken place in that little line shack.

Quickly Maggie made her bed and picked up after herself. When the room was in order, she went to the kitchen, where Rosita was already beginning to prepare Ruben's favorite dishes. There would be no presents, everyone knew, because years ago Ruben had declared that all he wanted on his birthday was one of Rosita's delicious dinners.

"Good morning, Mama," Maggie said brightly.

Rosita looked up and smiled. "Well, you're in a good mood this morning. Is Travis up, too?"

"Not yet. Tell me what I can do to help."

And that was how the day began, with Maggie pretending a cheerfulness she was far from feeling and wondering uneasily if she could maintain that facade for hours and hours.

Cruz and Savannah arrived around noon. Incredible aromas had filled the house, and Cruz's first remark was, "Hey, it smells terrific in here. When do we eat?"

After laughter, greetings and hugs, Cruz sat in the living room with Ruben—who had the TV turned to a football game—and with Travis, who was lying on the carpet playing with a toy truck. Savannah went to the kitchen to help. Rosita assigned her the task of setting the table with the good china, and Maggie did her best to contribute to the lighthearted conversation going on while the three women worked.

In her heart Maggie was so downcast—and tense because Dallas should be coming along any minute—that she marveled at her own acting ability. Thus far no one had caught on to her true state of mind, thank God, and she laughed heartily over everything that was said that was even slightly funny.

What she didn't realize was that she was going overboard in the good-cheer department. Every so often Rosita would send her a perplexed glance, but Maggie was so determined to appear normal that she didn't notice her mother's curious glances.

Then she heard Dallas in the living room, and she stiffened. But she immediately fell back into her role-playing and went to greet him along with Rosita and Savannah. As was Rosita's way, she greeted him with a big hug and a kiss on the cheek. "We're so glad you came," she told him.

Savannah smiled at him. "Yes, Dallas, we're all very glad you could join us."

It was Maggie's broad smile that threw Dallas. She had never smiled at him like that before. When she offered her hand, he took it and gave it an intimate little squeeze, thinking to himself that she had finally decided to let herself like him. Elated over what he considered a remarkable turnabout, Dallas held her hand until she pulled it back.

Then he turned to Ruben. "Happy birthday, Ruben."

Maggie returned to the kitchen with a throbbing headache and a nervous stomach. She knew without the slightest doubt that her mother had noticed that ridiculous handholding at the front door, and probably everyone else had, as well. Once again Dallas had taken advantage of a situation, and she had been stupid enough to create one.

How was she going to keep up this charade all day?

Maggie was so relieved when the birthday cake had finally been cut and eaten that she told her mother and Savannah to join the men in the living room. "I'll clean up, Mama. You and Savannah go and enjoy the rest of the day."

Savannah said, "Maggie, there's an awful lot of cleaning up to do. Why should you do it all?"

"Because I want to. Please, Savannah, join your husband and Papa, and enjoy yourself."

Savannah remained hesitant, and Rosita murmured quietly, "Yes, Savannah, you go and sit with Cruz. I'll join you all in a minute."

"Well...all right," Savannah said reluctantly, and left the kitchen.

Maggie immediately turned to the sink and started rinsing plates for the dishwasher. She felt her mother's eyes on her back and said in the most casual way she could manage, "Really, Mama, you worked very hard cooking a wonderful dinner. You deserve a few hours of relaxation."

"All right, Maggie, out with it," Rosita said sternly. "You've been behaving strangely all day. I want to know what's going on."

"Nothing's going on," Maggie said with a laugh, and forced herself to turn around and face her mother. "And I haven't been behaving strangely. Goodness, why would you think such a thing?"

"Because I know you, Maggie, and I can tell when something is bothering you. Are you upset because Dallas is here? I know you weren't happy when I told you he was coming to dinner."

"Oh, I got over that, Mama."

"Did you really," Rosita said musingly. It wasn't a question; it was Rosita's way of conveying doubt. After a moment she said, "You hardly ate any dinner. Did you think I wouldn't notice? Maggie, if you can't talk to me, who *can* you talk to?"

"No one," Maggie said quietly as her heart sank clear to her toes. Rarely did anyone pull the wool over her mother's eyes, Maggie knew. But she couldn't stop trying to do exactly that. Picturing herself telling anyone, especially her mother, the truth of her and Dallas's relationship was a horrifying image. Besides, Maggie wasn't all that sure of what the truth really was, other than that she had given in much too easily at the line shack.

"Okay," Maggie said. "I guess I am a bit overwrought. Time is going by so fast, Mama, and I've been thinking about how long I've been here."

"So?" Rosita said suspiciously. "Why would that concern you?"

"Mama, I know that you and Papa want me and Travis to live here with you, and I know it's going to upset you both when we leave, but it has to happen. I need my own home, and…and I need a job.''

''For heaven's sake,'' Rosita exclaimed heatedly. ''*This* is your home!''

''No, Mama, it's not. This is *your* home,'' Maggie said gently.

Rosita fell silent, but looked at her daughter for a long time. She finally said, ''Your father and I are only trying to help you, Maggie. You've had a rough time of it, and we would both like to see you happy.''

''I know you would, Mama.'' Maggie smiled wistfully. ''*I'd* like to see myself happy.''

Rosita dropped her voice. ''There's a man in the next room who could make you happy, if you'd give him half a chance.''

''I'm not looking for a man to make me happy!''

''Well, maybe you should be,'' Rosita said calmly. ''Think about it. I'll go and sit in the living room so you *can* think about it.''

Groaning under her breath—she would never have the last word with her mother—Maggie tackled the stacks of dirty dishes.

When the dishwasher was crammed full, Maggie started washing the pots and pans by hand. She worked slowly, because she dreaded the moment when there would be nothing left to do in the kitchen and she would have to join the others in the living room.

She could pick up bits and pieces of conversation. The men seemed to be comparing the pros and cons of various breeds of horses, and Rosita and Savannah were chitchatting about everything from recipes to Ryan and Lily's Bermuda trip. Occasionally Travis's voice could be heard. Obviously everyone was lazily relaxed after the big meal, and enjoying themselves.

Everyone but her, Maggie thought with a soulful sigh as she began scrubbing a huge roasting pan. If her family had the slightest inkling of just how far things had gone between her and Dallas, they would be sorely disappointed in her. *She* was disappointed—why wouldn't they be?

Dammit, why had Dallas accepted Ruben's dinner invitation in the first place? What did Dallas think was going to happen between them now? Lord, he certainly wasn't hoping for more lovemaking, was he?

Maggie's stomach sank. She had to get away from him before something else did happen. Calculating her funds, she mentally split them into rent and deposits for an apartment or small house in Houston. She had enough money for that, but then what would she do for food and other essentials while she looked for a job? If it was just herself she might get by, but she couldn't let Travis go hungry, nor could she leave him alone while she job-hunted, which meant that she had to factor in the cost of an after-school baby-sitter. No, there was no way around it; she simply did not have enough money to cover it all.

Maggie was so busy thinking in painful circles and furiously scrubbing the roaster that she nearly jumped out of her skin when she heard Dallas say, "You're working awfully hard in here." He leaned his hip against the counter next to the sink so he could see her face, and he was smiling!

He thinks because I said a decent "hello" when he arrived that I'm fair game again! Maggie held back the sharp retort on the tip of her tongue, and, just to keep peace in the house, managed a smile of her own, although it was a weak effort at best.

"Someone had to do it," she said rather frostily.

Although Dallas noticed the chill in her voice, his smile never wavered. "I was thinking of taking a walk to burn off some of the calories from that huge meal. How about going with me?"

"Uh…" Now there was an intelligent response, Maggie thought disgustedly. She lifted her chin. "I really shouldn't."

"Why not?"

She took a breath. "I should spend the rest of the day with my family. With Papa. It is his birthday, you know."

"I'm sure Ruben won't mind if you're gone for an hour or so. Come on, grab a sweater or light jacket and take a walk with me."

Maggie frowned uneasily. How was she going to get out of this gracefully? If her family wasn't in the next room, she wouldn't concern herself with "graceful." She would tell Dallas in no uncertain terms that her plans for the remainder of the day did not include spending time alone with him. She might even raise her voice and ask him where in hell he got his nerve.

Searching her brain for a sensible refusal that would keep her from shrieking at him, she fell back on the promise he'd made to her in the line shack. "You said you would give me some time." The roaster was clean, she realized, and she rinsed the soap from it under the faucet and laid it facedown on the dish drainer to dry.

"Which I've done," Dallas said calmly.

Maggie dried her hands on a paper towel and then dropped it into the trash container under the sink. She reached for the bottle of lotion on the counter. "I was talking about a lot more time than a week," she said, keeping her voice down so no one in the living room would be able to hear this unnerving discussion. She would bet anything that her mother had her ear cocked, hoping to hear signs of a big romance blossoming in her kitchen.

"More time than a week," Dallas repeated thoughtfully.

"Did you mean a month? A year? Maggie, time is a precious commodity, and each day that passes is gone forever."

Maggie couldn't hold back a sarcastic retort. "Thank you for telling me that. It's something I never would have figured out for myself."

"Sorry if I sounded patronizing. I didn't mean to. I guess what I was trying to say is that people waste a lot more time than they should."

Maggie couldn't disagree with that remark—God knew how the passage of time was affecting her!—even though she knew that Dallas was not referring to her homeless, jobless predicament. In fact, unless someone in her family had told him about her dire financial straits, which she doubted, Dallas couldn't possibly know anything about her situation beyond the fact that she had come home. Didn't he ever wonder *why* she'd come home? More to the point, didn't he wonder why she was staying so long? Surely he couldn't think—as her parents insisted on believing—that she intended to live here permanently.

But wait a minute. Hadn't she mentioned that she was here on a temporary basis the very first time they had talked? Maggie tried to remember that conversation, and decided that if she had said *temporarily* to Dallas, then it hadn't sunk in. Maybe she should say it again, and do it in such a way that she was positive he got the message this time. Learning that she was going to leave at the first opportunity just might diminish his determination to further their relationship. Their *affair,* Maggie amended with a strong sense of resentment.

"Okay, fine," she said coolly. "I'll take a walk with you."

"Even though it worries you." Dallas sighed quietly. He'd thought Maggie's big smile when he'd arrived had meant something. Apparently not. But he knew exactly how to ease her concern about being alone with him. "Maggie, Travis can go with us. That should prove to you that I have nothing in mind but a pleasant walk together."

Maggie was taken aback. "You really wouldn't care if Travis went with us?" That certainly would preclude any nonsense from Dallas, all right.

"Not at all," Dallas said firmly.

Maggie's mind raced. With Travis along, would she be able to talk freely about her plans to leave the ranch the very minute that departure was feasible? On the other hand, Travis didn't just walk during a stroll. He ran this way and that, picking up and flinging rocks, running ahead, or stopping to inspect an anthill or anything else that caught his eye. And it wouldn't take long for her to tell Dallas the facts of her life—probably no more than a couple of minutes.

"All right," she said. "I'll go and get jackets for Travis and me." She left Dallas alone in the kitchen and hurried to her son's bedroom, then her own. Actually, she reasoned, taking a walk would be better than sitting in the living room with everyone hanging on her and Dallas's every word and gesture. By now Rosita had probably hinted to Cruz and Savannah—or even told them outright—about her hope of a romance developing between Dallas and Maggie.

Carrying the two jackets, Maggie returned to the kitchen. Dallas smiled and followed her to the living room. Instantly Maggie saw Travis sleeping on the sofa, and she stopped in her tracks.

Rosita held a finger to her lips. "Speak quietly. He just fell asleep a few minutes ago, and we shouldn't wake him." Her gaze fell on the jackets Maggie was holding, and she smiled brightly. "Are you going somewhere?"

"For a walk," Dallas said.

"Wonderful! I hope you have a nice time. Maggie, give me Travis's jacket. I'll put it away."

Maggie experienced a sudden desire to cancel the walk, but decided that doing so now would only make her look foolish. Dammit, why did everything work out to Dallas's benefit? Now he would be able to say anything he wanted to her, or to try anything. But the worst part of being alone with him was that she didn't trust herself any more than she trusted him.

Ten

Once outside and walking, Maggie was glad she'd agreed to accompany Dallas, whatever his motive. The big storm had ushered in a weather change; there'd been a definite chill in the air ever since. But after the warmth of the kitchen, the cooler temperature felt good to Maggie, and she breathed deeply of the revitalizing fresh air. Dallas headed down the Perez driveway, and since Maggie didn't care in which direction they walked, she kept stride.

It surprised her that Dallas didn't immediately strike up a conversation, and, in fact, seemed content to merely walk along beside her. But Dallas's silence gave her the time to think of how best to introduce the topic of her pending departure. *Just say it and get it over with.* Of course that was what she should do, she thought. So why did she suddenly feel as though it was a subject that should be tactfully broached? Did she care how he might take her news?

And then, for some reason, she remembered that he hadn't only saved *her* life; it was quite likely that he'd saved Travis's that first day. At the very least he had prevented possible injury for each of them. Of course both incidents had been purely accidental. That was to say, Dallas's Johnny-on-the-spot rescues certainly hadn't been planned. It had been pure chance that he'd happened along when Travis climbed to the top rail of the corral fence, and then again when she'd been on foot during the worst electrical storm of the year.

Oh, it was all so confusing, Maggie thought unhappily. The gratitude she felt for Dallas's having saved her son from what could have been a disastrous fall, and then for his generous disregard for his own safety to get her under cover during the storm was all mixed up with regret that she'd made love with Dallas. Why *wouldn't* he believe that her response that day had been the start of an affair between them? Yes, she'd tried to rectify the damage afterward by doing some fast talking, but babbling about needing time to sort through her feelings had really been nothing more than a ruse to keep him from catching on to just how mortified she'd been by her own behavior.

And now she was involved—with a Fortune! It really didn't seem possible. Sneaking a quick glance at Dallas, Maggie's spirits dropped another notch. It hurt terribly to realize that if he wasn't a Fortune and one of the wealthiest men in Texas she just might be thrilled with their involvement. If he were an ordinary man she might even be thinking of a future together.

But there was nothing ordinary about Dallas. Not only was he rich beyond belief, but he was a member of a family that wielded enormous power in the state, and he was also the most handsome man she'd ever known. He had everything going for him—why on earth had he even noticed her? *To take you to bed, you ninny! And you let it happen. Not only that, but you'd like it to happen again.*

It was the painful truth. That almost constant ache in the pit of her stomach could not be construed as anything but what it was: desire for a man she could never have. Her, Maggie Perez, join the Fortune clan? What a laugh that idea was. She would never fit in. She wouldn't even know how to *try* to fit in.

Sighing to herself, she sent Dallas another glance. This time she took note of his clothes—great-looking western-cut pants and shirt—and frowned. "Aren't you chilly? Where's your jacket?"

"I didn't bring one with me. Since I drove over, I didn't think I would need one. It is a little chilly, all right. Maybe we should detour to my house so I can pick one up."

"Fine," Maggie agreed. It still didn't matter to her where their walk took them. She made up her mind. Right after Dallas picked up his jacket, she would tell him how determined she was to leave the ranch and get back to her own life. He really had no choice but to accept her plans, so it was silly of her to even wonder how he might take hearing about them.

Dallas interrupted her thoughts. "I'd like to repay your parents for inviting me to dinner today," he said. "Do you have any suggestions as to how I could do that?"

"Repay them? I'm sure neither of them are expecting any sort of payment for a simple dinner invitation. And Papa frowns on birthday gifts."

"I don't consider their generosity simple, Maggie, and I know Ruben's views on birthday gifts. It's why I didn't bring one with me. But I still think some sort of thanks for dinner is called for. Do they enjoy good wine? I could bring them a bottle. Or flowers? Maybe Rosita would enjoy a nice bouquet of flowers. I could phone a florist in Red Rock and have them delivered."

"I suppose Mama would be pleased to receive flowers, but, believe me, it's not at all necessary."

"Maybe I should do both—wine for Ruben and flowers for Rosita. Yes, that makes sense. I'll see to it tomorrow." *And maybe something for Maggie, as well. And for Travis.* Dallas was glad he'd thought of it. If he entertained at home, he would ask them all to his house for a meal, but since he hadn't invited even one person to his home since

Sara's death, he was so out of practice that he wasn't sure he would even remember how to be a good host.

Approaching Dallas's home, Maggie couldn't help admiring it. It was a lovely house with beautiful landscaping and that lovely little gazebo. She wouldn't let herself even dream of living in a house like this one day, because she knew in her heart it would never happen. Actually, her dreams were as ordinary as she was, she realized—just a nice little house, a good job and maybe someday a second marriage to a decent man. A decent, *ordinary* man.

"I'll wait in the gazebo while you get your jacket," she told Dallas.

There was no good reason for her to wait outside that he could think of. "Maggie, please come inside while I get a jacket." There was something in her eyes—a reluctance— and he added, "You're not afraid to be alone with me, are you?"

"Don't be absurd," she snapped.

"Yes, it would be absurd, wouldn't it? Come inside. I'll only be a minute."

Bravely lifting her chin to prove how absurd the idea of her being afraid to be alone with him really was, she followed him in. It was a gorgeous house right from the front door, and she furtively looked at everything she could see as he brought her to the living room.

"Go ahead and sit down," he told her. "Would you like something to drink?"

"No, I'm fine." Maggie sat on the sofa, and when Dallas left the room she permitted her gaze to wander. It was tastefully furnished and decorated, but she had expected that. What really caught her eye was the painting hanging above the fireplace: a portrait of a lovely young blond woman. *Sara,* Maggie thought, feeling as though the last drop of blood had just drained from her body. Dallas was still in love with his deceased wife. It wasn't just her, Maggie Perez, who didn't stand a chance with Dallas Fortune. No woman did!

Oh, she was so right not to look for anything real or enduring from Dallas. And she'd been such a fool with him, such a terrible fool. But never again, no matter how long she was trapped at the ranch.

Dallas returned with his jacket and was shaken by the resentful look Maggie laid on him. He could not stop himself from asking, "Maggie, are you still angry with me? I thought from the way you greeted me today that that was over, but it isn't, is it?"

Honesty was all she had left. "No," she said dully, "it's not over. But let me add something to that statement. I'm also angry with myself, probably even more so than I am with you. And my anger doesn't stop there, either. I'm angry because the bank I was working for in Phoenix laid me off. Not because I was a bad employee, but because the new owners of the bank were bringing in their own people. And I'm angry because none of the banks in Houston to which I sent my résumé have contacted me with a job offer. I could go on," Maggie said bitterly.

"Go ahead," Dallas said quietly as he sat on a chair facing the sofa. He wanted to hear it all, everything that made Maggie the distant, angry woman she persisted in being.

"All right, but don't say you weren't warned. I'm angry because my marriage was such a bust, and because my ex-husband didn't love his son enough to pay child support. Instead he chose to give up all parental rights to Travis."

"You don't mean it!" Dallas looked stunned.

"Oh, don't look so shocked. There are lots of deadbeat parents in this miserable world, both mothers and fathers.

Good grief, what kind of cocoon have you been living in?''
Maggie looked scornful.

"You're right, you know. I have been living in a co-coon,'' Dallas said with a troubled frown. "Or rather, I was. Until I met you again, I was.''

"And now I'm supposed to believe that meeting me again made some kind of difference? For heaven's sake, Dallas, I wasn't born yesterday,'' Maggie said disgustedly. "You let me know from the first what you wanted from me, and it was hardly an indication of a high-minded trans-formation.''

"It was one of the worst mistakes of my life, and I'd give anything if you could forget the way I talked to you that day.''

"Sorry, but some things just aren't forgettable.''

"True,'' Dallas murmured. "For instance, I could never forget you.''

"Well, that statement is going to be put to the test,'' she drawled sardonically. "When I find a job in Houston, Travis and I will be moving.''

"Cruz thinks you came home to stay.''

"So do my parents. Even though I told them that this was just a visit, they refuse to face it. There's another rea-son for my anger,'' Maggie said harshly. "I'm living off my folks, and I feel guilty as hell about it.''

Dallas sat back in his chair and tented his fingers about chest level. "So, what it boils down to is that you're angry at just about everyone and everything.''

"Close,'' Maggie admitted.

"Well, at least you didn't single me out.''

"No, you singled *me* out, and you managed to get what you wanted, didn't you? How is it that even nature is on your side? Without that storm I would never have gone to that line shack, and we never would have——'' Maggie stopped short of using an explicit vulgarity.

"We made love," Dallas said softly. "Don't you dare call it anything else."

Maggie's face got red, but her courage wasn't yet entirely destroyed. "Whatever name you give it, we did it without protection," she said defiantly, suddenly hit with an incredibly strong urge to scorch him with the facts.

But she'd already told Dallas more than she should have——spewing her anger had been especially unnecessary——when all she'd planned to say was one thing: I'll be leaving the ranch. While she'd emphasized that point, it hadn't seemed to affect Dallas all that much. Obviously he didn't believe it, just as her family didn't believe it. What was wrong with everyone? Did they think she was talking just to hear her own voice? Couldn't anyone grasp how important self-sufficiency was to her?

"Yes," Dallas said thoughtfully. "We did take a chance, didn't we?"

Maggie's thoughts had gone so far afield that it took a moment for her to align them with Dallas's comment. "Uh...yes, we did," she stammered. She fell silent when she saw how hard Dallas was thinking. It could only be about them, and she didn't want to hear any phoney excuses or remarks. Hastily she got up from the sofa. "I'm going to go," she said, wishing she hadn't come into his house for even a minute.

Frowning, Dallas got to his feet. "I'll go with you."

"I'd rather do a little walking by myself, if you don't mind." Her tone of voice indicated that she didn't care if he did mind.

Maggie started to leave, and all Dallas saw was her walking out of his life again. He rushed forward, took her arm in a firm grasp and forcibly turned her around to face him.

The look of surprise on her face was too apparent to miss, but he couldn't just let her leave with nothing resolved between them. He'd thought he'd been making some real headway when she opened up and talked about her reasons for being angry, but Maggie could turn on a dime, he realized, and he still had no idea why she was so angry with him. Oh, he had a few vague suspicions, like the fact he was a Fortune, for instance. But they'd talked about that in the line shack, and it was such a ludicrous reason for anger that he couldn't accept it.

"I don't want you leaving yet," he said, looking directly into her face. He loved her beautiful dark eyes, but probing their seemingly endless depths provided few clues to her inner self. Then he noticed the sardonic twist to her lips.

"And, of course, you always get what you want," Maggie retorted. He was too close to her, and she tried to shake off his hand. "Let go of me, Dallas," she said threateningly, worried sick that if he didn't let go of her, she might do something foolish again. He had a powerful hold on her emotions. It was bad enough that she had admitted to herself her physical attraction to him; she certainly didn't want to do so with him all but breathing in her face.

"No, I do not always get what I want. Dammit, Maggie, where do you get such crazy notions?"

"So now I'm crazy?" she shot back. "Is everyone crazy who doesn't snap to when you want something, Dallas, or is it just me?"

"I can tell you one thing, Maggie. You're the only person driving me crazy!"

"Thank you. You're very kind."

"Cut the sarcasm, Maggie. I know now that it's something you retreat behind when you don't know how to deal with a situation. Am I making you nervous, Maggie? Am

I standing too close to you? Are you remembering what making love with me was like?"

She gasped. "That's ridiculous!"

"Like hell it is. We got along great in bed, and you know it. What I can't figure out is why we don't get along as well out of bed."

"Don't strain yourself with that one, Dallas. I simply do not like you." Her own words stunned her, but what could she do about them now? They'd been said, and she could see in Dallas's eyes that the possibility had never occurred to him. She felt awful for saying something that wasn't even remotely true, and she looked away from the pain on his face, the pain she had inflicted with a lie.

It took Dallas a few moments to recover from the blow she'd just dealt him, and he came out of it a different person. Suddenly he was a man who could fight back, who could say things that he knew would hurt her as badly as she'd hurt him.

"In that case, I guess I should assume that you don't have to like a man to sleep with him," he said, jerking her forward so that she was pressed tightly against his chest.

"Don't!" she cried.

"Why in hell not? We had fun that day in the line shack, didn't we? Don't bother to lie about it. A man knows, Maggie, and you were with me every step of the way that day. Let me say it plainly. I'm good and ready for a rerun. How about you?" His mouth covered hers in a rough and punishing kiss; he'd given her no chance to answer.

Maggie's heart started pounding. She knew she should be furious and fighting him, but all she wanted to do was to lose herself in his arms. Hadn't she thought of this a hundred times since the first time? Hadn't she restlessly rolled and tossed in her bed at night, remembering every detail of his body and how it had felt against hers? How he felt inside her?

When Dallas realized that she was kissing him back with the same abandonment she'd shown him in the line shack, he gentled his kisses. That was Maggie's undoing. She tried to get rid of her jacket without disrupting the passion between them. Dallas caught on to what she was doing and helped her shed the garment. Then, without one word of warning, he picked her up and started carrying her toward his bedroom.

Keeping her eyes tightly shut, Maggie said nothing. She couldn't. She wanted what Dallas did, and she feared that if she said anything at all, it would be something negative. In her soul she knew she shouldn't be doing this and that she would regret it horribly after it was over. But as inundated with desire as she was right then, regret seemed like a small price to pay for another glimpse of heaven.

And then Maggie opened her eyes at a fateful moment. Dallas was carrying her past the fireplace, and above it, the portrait of Sara Fortune seemed to be looking directly at them. Maggie's heart nearly stopped beating, and she started struggling.

Perplexed, Dallas stopped walking. "What's wrong?"

It took Maggie a second to catch her breath. But then she spoke pleadingly, "Please put me down. I—I can't do this. Not with—with her...watching us."

"What are you talking about? Who's watching us?" Dallas actually looked around the room, half expecting to see someone there. Then he caught on: Sara's portrait.

The steam he'd worked up suddenly deserted him, and he let Maggie's feet slip to the floor. She teetered a moment, then turned and walked away from him. Dallas stood where he was and looked up at the portrait. Heaving a long, soulful sigh, he moved closer to Maggie, who was fumbling with her jacket, trying to put it on.

He helped her into it, then dropped his hands and stepped back. "I don't think I'll be going back with you," he said quietly.

She nodded and wished to God that she could stop the tears that were threatening. Dallas disappeared for a minute and returned with a handful of tissues, which she gladly accepted. Wiping her eyes, she managed a few hesitant words. "I—I'm terribly embarrassed."

"You're embarrassed and I'm sorry. We're a fine pair, Maggie. It appears that neither of us is ready for a new relationship, doesn't it?"

He sounded sad and a little lost to Maggie's ears, and she realized that she felt almost the same sense of desolation.

"It...appears so," she whispered hoarsely. Wiping her eyes again, she stuck the damp tissues in a pocket of her jacket. "It's best if I leave now."

Dallas didn't disagree. "Would you tell your folks 'thanks' for me? And if they wonder why I didn't return with you, tell them..." Dallas paused to think, then said, "Tell them the truth, if you want."

"The truth? No, I don't think so." Maggie started for the door.

"'Bye, Maggie," Dallas said in that same saddened voice.

She left Dallas's house without answering, and she walked away from it with her head down.

Maggie hiked around until the chill in the air began penetrating her clothes. Then she returned to her parents' house and went in by the back door. Quietly she tiptoed to her bedroom and silently shut herself in. Placing her jacket on a chair, she lay on the bed and stared at the ceiling.

A burst of laughter in the living room breached the walls of her private domain. Obviously her family was still having a good time, still enjoying the day.

Maggie heaved a sorrowful sigh. She'd never felt more alone than she did at this moment. Her list of worries and problems could only be solved by her. She could not burden her family with her troubles, especially her parents. They were good and honest people, and they would never understand why she wasn't the same. They especially would not understand why she had made love with Dallas if she wasn't in love with him.

Tears filled her eyes again. All along she had known—or at least suspected—that Dallas felt nothing for her but lust. Now there was no room at all for doubt; he'd said it right to her face. *It appears that neither of us is ready for a new relationship.*

And she hadn't had the courage to refute his observation by telling him that she ardently hoped someday to find the right man and marry again. There really would have been nothing wrong with saying, *Speak for yourself, Dallas. You might be satisfied living with memories of your deceased wife, but I do not intend to spend the rest of* my *life alone.*

''Oh, God,'' she whispered as anguish inundated her system. As difficult and painful as it was to face, she had fallen in love with Dallas Fortune. She was in love with a man who didn't now nor ever would love her. She could no longer argue herself out of the feeling; she would just have to learn to live with it, because she knew in her soul that it wasn't going to disappear just because she wished it would.

Some way, somehow, she had to find the means to leave the ranch. Just because Dallas couldn't commit to any sort

of permanent relationship didn't mean that he might not try
to further their sexual entanglement.

After all, he was still a Fortune and accustomed to having
things go his way.

Eleven

Long after Maggie had gone, Dallas sat in his living room and looked at the portrait of Sara. It was an excellent likeness and a good piece of art. He remembered when Sara had sat for it, at his request, and how she had complained about doing nothing for hours on end while the artist worked. Dallas also recalled teasing her and making her laugh over her own complaints, but tonight, dredging up memories while studying the portrait, he finally admitted that Sara's impatience with inactivity had caused her own death.

It was a chilling thought, but if she had listened to her doctors and heeded their advice to stay off the horses, to stop rushing around at top speed and to spend most of her time in bed, or at least resting, she would be alive today. And, in all likelihood, so would his son.

For the first time since the double tragedy, Dallas let a clearly defined resentment roll through his system. An anger that Sara and their child had died needlessly. For the first time he admitted that Sara had *not* been perfect. She'd been stubborn and willful and defiant, all but daring fate every time she'd climbed on a horse, or played a rousing game of tennis, or dived into chores that she'd had no business even worrying about. How many times had he reminded her that she shouldn't be doing something, and how many times had she told him that she was fine, and for him to stop mother-henning her?

Why in heaven's name had she believed in her own immortality, and treated her pregnancy so cavalierly? They had wanted to have children so much, and when she'd finally become pregnant, they had celebrated and made wonderful, enthusiastic plans for their child's future, telling each other that this baby would be the first of many. But then when it became apparent that her pregnancy was not normal, and Dallas had pleaded with her to stay in bed, she'd ignored everything he and her doctors said to her. She'd done exactly as she pleased.

Dallas realized that he was undergoing some sort of metamorphosis, and he broodingly stared at the portrait while facing the truth, after two years of pain-studded, guilt-ridden grief. It hurt, it hurt terribly, but he could no longer think of Sara without resenting her selfish disregard for their child and for him.

But he didn't want to live with resentment any more than he wanted to live with grief, and he forced it from his mind. What good would it do to resent Sara now? That chapter of his life was over. It was time he moved on.

Dallas took a sip from his glass of scotch and water, and wondered what had caused this incredible change in him. Maggie? Yes, it had to be Maggie, he decided. Maggie—so beautiful and passionate...and so filled with anger over life's inequities that she couldn't see the forest for the trees. He'd been the same—or almost the same. Their reasons for misery were different, but the results were similar.

Or they had been, Dallas amended. He was no longer angry, guilty or remorseful over Sara's death. It hadn't been his fault, it had been hers. He realized that he felt alive again, and it was an exhilarating sensation.

He sat there for a few more minutes, then made a decision that was long overdue. Setting his glass on the table next to his chair, he got up, went to the garage and returned with a stepladder and a box of oversize trash bags. When the painting was down and in one of the trash bags, he took the box and went to the second walk-in closet in the master bedroom. It was full of Sara's things, exactly as it had been the day she died. He started filling bags, and he didn't stop until the closet was empty.

His final chore was to comb the house and remove every other reminder of Sara. When he was finished, he toted a dozen bulging bags to the garage. He would dispose of them tomorrow.

He would remember the good and forget the bad, he vowed. And he slept better that night than he had in years.

Dallas was more fortunate than Maggie; she slept fretfully that night. Her mind wouldn't shut down, and her many problems and worries kept going around and around in her brain until she thought she would scream. Just before dawn an idea came to her, and she hopped out of bed, got dressed and left the house.

Maggie caught Cruz just as he was climbing into his pickup to go to work. Out of breath from running between her parents' house and Cruz's cabin, she asked, "Cruz, could you spare me a few minutes? I need to talk to you about something."

Cruz glanced at his watch, then nodded. "Sure. What's up?"

"I—I need to borrow some money."

A serious light entered Cruz's dark eyes. "How much money, Maggie?"

"A thousand dollars." Quickly she added, "I could probably get by on eight hundred. I would pay you back, Cruz. Not right away but...eventually." *Eventually* was such a nebulous word, she realized uneasily, but what other word could she use when getting started in Houston was such an unknown? It could be months before she reached the point of having extra money to start paying off a loan.

Cruz looked away for a moment, then brought his gaze back to his sister. "I could get the money for you, Maggie, and I will if it's really necessary, but Savannah and I have been saving every dollar for our own ranch and horse-breeding operation. Even with Dallas's investment, it's going to take everything we can scrape together to stay afloat until the ranch starts showing a profit."

Maggie's stomach sank. "I understand. I shouldn't have laid this on you, Cruz, and I'm sorry I did." She smiled at her brother, a weak effort at best. "Thanks for listening, though." She started to walk away.

"Maggie, what do you need the money for?" Cruz called.

"Nothing important. Please forget I even mentioned it." She could feel her brother's eyes on her back and knew that she'd troubled him, which in turn troubled her.

She could only hope that Cruz was too busy to look for the real reason she'd asked for a loan, because she didn't want their parents hearing about it. Rosita and Ruben were both so firmly set against her leaving at all.

She couldn't give up, though. She had to find a way to get away from the Double Crown Ranch.

And away from Dallas Fortune.

During breakfast with her mother and Travis—Ruben had eaten much earlier—the urge to get away from the ranch became so strong that even a short drive looked good to Maggie.

When Travis had finished his cereal and run outside to play, Maggie broached the subject. "Mama, I know you're very busy, but would you mind keeping an eye on Travis for a few hours while I take a drive to Red Rock? I'd have to borrow your car, of course. If you have plans of your own, please don't hesitate to say so.''

''I have no plans and I wouldn't mind watching Travis in the least,'' Rosita replied with a smile. ''Feel free to take the car and enjoy yourself. You've hardly gone anywhere since you came home.''

''Thank you, Mama.'' Maggie sighed. It was going to feel so good to go off by herself for a few hours, and maybe a change of scene would open her mind to new and feasible solutions for her financial quandary.

''Maggie, where did you and Dallas go yesterday? I wanted to ask about your walk when you got back, but not in front of Cruz and Savannah. And then the day just sort of slipped away.''

Maggie thought a moment. There really was no reason to lie about yesterday's walk; she'd done nothing wrong, after all, even if she had come close to another mistake with Dallas. ''Well, we hadn't walked very far when Dallas decided to go to his house and pick up a jacket.''

''Oh, you went to his house?'' Rosita looked extremely pleased. ''Did you go inside?''

Maggie cleared her throat. ''Just for a few minutes.''

''Isn't it grand?'' Rosita asked, sounding as proud of Dallas's beautiful house as if it were her own.

''It's very nice,'' Maggie said quietly. And then she added, probably because it had remained in her mind, ''His wife's portrait is still hanging above the fireplace in the living room.''

Rosita sipped her coffee, frowned a bit and then said, ''Yes, I know. For his own peace of mind Dallas should have taken that painting down a long time ago.''

''Why would he do that when he's still in love with Sara? Mama, he's never going to get over Sara. You really should accept that and stop trying to throw Dallas and me together.''

''I can't accept it, Maggie. Dallas is too young a man to give up on life. Losing Sara and his child was a terrible tragedy, and I fully understand why it hit him so hard. But he almost completely withdrew into himself, and that's wrong for anyone to do. Yes, he had every right to mourn, but there's a limit, Maggie, and I firmly believe he finally reached it.'' Rosita smiled. ''I think he realized it himself when he met you again.''

''If he did, why didn't he take down Sara's portrait? No, Mama, in this case you're very wrong. No one is ever going to replace Sara for Dallas. Especially not me,'' she added after a brief pause.

''There you go again, thinking you're not good enough for a Fortune! Maggie, you're good enough for any man, and I will never understand why you feel that you're not. Goodness, the Fortunes might be wealthy, but they're not snobs. And if Dallas felt the way you do, do you think he would invest in Cruz's future, or even set foot in this house? If Dallas had never had a penny, he'd be the same man that he is today.''

''I'm sorry, but I don't agree,'' Maggie said quietly. She got up and started to clear the table.

''Leave this. I'll take care of it later,'' Rosita said rather sharply, startling Maggie into sitting down again. ''Now you listen to me, young woman. I know Dallas much better than you do, and he did not suddenly start coming to this house because of your papa or me. He came because of you. And because of Travis. He likes both of you, Maggie, and it's just as important for a man to like your son as it is for him to like you.''

''Mama,'' Maggie said with a long-suffering sigh. ''We've already had this conversation.''

"Yes, we have, but apparently it did no good the first time around. You've got some very silly notions about what makes Dallas tick, Maggie, and you're so wrong that it breaks my heart."

Maggie lifted her chin. "That portrait of Sara is not a figment of my imagination, Mama."

"Of course it's not, but until you came along Dallas had no reason to stop living in the past. Goodness, child, Dallas doesn't think you're not good enough for him. That ridiculous idea is only in your own head and is a figment of your imagination."

Maggie wanted to say, *Dallas thinks I'm good enough to take to bed, Mama, and that's all he wants from me. Knowing that, do you still believe he's so wonderful?* But she couldn't, because if she did, Rosita would ask why she felt that way, and Maggie would have some tall explaining to do.

"Mama," she said wearily, "let's not talk about it any more this morning. I'm sorry, but I simply cannot see Dallas the way you do."

"You're making a mistake, Maggie."

Maggie got to her feet. "It wouldn't be my first, Mama."

"She means well," Maggie said under her breath while driving toward the town of Red Rock. In all her life Maggie had never doubted her mother's love, and even though she wished her mother would stay out of it, she understood Rosita's reason for pushing her about Dallas. Rosita wanted very much to see Maggie happy, and she also wanted to see Dallas happy. In Rosita's mind, her daughter and Dallas Fortune were perfect for each other, and Rosita Perez had never been shy about speaking her mind.

"But she doesn't know Dallas as I do, and I can't explain his true colors," Maggie mumbled.

She was almost to Red Rock before she was able to shake off the aftermath of that disturbing breakfast-table discussion. But finally she was able to enjoy seeing the passing countryside, and her burden of worries seemed to get a bit lighter.

It was a sunny day, cool but pleasantly bright. Maggie had worn her dark glasses for the drive, and she had on a dress that she liked. It was a straight-line dress from shoulders to hem, nothing fancy, but Maggie loved the deep rose color and the fact that it had a matching jacket. She really didn't know why she had dressed up for just a simple drive, but she felt good about looking good, and by the time she reached the outskirts of Red Rock, her entire mood had mellowed.

Slowly she cruised the streets of Red Rock, noticing that the town had changed very little during her absence. There were a few new buildings on the main business thoroughfare, and when she drove through some residential areas, she saw several new housing developments. But on the whole Red Rock was the same pleasant little town she remembered it to be. Returning to the business area, Maggie found a parking place and got out to stroll and to look into store windows.

Passing a restaurant, she stopped to read the sign in its window: Waitress Wanted—Come inside and ask for Joe.

Maggie's heart skipped a beat. There were jobs to be had in Red Rock! Here was one staring her right in the face. If she had any kind of job, wouldn't she be able to save enough money to eventually make the move to Houston?

But then reality struck. Her mother worked; there was no one to take care of Travis. And if Maggie had to pay for child care, how much would she be able to save from a waitress's income? She had worked as a waitress during her college years, and without very good tips, waitresses didn't make much money. Besides, she had no transportation of her own, and she couldn't separate Rosita from her car by borrowing it five days a week.

Frowning intently, Maggie continued on down the sidewalk. She'd been so thrilled to come home and see her family, and her visit had backfired dreadfully. Now she was trapped on the ranch, and no matter how hard she tried to find a way to get back to her former independence, every solution she came up with had its own set of drawbacks.

It was not fair—not fair at all.

The first thing Maggie saw when she got home was Dallas and Travis playing in the yard with an adorable little cream-colored puppy. Travis was rolling around on the ground, giggling almost hysterically as the puppy leaped on top of him and licked his face.

A discomfiting premonition suddenly felt like a fist in Maggie's stomach, but she couldn't let herself quite believe it, and she climbed out of the car, calling a ''hello'' to her son. Travis was giggling too hard to answer, but Dallas waved, grinned and returned her greeting. Maggie walked up to the trio with a forced smile.

''Looks like you're having fun,'' she said coolly to Dallas. ''I hope this is your puppy.''

''He's mine, Mama,'' Travis gasped between giggles. ''Dallas gave him to me.''

If looks could kill, the one Maggie laid on Dallas would have withered him into a small pile of ashes. ''How dare you?'' she whispered furiously.

''Every boy needs a dog,'' Dallas said congenially.

''But not every mother does, you...you...'' She couldn't think of a vile enough name to call him. Now she had a dog to contend with, and most rental agencies and homeowners demanded a very high deposit if a would-be renter had a pet. "Take it back," she hissed through clenched teeth.

"Take that puppy away from Travis? *You* tell him he can't have Baron. That's the pup's name."

"I don't give a damn what his name is. You had no right to give my son a puppy without first talking to me about it."

"Oh, give it a break, Maggie," Dallas said disgustedly. "If you're not mad at me for one reason, you're mad about something else. Look at how happy that puppy is making Travis. Doesn't that count for anything?" Before Maggie could answer, he changed the tone of his voice. "You look very beautiful in that dress, sweetheart. Would you do me the honor of having dinner with me tonight?"

Sweetheart? Dinner? Maggie suddenly felt like screaming. Despite her ongoing objections, Dallas continued his invasive tactics. Giving Travis that puppy was unforgivable. But of course she couldn't take the puppy away from her son now. Any fool could see that Travis was already madly in love with the wiggly little pup.

She almost said, "Don't call me sweetheart," but what good would it do? Dallas did as he pleased, and apparently—at this particular time—his pleasure was derived from making her crazy. All she could really do was to suffer his attentions until he found someone else to torment.

But dinner? No, she didn't think so.

"Sorry, but dinner is out," she said coldly, and spun on her heel to march into the house.

Rosita rushed her. "Wait till you see! Everything's in the kitchen. Come along."

Maggie let herself be dragged by the hand to the kitchen. And there, on the kitchen table, were two immense bouquets of roses—one red, one white.

"Yours are the white ones," Rosita told her excitedly. "Read the card."

Reluctantly Maggie took the card and read it.

Maggie,
Maybe these roses will express my thanks for so many things, although nothing speaks as well as words from the heart. Please have dinner with me tonight. We have much to discuss.

                                                           Dallas

"Well?" Rosita said, grinning from ear to ear.

"You already read it?"

"I couldn't resist. And look, Maggie, he brought me the red roses and your papa three bottles of excellent red wine. My, he's a generous young man."

"He also brought that puppy for Travis," Maggie said dully.

"Isn't Baron the cutest thing you've ever seen?"

"Adorable."

Rosita sighed. "Doesn't anything make you happy anymore, Maggie? Goodness, when you first came home you were so different."

"Call it Post-Dallas Fortune Syndrome." Maggie plopped down on a chair. "I'm not having dinner with him, Mama, not tonight or any other night."

Rosita's forehead creased into a serious frown. "I simply do not understand you, Maggie. The most eligible bachelor in the county is doing his utmost to court you, and you keep saying no."

"Not always," Maggie muttered.

"What was that?"

"Nothing." Maggie got up. "I'm going to get out of this dress and into some jeans."

Rosita stared after Maggie with a puzzled expression, then shook her head sadly. As much as she hated admitting it, her daughter seemed to be her own worst enemy. What in heaven's name was wrong with that girl? She would never find another man to compare with Dallas Fortune. Did she want to sleep alone for the rest of her life? And what about a father for Travis? That boy needed a father, and Maggie needed a husband!

Clucking her tongue in disapproval, Rosita began arranging the roses in two large vases.

Outside, Dallas kept hoping that Maggie would come out again. But when the door finally opened, it was Rosita he saw.

Rosita motioned him over to the porch and spoke quietly, worriedly. "I'm sorry, Dallas, but Maggie went to her room to change clothes and she's still in there. I have the feeling that she intends to stay in there until you leave."

Dallas looked off across a field for a few moments, then brought his gaze back to Rosita. "I have to talk to her, Rosita. Would you mind if I went into her bedroom?"

"Mind?" Rosita's whole demeanor changed, and she grinned wickedly. "I wouldn't mind a bit. In fact, I'll stay outside with Travis and give you enough time and privacy to talk some sense into her. If you ask me, that's exactly what she needs. Oh, her bedroom is the second door on the left if you're heading for the bathroom."

"Thanks." Dallas bounded into the house, located the door to Maggie's bedroom and walked in without knocking.

Maggie honestly couldn't believe her eyes, and she became so furious that she forgot she was wearing only her underwear. In her left hand was a pair of jeans; she'd been looking in the closet for a top to put on. But everything fled her mind except Dallas's gall.

"You get the hell out of my room," she spat. "What will my mother think?"

"I happen to have Rosita's permission to be in here," Dallas retorted. "In fact, I have her blessing."

Maggie sneered. "Oh, yes, she thinks you're so wonderful. If I told her what you did to me in the line shack, she'd change her tune in the wink of an eye."

"What I did to you in the line shack? Have you actually been kidding yourself about what took place between us that day? My God, Maggie, get real. You were so hot that day your skin sizzled. And you were the same last night until you saw that painting." Dallas began advancing on her.

"Well, let me tell you what I did after you left," he said. "I took down the painting, and I emptied Sara's closet."

"Her things were still in a closet?" Maggie gasped. "After two years? Don't you think that's a little extreme?"

"No, I do not. I won't lie to you, Maggie. I loved Sara with all my heart, and I came close to dying myself when she did. But things started changing the day I saw you. *I* started changing. And after you left yesterday I had a lot of brand-new thoughts. I see it all much differently now than I did, and I know that I want to get on with life."

He put his hands on her bare shoulders, and that was when Maggie remembered that she was almost naked. Wide-eyed and nervous, she backed up a step, and Dallas took a forward step.

"I want you in my life, Maggie, but you have to help me out." When she took another backward step, he took another forward step, keeping the distance between them no more than a few inches. "If I swear an oath not to do anything that makes you uncomfortable, will you please have dinner with me tonight?"

Tears of frustration began stinging her eyes, and she said

raggedly, "You're making me uncomfortable right now, Dallas. Don't you realize that? I'm not even dressed."

His eyes flicked down her body. "You are seriously beautiful," he said hoarsely. "Oh, sweetheart, please don't keep us apart." He moved quickly and put his arms around her. In the next instant he was kissing her, and Maggie could feel her strength draining away, as surely as water runs downhill.

His tongue plunged into her mouth, and she moaned as her pulse went wild. She let her jeans fall to the floor, and both her hands were free to wander. Dazed by so much passion, she kissed back and sought a closer union by leaning into him.

Her response didn't surprise Dallas. He knew they had more chemistry than anyone had the power to deny. Kissing her again and again, he slid his hand into her panties and between her legs.

"Dallas," she whimpered when he began stroking her most sensitive spot. "Please...Mama and Travis are right outside."

He was so aroused that he could barely speak. "I know, baby, I know. Maggie, say you'll have dinner with me tonight. Or something. We need to talk."

"I...really don't feel that talking is what's on your mind," she whispered. When she attempted to disentangle their arms and bodies, he let her. On trembling legs she walked over to the dresser and held on to it for support. "I—I'm going to say no, Dallas. I have to."

"Dammit, you *don't* have to!"

"Get angry if you wish, but my answer is still no."

He felt helpless enough to cry. Instead, he whirled around and walked out. There was no way to get through to Maggie. He'd tried everything, and had failed. It was time he faced facts. Maggie might melt when he touched her, but that would forever be the extent of their relationship.

It wasn't enough. By damn, it wasn't *nearly* enough!

Twelve

The weekend passed, and on Monday Rosita went back to work. To keep herself busy, Maggie tore into the house. She took down curtains and washed them, and then washed the windows before hanging the curtains again. She moved the furniture in the living room to vacuum every inch of the carpet, and she scoured the two bathrooms until they shone.

While she worked she kept an eye on Travis, who was so enthralled with his puppy that he didn't even play with his lasso. And every time Maggie looked out a window and saw Baron, she thought of Dallas. He had not come by all weekend, not since Friday when she'd taken that drive to Red Rock. Apparently she had finally gotten her wish: Dallas had given up on her.

But instead of being glad about it, she felt a disconcerting emptiness. Why wasn't she relieved because Dallas was staying away? It was what she'd asked him to do—*demanded* he do—wasn't it? She should be elated. And the fact that she was neither elated nor relieved was terribly confusing.

Cleaning furiously, Maggie attempted to analyze herself. Since she had already admitted, if only to herself, that she had fallen in love with Dallas, it stood to reason that the emptiness she was feeling now was caused by his extended absence. Was this how she would feel for the rest of her life—empty because a man she could never really have,

and who obviously didn't want her—except for one thing—
had finally abided by her demands?

Pure and painful unhappiness brought tears to her eyes.
Would she ever be a happy woman? Why had she fallen
for Dallas Fortune, of all people?

Dashing away tears that she believed she had no right to
shed, Maggie prepared a bucket of hot water to scrub the
kitchen floor. She'd given Travis his lunch and he was
again outside with Baron. A boy and his dog, Maggie
thought poignantly. While she certainly didn't need a dog
to worry about, that puppy had put a permanent smile on
her son's face. How could she continue to resent Dallas for
bringing such joy into Travis's life?

Maggie sighed. Resenting Dallas just felt like wasted energy now. He wouldn't be back, she was sure of it. It was
entirely possible that she would never see him again. Eventually she would leave the ranch, and even when she came
home for visits it wasn't likely that she would run into
Dallas. Not unless she knocked on *his* door, which she
knew in her heart she would never do.

No, this was best, even if she did wish things could have
been different. No matter how she looked at their relationship, Dallas was still a Fortune. He would always be a
Fortune, and she would always be a Perez.

"And never the twain shall meet," Maggie muttered as
she hefted the bucket of water from the sink to the floor.

She would have liked to turn on the radio and listen to
some music while she worked, but she always kept an ear
cocked for Travis. There was one thing she knew about
herself that no one and nothing could alter: she was a good
mother. She loved her son unconditionally and had vowed
at his birth to raise him with high standards, just as she'd
been raised.

Maggie started to get down on her knees, and raised up

again when the front door opened and she heard Savannah's voice. "Maggie?"

"I'm in the kitchen." Maggie hurried to welcome her sister-in-law. "I'm glad you dropped in."

Savannah smiled. "Only for a minute. I'm really out walking, getting my daily exercise, and I wondered if you'd let Travis go with me. Baron, too, of course."

"Travis would probably love to go with you," Maggie said. "Did you mention it to him on your way in?"

"I thought I should ask you first."

"Well, feel free."

Savannah reached for the doorknob. "Thanks, Maggie."

"If you have time when your walk is over, come in and we'll have a cup of tea."

"Sounds good."

Maggie stood on the porch while Savannah invited Travis and Baron to walk with her, and then waved them off. Going back inside, she returned to the kitchen and started scrubbing the floor, working with a scrub brush, a bar of strong soap and a clean rag. Thirty minutes later the floor was spotless, and she got up with a feeling of a job well done.

She was at the sink, wiping out the bucket, when she heard the front door open again. "Savannah, please don't let Travis bring the puppy in. I'd like this floor to dry first!" she called.

"It's not Savannah or Travis!" Dallas called back. "It's me."

Maggie whirled. He was here! Pink spots stained her cheeks, and she opened her mouth to say something, then couldn't think of anything appropriate.

"Looks like you've been doing some cleaning," Dallas commented.

"Uh...yes." The expression on his face was so sober

that Maggie wondered what was on his mind. She'd been thinking that she might never see him again—and here he was. Why? Regardless of that disturbing question, something real and alive had ignited inside her. Dare she call it happiness? She certainly no longer felt empty.

Unnerved over her own ambiguity, Maggie turned back to the sink and finished wiping out the bucket.

Dallas stared at her. Was she just going to go on cleaning, and ignore him? Obviously he'd surprised her, but did she think he was just going to stand around and hope that she would deign to talk to him?

"Could you possibly force yourself to look at me?" he asked in a lethally quiet voice.

Maggie drew a long breath, folded the wet cleaning rag and draped it over the lip of the bucket. Then she turned and faced him.

"I can look at you, yes," she said, proud of the calmness she heard in her own voice. It was a good act, because she wasn't feeling calm on the inside.

"Thank you. There's something I want to ask you."

"Go ahead." His question undoubtedly had to do with Travis, she thought. Maybe he wanted to take Travis for a horseback ride, or give him another gift. Since she'd raised such hell about the puppy, Dallas probably figured he'd better check with her before giving Travis anything else.

Dallas cleared his throat. "I think we should get married. Would you marry me, Maggie?"

Her jaw dropped and her eyes went blank as a freshly cleaned blackboard. Surely he hadn't said what she'd thought she heard!

"Excuse me?" she mumbled.

"I just asked you to marry me."

She'd heard right! He had actually asked her to marry him. She was speechless.

"I know this is sudden," Dallas said, "but I've thought it through all weekend and it makes a lot of sense. First of all, we both need someone. You're alone and I'm alone. I know we've been at odds, but I think that's because you're too damn regretful about what happened between us in the line shack. I'm not one bit regretful about us making love, and I don't mind admitting that I can't stop wanting you.

"Second, there's Travis to consider. Maggie, I couldn't love him more if he were my own son. And that boy needs a father. I'd be a good father, Maggie, and I think you know it."

What about me? Do you love me? Oh, please say you do! Maggie realized at that crucial moment that she didn't care what Dallas's last name was. All that mattered was that he loved her.

He was ticking off his reasons for proposing marriage on his fingers. "Third, I've figured out your financial situation, and from the hints you gave me at my house the evening of Ruben's birthday, I've also figured out that you'd like to stop living off your folks. Marrying me would solve all your problems, Maggie. Every single one of them."

Yes, but do you love me?

"So there you have it," Dallas said. "There are a lot of good reasons for us to marry. Sound reasons, Maggie. What do you say? Should we set the date?"

"Gi—give me a minute," Maggie whispered shakily. He was right. Marrying Dallas *would* solve all her problems. She would never have to worry about money again...or a job...or a home of her own.

And yet he'd not said one word about love, except with regard to Travis. Not one word about loving her. Wanting her, yes, but she'd already known that. How could he marry a woman he didn't love? And how long would her love for him last when there would never be anything except sex between them?

This wasn't exactly like her first marriage proposal, but it was close. And so would the marriage itself be, if she said yes.

She wanted to marry again very much, but she wanted a husband who adored her. She wanted what her parents had, and what Cruz and Savannah had. They all worked hard to earn their keep—why should she give up her dream of a truly happy marriage just to put an end to her problems?

She couldn't do it. Whatever the future held for her, she could not marry a man for his money. And that's all it would be when Dallas couldn't even say that he loved her. He couldn't say it because he *didn't* love her, she thought as a burst of adrenaline hit her. His proposal was offensive. She suddenly had no qualms at all in telling him.

Facing him head on, she said it. "No."

Dallas looked slightly shell-shocked, incredulous. "You're saying no?"

"Yes, sir, that's the word."

"But…but why? Maggie, it makes so much sense."

"Maybe to you it does. Sorry, but the whole idea leaves me cold."

"It leaves you cold! What the hell do you want from a man? I've offered you everything I have. What more could you want?"

"You know, Dallas, in spite of our many disagreements, I've always thought of you as an intelligent man. Obviously I was wrong."

"That's a damn low blow," Dallas growled.

"So was your marriage proposal," she snapped.

"You're insulted by a serious proposal of marriage? What in hell's wrong with you?"

"What in hell's wrong with *you?*" she shouted. "All

you did was try to buy me. Well, let me tell you something, Dallas—you can buy what you need from a woman in any town in Texas. I do not happen to be for sale!''

Dallas was so angry that she would bring his marriage proposal down to such a degrading level that he grabbed her by the upper arms with the intention of shaking some sense into her. He hadn't thought that sort of physical behavior through, however, and the second his hands were on her his thoughts went in an entirely different direction. Yanking her forward, he kissed her until her whole body was trembling against his, and when they were both gasping for air he raised his head and looked into her eyes.

"How can you refuse me when we've got this?" he demanded hoarsely, and before she could do more than blink, he kissed her again.

As happened every single time he touched her, Maggie felt her resistance slipping away. He was right; in this they connected. In truth she had never felt so connected to a man as she did to Dallas when he kissed her. Lord help her if this was the reason she'd fallen in love with him, she thought in the back of her mind, but that unsettling concept didn't prevent her from responding.

She honestly didn't know how it happened so fast, but she suddenly found herself naked from the waist down and sitting on her mother's kitchen counter, with Dallas just naked enough and thrusting into her.

It was wild and crazy and so exciting that she could think of nothing else. The whole thing happened so fast that Dallas was surprised when she cried out and dug her fingernails into his back. But it pleased him more, and he let go completely and went over the edge with her.

Burying his face in the curve of her throat, he heavily breathed her name. "Maggie…Maggie…" And after a minute he was able to speak more coherently, and he whispered raggedly, "After this, can you still say no?"

Reality hit Maggie hard, and she pushed him away, got off the counter, hurriedly picked up her panties and jeans and ran for the bathroom.

Straightening his own clothes, Dallas called after her, "Can you?"

She shouted, "Yes, I can still say no! Now, go away and leave me alone!"

She heard him yell, "Damn you!" Then she heard the hard slam of the front door, and knew he'd gone. Shaking from head to foot, she turned on the shower, threw off the rest of her clothes and stepped into the stall.

It was while she was drying off that she remembered they had again made love without protection.

Rosita was spitting mad when she got home that afternoon. "How did Sophia know that the big house was empty for the weekend? How *could* she have known?"

"Mama," Maggie said wearily, "what are you talking about?"

"I'm talking about Sophia Fortune, that...that... Well, I don't use bad language, but think the worst and you'll know what I'm thinking. Maggie, sometime during the holiday weekend, Sophia went into the house and took china, silver, cash and paintings right off the walls."

"How do you know it was Sophia?"

"Who else would have such gall?"

"A thief?"

"Oh, yes, it was a thief, all right, and her name is Sophia Fortune! Didn't you notice the sheriff's car parked near the big house all afternoon?"

"No, I didn't. Is there proof that the thief was Sophia?"

Rosita sighed. "I don't think so. Not the kind of proof

that would put her in jail, at any rate. But it was her, everyone knows it.''

"Mama, how would she know that no one was home? She wouldn't dare come by when someone was in the house, and who would tell her that everyone had gone away for the weekend?''

"That's the sixty-four-thousand-dollar question, Maggie. Who on this ranch would tell Sophia anything? Even the household help only put up with her imperial attitude and self-centered demands because of Ryan. She wasn't even nice to Ryan's kids. I remember very well when Ryan married her, and she never once attempted to mother those children, and they were terribly distraught over their own mother's death, I can tell you. If Sophia had shown the least bit of compassion or affection for Ryan's children, things might have turned out much differently than they did in that marriage. But Sophia's concern was always for herself. I doubt very much if she ever loved Ryan at all. She saw a good catch while she was nursing Janine, and the minute Janine passed away, Sophia moved in on Ryan.''

"She married him for his money," Maggie said quietly, comparing what Sophia had done to what *she* could have done this very day. If she had said yes to Dallas's marriage proposal, she would be no better than Sophia. Thank goodness she was not a crass opportunist, as Sophia obviously had been.

Rosita was glancing around. "Gracious, what did you do, clean all day?''

"Just about.''

"Well, the house looks wonderful, but—'' Rosita eyed her daughter "—you don't. You wore yourself out, didn't you? Maggie, I appreciate a clean house, but not at your expense. You look pale and drawn. You don't feel well, do you?''

"It's natural at this time of the month, Mama." It seemed like a good excuse for looking ''pale and drawn.''

"Oh, I see. Well, getting back to the robbery..."

In spite of the tackiness of their room in that horrid little off-road motel, Sophia was in high spirits. "It was so easy," she said with a self-satisfied laugh. "When you told me everyone was going away for the holiday weekend, and that even the household staff wouldn't be on the premises, I knew immediately that I'd been handed a golden opportunity."

Clint wore his usual brooding expression. "So, what did you take?"

Sophia airily waved her hand. "Just a few things...my favorite set of china, for one. Nothing I dare sell, of course. I'm sure Ryan has called in the law by now, so we must be very careful. If I'd known the combination to Ryan's safe, you and I would be in tall cotton tonight. That cheapskate never would give me the combination," she said with a disgusted roll of her eyes.

"Obviously he didn't trust you," Clint drawled, adding, "With good reason." Then he asked, "Did you find any cash?"

"About five hundred dollars." Sophia opened her purse and pulled out a small wad bills. "Here's your share."

Clint was disappointed. "Five hundred was it?"

''I found that in a drawer of his desk.'' Actually she'd found two thousand plus change in Ryan's desk, but she felt that she needed the cash a whole lot more than Clint did.

"The sheriff was at the ranch all afternoon," Clint said. "Rumor has it that the thief got away with a lot more than a set of china. Let me take the stuff to Houston and pawn it. I know one pawnshop owner that would take anything I brought in without notifying the law, even if he did recognize it as stolen property."

"No," Sophia said flatly. "I won't take that risk, Clint. My divorce settlement with Ryan is far more important than the few measly bucks a pawnshop owner would pay for stolen goods."

"I'm getting damn tired of waiting for those negotiations to be finalized," Clint snapped.

"Do you think I'm not?" Sophia bit back. She was also getting tired of Clint pressuring her for money. If she didn't need the information he provided about daily occurrences at the ranch, she would shed him like a dirty shirt.

But theirs was a liaison she couldn't yet discard, and she forced herself to smile at him. "Let's forget all that for now and have a drink. I brought your favorite whiskey with me. How about it?"

Clint felt another moment of intense dislike. Small wonder that Ryan hadn't trusted his wife enough to give her the combination to his safe, Clint thought. *He* didn't trust Sophia either: he would bet anything that she'd found a lot more cash during her midnight raid than she'd told him about.

His hands were tied for the present, but he wouldn't always have to play the fool, he told himself. Sophia held all the cards right now, but once the divorce was behind them and he'd gotten his share of the Fortune wealth, Sophia had just better watch her step around him.

"Sure," he said with a casualness that was phonier than a three-dollar bill. "Go ahead and pour the drinks."

Maria Cassidy was sitting on the sagging sofa in the minuscule living room of her rented trailer on the outskirts of the town of Leather Bucket. Her expression was brooding and bitter. Baby Bryan Fortune was sleeping peacefully in the small crib she had bought for her own son, James. While she was relieved that James had been plucked from the kidnappers' hands, it galled Maria that Matthew and Claudia had taken over his care and had named him Taylor.

But Maria was the first to admit that everything about the Fortunes bothered her. She didn't trust any of them, nor did she like them—with the possible exception of the baby boy she had taken upon discovering that kidnappers had taken her own son, stupidly thinking that James was Bryan.

Whoever the kidnappers were, though, they weren't the only stupid people in this part of the world. Maria felt that her own mother, Lily, was appallingly stupid. Lily actually believed that Ryan Fortune was going to marry her when his divorce from Sophia became final—which, to Maria, was the laugh of the century.

The thing was, though, no one else thought it was a laughing matter. Maria had tried talking to her sister, Hannah, about it, and normally mealymouthed Hannah had actually snapped at her. "Mother is happy, Maria, and don't you dare do anything to ruin it for her."

Her brother, Cole, was as unapproachable on the subject as Hannah was. Maria felt that she was the only one who had the nerve to face the truth of that ridiculous liaison: Ryan Fortune would use Lily until he tired of her, then he'd toss her out. Maria could hardly wait for that day, and she often fantasized how she would triumphantly say, *Told you so!*

Maria had other fantasies, as well. She knew that the Fortunes would do just about anything to get baby Bryan back. That beautiful sleeping child was worth millions, but how did one go about converting a kidnapped child to hard cash? Without getting caught, of course.

Maria let her imagination take over. Obviously some sort of contact would be necessary. A telephone call? No, a phone call was too risky. Even if she disguised her voice, someone might recognize it. It would have to be a letter.

How much should she ask for? My Lord, she would be rich! She fantasized about living with more money than she could spend. First-class travel accommodations, designer clothes, the best hotels and restaurants, elegant resorts, elbow-rubbing with rich and famous people—all this ran through her mind.

And then her lips twisted with renewed bitterness. Money would permit her to get out of Texas and away from the Fortunes and her own dumb family. Nothing she could buy with that money would please her more.

Now, exactly when should she write that letter? And how should she deliver it without leaving a trail of clues that would lead investigators back to her?

She had a lot to think about. This was going to take some very careful planning.

The day had been trying. Dallas had been at the big house since around two that afternoon with his father, Lily, Parker Malone—Ryan's lawyer—and the sheriff. They'd gone through the house with a fine-tooth comb, making a list of missing items. Ryan had been mad as hell and distraught, and Dallas had apologized for not putting a night guard on the place.

"It's not your fault," Ryan had told him. "I should have thought of it myself. Hell's bells, we've got two bodyguards, and one of them went with Matthew and Claudia, and the other went to Bermuda with Lily and me. I should have left one of them behind to keep an eye on the house, or hired a third man to do it. So stop blaming yourself, Dallas. It was my oversight, not yours."

They had discussed Sophia. "Dad, I realize she's the most likely candidate, but how would she have known that everyone was gone?"

"That's what none of us can figure out," Ryan had said grimly. "Parker came up with an idea that's been eating at me—the possibility of Sophia having an ally among the hired help. Someone who tells her everything we do. What do you think?"

"I guess it's possible," Dallas had said slowly, thinking of the ranch's cadre of hired help. No one person stood out in his mind. "But I can't imagine who it would be."

"Neither can I," Ryan had admitted. "Which only makes that idea doubly worrisome. If there really is someone among our ranks who's spying on every move we make and carrying the information to Sophia, who do we dare trust?"

When Dallas went home after dinner at the main house that night, he was still thinking about it. Who, among all the people who worked on the ranch, would carry tales to Sophia? Had she ever been particularly friendly with any of the hired help? If she had been, Dallas thought, he'd certainly never witnessed it.

After a shower, Dallas doused the lights and climbed into bed. The robbery fled his mind as Maggie's image filled it. He'd made a damn fool of himself again with Maggie. He never could have imagined her taking his proposal of marriage as an insult—and it hurt like hell that she had.

And yet she'd told him straight out one time that she didn't like him. Why in heaven's name couldn't he just believe her and let it go at that? Was it because she physically responded to him? Damn, she was a confusing woman. After flatly refusing to marry him, she'd made love with him, then told him no again. If only there was a way to crawl into her brain and really get a grasp on her thoughts and feelings.

Well, that was an inane wish, Dallas thought. He would never understand Maggie, and he might as well face it.

Thirteen

The furor caused by the robbery gradually died down. Suspicions were not enough to legally lay the blame on Sophia, and even the question of how a thief—be it Sophia or someone else—could have pulled it off without anyone on the ranch catching on lost impetus.

Christmas was getting close and uppermost in everyone's mind. Since the day of his proposal, Dallas had stayed away from Maggie. She knew that he came by every so often to see Travis, but he never once attempted to see her. Every time Maggie realized that Dallas was in the yard talking to Travis, she chanced a peek out a window at him. The sight of Dallas never failed to upset her, but she couldn't stop herself from taking that furtive look. And, perversely, he seemed to be more handsome each time she saw him. Obviously, as long as she was in a position *to* see him, her feelings were only going to keep digging deeper into her psyche.

She'd stopped telling herself that she had to leave the ranch, because there was no way to accomplish it. She couldn't accept her fate graciously, however, and, as Maggie should have known would happen, Rosita noticed her daughter's down-in-the-mouth mood.

"Maggie, if you're worrying about paying for Christmas gifts, your papa and I will give you the money to do your shopping."

"Thank you, Mama, but I have enough money for gifts."

She figured she might as well spend what money she did have in giving Travis a wonderful Christmas; it wasn't enough for anything else. Then Rosita's generous offer sank in. Her parents would give her money for everything but what she really wanted: a move to Houston.

Rosita and Ruben were happy that she and Travis were living with them, and they would never agree to finance a move that they so rigidly disapproved of. To their way of thinking, a daughter alone *should* move back home. It was an old world attitude, but Maggie knew there was no way to convince her parents that she was perfectly capable of living independently, not even if she pointed out that she had done exactly that in Phoenix since her divorce.

But in spite of her decision to use her money for Christmas gifts, Maggie procrastinated on the actual shopping. Every day she walked down to the mailbox with hope in her heart that this would be the day that she would receive a letter from a Houston bank, and every day she walked back to the house disappointed.

Until Friday, the eighteenth of December. There was a handful of mail that day, and she thumbed through it, looking for an envelope addressed to her. When she saw one, she gasped out loud at the return address: Texas Bank of Commerce and Industry. So excited that her heart was pounding, she ran all the way back to the house.

Travis called, "Mama, why are you running?"

Maggie laughed gaily. "Just for the fun of it, son." Most days Travis walked to the mailbox with her, but today he'd been frolicking with Baron and hadn't wanted to go. Maggie had told him he didn't have to go, but to be sure that he stayed in the yard. In one notable way the puppy had been a blessing, because from the day Dallas had given Baron to Travis, the little boy had stayed close to the house, apparently content to play with his pet.

Inside, Maggie breathlessly tore open the envelope and extracted a single page, which she unfolded and eagerly read.

Dear Ms. Perez Randall,
We have an opening in our commercial loan department that may interest you. We will be holding interviews for the position the first two days of next week, so if you are still seeking employment, please call the following phone number and we will schedule an interview for you. The number is 555-6261.

The letter was signed by a Karen Johnson with the title of Director of Personnel.

Maggie was beside herself, and she immediately went to the phone and dialed the number. In ten minutes she had an interview lined up for Monday morning at 9:00 a.m.

Something told Maggie that she was going to get that job. But even before the interview, sometime this weekend, in fact, she had to express to her parents her unshakable determination to get back on her own two feet. She knew in her heart that it wasn't going to be an easy discussion, but there simply was no way around it.

A short time later her initial excitement over the letter began dissipating. An early-morning interview presented its own set of problems. Transportation to Houston was one of them, of course, and another was what she would do with Travis on Monday.

While going through her closet to choose the perfect outfit for the interview, Maggie decided she could catch a ride to Red Rock with someone from the ranch; people were always going to town for one reason or another. Then, in Red Rock, she could take a bus to Houston. Though that plan seemed feasible, its success depended on bus schedules and whether or not someone would be taking an early-morning run into Red Rock on Monday. It would be far, far better if she could arrive in Houston on Sunday night and rent a motel room close to the Texas Bank of Commerce and Industry. At least she would be on time for her appointment with Karen Johnson. First impressions were crucial in job interviews, and showing up late wouldn't be wise.

But then there was Travis, who was much too young to leave alone in a motel room while she went to the interview. Remembering that there were motels and hotels in Phoenix that advertised bonded baby-sitting services for their guests, Maggie began searching for the Houston telephone directory that she was positive she had seen in one drawer or another since coming home.

When she finally found it, she flipped through the *Yellow Pages* and read the dozens of hotel and motel ads. Some mentioned reliable baby-sitting as part of their service, so her next task was to locate one situated near the bank. Using the map of Houston in the phone book, she finally pinpointed a hotel in the general vicinity. Deciding that was the best she could do, she phoned and made a reservation for Sunday night, emphasizing her need for child care on Monday morning. The clerk promised to line up a sitter, and Maggie put down the phone feeling greatly relieved.

Surely someone would give her and Travis a ride to Red Rock on Sunday, and the rest of her plan would fall into place after that. On Monday she would arrive at the interview on time, bright-eyed from a good night's sleep, and not worried about her son.

Maggie suddenly noticed the clock—almost two hours had passed since she had talked to Travis on her way into the house! Darn it, how had she let so much time go by without checking on her son? It was strange that he hadn't run in for a drink of water, a snack or a potty break.

Jumping up, Maggie hastened to the door and stepped out onto the porch. When she didn't immediately see Travis in the front or side yard, she started calling his name. Leaving the porch she walked to the back of the house, where he often played. He wasn't there, nor was he on the other side of the house. He was, in fact, nowhere to be seen. Nor was the puppy. Maggie's heart sank clear to her toes. Scanning fields and the ranch, her eyes darting in every direction, she felt the same dread every time Travis had taken a notion to wander.

Recalling that Cruz had found him playing in a haystack the last time Travis had left the yard, Maggie took off running in that direction. This time, she told herself, Travis was going to have to be punished. Maybe if he sat on a chair in the house for a full day, he would remember his promise to stay in the yard.

Dallas, on Vic, was heading for the ranch. As always when he rode alone, his thoughts were jumping from one thing to another. Chores and projects on the ranch, as well as his father's many personal problems, occupied his brain. Behind every thought, though, was Maggie and her cruel, incomprehensible rejection of his marriage proposal.

He had forced himself to stay away from her, but obviously that old adage about absence making the heart grow fonder was true, because no matter how busy he kept himself he couldn't stop thinking of her. Sometimes he resented her with every fiber of his being; he told himself that she simply wasn't the woman he'd thought she was, and that he was better off without her.

But there were also unnerving moments when he blamed himself for her attitude, when he remembered in torturous detail how crudely he'd first approached her. That invariably led to other memories, most of which were heart-wrenchingly disturbing. A constant question tingled: If she hadn't liked him from the get-go, why had she made love with him, not once but twice?

Deep in thought, Dallas barely noticed the childish voice that came out of nowhere. But after a few minutes that high-pitched sound zigzagged through his thoughts and finally registered. Pulling Vic to a halt, Dallas frowned and looked around.

Way off in the distance he could see a child and a small dog. The child appeared to be chasing the dog, and the dog playfully kept dodging the child's hands. Dallas's frown deepened. Surely he wasn't seeing Travis and Baron this far from their house. Good God, Maggie would pitch a fit.

Nudging Vic into a quick gallop, Dallas rode toward the scene that became clearer the closer he got. It *was* Travis and Baron, and what was going on was pretty damn funny. The puppy would dart ahead, then stop and wait for Travis to try and catch him. The second Travis reached out for the pup, off Baron would go again.

Dallas couldn't help laughing. "Hey, Trav!" he shouted when he figured the boy was within earshot.

Travis stopped running and waited for Dallas to ride up to him. Dallas immediately saw how hot and sweaty Travis was, even though the day was cool. While Dallas dismounted, Travis said forlornly, "He ran away, and I can't catch him, Dallas."

"He's just playing with you, Trav. Come on. I'll give you a ride home, and you just wait and see. Baron will realize the game is over and follow us."

Travis looked worried. "What if he doesn't? What if he keeps on going and I never get him back?"

Dallas looked at the puppy, who was lying down about

ten feet away with his nose on his front paws. "If he doesn't follow, then I'll catch him and bring him back to you. Come on, Trav, if your mother has noticed your absence, you're going to be in big trouble. Let's get you home before she does notice."

Travis visibly gulped. "Gosh, I didn't think of that."

"You should have, son," Dallas said gently. "An honorable man keeps his promises."

"Yeah, but—but Baron ran away and…and I had to catch him."

Dallas lifted the boy to Vic's back, then climbed up behind Travis. "If you hadn't chased Baron, he probably wouldn't have gone far. He's a playful little guy, Trav, and you can't let having fun interfere with a promise." Dallas urged Vic into a fast walk.

"Mama's gonna be mad at me, ain't she?"

"If she discovered your absence, I wouldn't doubt it." Dallas looked behind them. "Take a look for yourself, Trav. Baron's following us."

Travis peered around Dallas and said dispiritedly, "Yeah, he is. How'd you know he would?"

"Because he doesn't want to be way out here by himself, Trav. He's your puppy and you're his boy."

Travis cheered up and giggled. "I'm his boy?"

"Yes, but before you're Baron's boy, you are your mother's boy. That's what you have to remember the next time Baron tries to lure you out of the yard. Your mother loves you very much, and she worries about you."

"I love her too, Dallas."

"I know you do, son. I know you do," Dallas said quietly.

Maggie was getting frantic. Travis was not playing in one of the haystacks, and she didn't know where to look for him next. The ranch was so big. The buildings were

big, and there were so many of them. And what if he'd
wandered far enough away that he had ended up in the
bulls' pasture? In two hours he could have covered a lot of
ground. How could she have let herself get so involved in
her plans that she'd forgotten to check on him? He was
only five years old, and if anything happened to him it
would be her fault.

Maggie shuddered. She couldn't start thinking that way.
She had to believe that Travis was all right or she would
collapse on the spot. She began running again, this way
and that, and shouting his name.

Then she heard someone shouting *her* name. Wild-eyed
she stopped running and looked around. Relief weakened
her knees. Coming toward her were Dallas and Travis, both
riding Vic.

"Here I am, Mama!" Travis yelled.

Maggie had no strength to answer. Apparently Dallas had
once again been in the right place at the right time. Why
did this keep happening? It was as though he'd been ap-
pointed her and her son's keeper. Any time either of them
was in some kind of trouble, Dallas was always there.

As grateful as she was that Travis was safe and sound,
Maggie wasn't happy about being forced into talking to
Dallas. She vowed to keep any conversation between them
strictly impersonal.

"Where was he?" she asked dully, as Dallas dismounted
and then lifted Travis to the ground. The second Travis was
down, he ran back to Baron to hug and pet his puppy.

"About a quarter-mile from here," Dallas said quietly.
"He was chasing Baron. Apparently the puppy ran away
and Travis kept trying to catch him. No harm was done,
Maggie, and I hope you're not too angry with the boy."

She turned hard eyes on Dallas. "Who should I be angry

with, in that case? Should it be you for giving the puppy to Travis in the first place?"

Dallas's own eyes became steely. "I never do anything right, do I, Maggie? Well, the anger I see in your eyes right now is no more than what I've come to expect from you." He climbed back on his horse. "See you later, Trav," he called. "Remember what I told you about keeping promises."

"I will, Dallas," Travis called back. "See ya."

Too late, Maggie realized that she hadn't even tried to thank Dallas. His coolness had matched her own, and, in fact, he had gotten the last word.

Disheartened by circumstances that she honestly believed were beyond her control, she said listlessly, "Come on, Travis, let's go home."

The boy got to his feet. "Are you mad at me, Mama?"

Maggie sighed. "You left the yard again, son."

"But I couldn't help it, Mama. I was afraid that Baron was running away." Travis frowned then. "Dallas said that 'hobornal' men keep their promises. What does hobornal mean, Mama?"

"The word is *honorable*, son. An honorable person has a strong sense of right and wrong, and he's honest and trustworthy."

They held hands for a quite solemn walk to the Perez house. Baron followed with his little tail between his hind legs and his head down, acting as chagrined as his pint-size master.

All through dinner that evening Maggie was on pins and needles. Both her parents were present; it was an opportune time to talk to them. Besides, putting off the necessary discussion about her job interview was childish. She should just introduce the topic, say her piece and get it over with.

But Travis was also present, and her father—appearing to be more tired than usual after a day's work—ate without saying much. So Maggie decided to wait until Travis was in bed. That didn't work out, because Ruben went to bed while Maggie was tucking in her son for the night. Rosita stayed up for another hour or so, but by nine-thirty everyone had gone to bed. Maggie lay in hers and worried until she fell asleep.

When Maggie got up the next morning, Rosita was in the kitchen. It was early, and Travis, Maggie knew, would sleep for at least another hour. "Good morning, Mama. Where's Papa?"

"He left about an hour ago," Rosita said. "He and Cruz are going to a horse auction. I don't think Cruz is ready to start buying stock yet, but he wants to keep up on the price of good horseflesh."

"Makes sense," Maggie murmured as she poured herself a cup of coffee. She joined her mother at the table. "Will Papa be gone all day?"

"Most of it. Why, Maggie?"

"Just curious," she replied vaguely. Then she really looked at her mother. "You look tired, Mama. Didn't you sleep well?"

"I had one of those nights with too many dreams," Rosita replied. "The one that is still bothering me was about Logan Fortune. You remember Logan, don't you?"

"I haven't seen him for years, but yes, I remember him. His father is Cameron Fortune, Ryan's brother, am I right?"

"Yes, and Cameron was killed in a terrible collision with a truck about five years ago. A young woman was in the car with him, and she died, too."

"Oh, yes, I remember that now. If I recall correctly, Cameron was quite a lady's man."

"Judging from some of the things I've heard about Logan, he is a lot like his father where women are concerned," Rosita said with a sigh. "Not that flitting from woman to woman is a crime. He is a single man, after all, and he's also very dedicated to the company. He's the CEO of Fortune TX in San Antonio and a hard worker, or so I've heard. But…"

"But what, Mama?" Maggie asked. She really wasn't interested in Logan Fortune's history or present life-style, but she could tell that Rosita wanted to talk about her dream. "Why did dreaming about Logan trouble you?"

"Because it was more like a premonition than a dream," Rosita said.

Maggie had grown up with her mother's premonitions, visions and dreams, and knew that many times Rosita's predictions had been amazingly accurate and had actually taken place, in one form or another.

"Tell me about it," Maggie urged.

"Well, it was a very strange dream. Logan was sitting on a chair under a spotlight. The rest of the room was dark, and there were voices coming out of the dark, as though Logan was being questioned. I couldn't make out what the voices were saying, but there was a very eerie quality about the whole thing." Rosita paused a moment, then said quietly, "I believe it means that there's trouble on the horizon for Logan."

"Maybe he's going to be arrested for some reason. If he was being questioned—"

"No," Rosita said with a shake of her head. "My feeling is that he's going to be forced into facing something."

"Yes, well, that can certainly be troubling," Maggie said, thinking of herself in that context. Maybe this was the moment to speak, she thought. Maybe it was best if she talked to her mother first, who would be the most vocal of her parents during a discussion, anyway.

"Mama, there's something I have to tell you," Maggie said. She lifted her eyes from her cup of coffee to look across the table at Rosita. "I have a job interview with a bank in Houston on Monday morning."

Rosita frowned and fidgeted for a few moments, then asked, "Why, Maggie? Why aren't you content to be living at home?"

"I have to pay my own way," Maggie said softly. "Please try to understand."

"What I understand is that you'll be raising Travis in a big city, and he's so happy here."

"I know he is, but he was also happy in Phoenix, Mama. Young children are very adaptable, and as long as I provide a secure environment for him, and I'm there for him when he needs me, he will adjust to city life again."

"Maggie, how can you be there for him when you're working?"

"The same way you were here for us when you were working. Mama, you always worked, and did it hurt any of us kids? Not a bit, and it was because we always knew we could come to you with anything, good or bad. We always knew you loved us, Mama. Well, I've nourished the same kind of relationship with Travis. He *knows* I love him."

"Yes, I'm sure he does, but you still can't compare my life to yours. My work was always right here on the ranch, and I remember many occasions when one of you kids came running to the big house to talk to me about something. That's a far cry from your working in a bank and Travis being cared for by strangers."

"Today's world is a far cry from what it was during those years, Mama."

"My point exactly," Rosita said. "Don't go, Maggie.

Stay here where you're loved and wanted, and where Travis will never have to go without." Rosita's eyes suddenly narrowed. "What does that job pay?"

Maggie could only be honest on that point. "I don't know. I won't know until the interview. Mama, I understand why you feel the way you do. You haven't lived anywhere else since you were fourteen years old. I'm sure that for you the world beyond this ranch looks very big and frightening."

"I watch the news. I know what's going on out there, Maggie. I want no part of it, and I wish you felt the same."

"I'm sorry, Mama," Maggie said gently. "But I have to do this."

"Your papa is not going to like it."

"I know that."

"What about Dallas?"

Maggie's heart lurched. "Dallas has his life, I have mine. It's as simple as that, Mama."

"You never gave him a chance."

Maggie became thoughtful, then said quietly, "Maybe he never deserved a chance."

"Maggie!" Rosita gasped. "How can you say such a thing? Dallas is a wonderful man. Why wouldn't he deserve a chance?"

Maggie could not take this conversation any further. Not without explaining her and Dallas's perfectly awful relationship.

Pushing back her chair, she got up. "I don't want to talk about Dallas, Mama. I'm going to go and see if Travis is awake."

Fourteen

Maggie fidgeted nervously when she realized that her parents were discussing her plans in their bedroom shortly after her father got home from the horse auction. But after about an hour they came out all smiles, and their change of attitude was surprising. Maggie had expected, at the very least, to hear a lecture from her father.

"I'll watch Travis for you on Monday," Rosita told her.

Startled by such a complete turnabout, Maggie objected. "Mama, I appreciate your offer, but the hotel I'll be staying at is arranging a baby-sitter for me."

"I know, but I would really like to do this."

"Well, if you're sure." Maggie was so relieved that her parents were now on her team that her heart swelled with love for them. They had always been kind, generous people, and she should have known they would eventually grasp her need for independence, and maybe even admire her spunk.

Her father offered to drive her to town to catch the bus to Houston on Sunday, and she threw her arms around him and hugged him. "Thank you, Papa."

The evening passed normally—they talked quite a lot about Christmas—and no one mentioned her interview again. In bed that night, again thinking how lucky she was to have two such great parents, Maggie suddenly felt the strangest sense of something awry. The sensation hit her from out of the blue and bothered her unmercifully. Something was wrong. Rather, something wasn't quite right, but what on earth could it be?

And then she realized that along with not mentioning her interview again, her mother had also not mentioned Dallas. Not even after her father and Travis had gone to bed and Maggie and her mother had been alone. In fact, her mother had projected unusually high spirits while they chatted about Christmas and other things. And, thinking about it now, Maggie found it hard to believe that her mother had so easily given up on bringing her and Dallas together.

"That is strange," Maggie whispered to herself uneasily. Rosita Perez did not give up on anything she'd set her mind to. At least she didn't until she had tried every possible way to make things work out as she believed they should.

Unless her father had told her to lay off, Maggie mused. The only times in her memory that her mother had backed away from something were if her husband had put his foot down and demanded that she mind her own business. Her mother made most of the decisions in the family, but she never argued with her husband if *he* made a decision.

"Hmm," Maggie murmured, wondering if Dallas had been a part of her parents' private discussion in their bedroom. It was entirely possible that her father had told his wife to leave Dallas be. In fact, it seemed to be the most likely reason why her mother hadn't brought up his name this evening when she and Maggie were alone.

That line of thought led Maggie to Dallas himself. With his image clearly defined in her mind's eye, she sighed ponderously. If he had fallen in love with her, as she had with him, they would now be in the process of planning their wedding. How sad it was that he couldn't forget Sara and let himself love another woman.

It even seemed petty to her now that she had once found his name and position to be such a deterrent to a lasting relationship. She loved Dallas Fortune and probably always would. She felt that she might as well forgo her hope of marrying again, because her feelings for Dallas were going to make it nearly impossible for her to love some other man.

Unshed tears began stinging her eyes, and she stopped herself from breaking down completely by thinking of her Monday morning interview. If she got that job she would concentrate on her career. There were other roads to happiness besides love and marriage, and she would find them. She and Travis were going to be happy. She swore it.

Maggie was packed and ready to leave when her father said, "Something's come up that I have to take care of, Maggie. Cruz is going to drive you to Red Rock."

Realizing that her father was not looking her in the eye, Maggie again felt that nagging suspicion that all was not as it seemed on the surface. But she merely said, "That's fine, Papa."

When Cruz arrived without his wife, Maggie said, "I thought that Savannah would be going with us."

"She's in the middle of something," Cruz said. "She told me to wish you luck with your interview. Are you ready to go?"

"All set." Maggie knelt by her son and gave him a big hug. "Now, you be a good boy for Grandma. I'll be back tomorrow afternoon." She kissed his soft cheek and hugged him again. Her father had disappeared, but her mother was waiting to see her off, and Maggie hugged her also. "I'll get back as quickly as I can," she said. "You have the name and phone number of the hotel I'll be staying at tonight. Don't hesitate to call me if...something happens." Maggie glanced at her son, making it clear where her concern lay.

Rosita smiled broadly. "Nothing is going to happen, Maggie, and I know in my heart that everything is going to turn out real well for you. See you tomorrow. And don't worry about Travis."

"Thank you, Mama." Cruz carried her small suitcase, and together they walked to his pickup. Maggie settled herself in the passenger seat and fastened her seat belt. She waved at her son and mother as Cruz drove away from the house.

On the highway, she said to her brother, "This is really nice of you, Cruz."

He sent her a grin. "Just remember you owe me a favor."

Maggie grinned too. "I'm sure you won't *let* me forget it." Her demeanor sobered. "Even if nothing comes of this interview, I will eventually find a job and move to Houston. When I'm finally settled, I would love it if you and Savannah came for a visit."

Cruz cleared his throat. "I think that's a safe enough bet. I know what good friends you and Savannah have become, and if you're ever really living in Houston, I'm sure she would insist that we go there to see you and Travis."

"Not 'if,' Cruz, *when*," Maggie reminded. "I really like Savannah. You're a lucky man, Cruz."

"I know I am," Cruz said quietly. He was looking straight ahead, watching the road as he drove. "Maggie, Papa asked me to take you to Red Rock so you and I could talk."

"He did? But he told me—" Cruz's words sank in "—What does he want us to talk about, Cruz?" After a second she added, "I already know, don't I? Mama and Papa want you to talk me out of taking this step." She sighed heavily. "They only pretended to agree with me, didn't they?"

"Maggie, you have to understand where they're coming from. They're worried about you and Travis living alone in a big city like Houston."

"Are you worried about it, as well?"

"Well, no. Personally, I believe you can take care of yourself."

"So this talk we're supposed to have is based strictly on Mama and Papa's worry. Cruz, Travis and I lived alone in Phoenix for a year after the divorce, and to be perfectly honest, we were alone most of the time *before* the divorce. Craig was rarely in town, and even when he was home he was running all over Phoenix. You must remember the night I called home to tell the family about Craig wanting a divorce because he'd fallen in love with someone else, because you got on the phone and threatened to come to Phoenix and beat him into the ground.

"Well, just how do you suppose I lived through all that? I wasn't a coward then, Cruz, nor am I one now. I am not afraid of starting a new life in Houston, and while I respect Mama and Papa's concern for their children, they have to realize that I haven't been a child for a very long time."

"I'm sorry I let Papa involve me in this, Maggie," Cruz said gently.

"Yes, well, it's obvious that it was their last-ditch effort to make me see the error of my ways. Tomorrow when I get home they'll greet me warmly and act as though nothing happened. I'll act the same, and everything will be fine. The last thing I could ever want is a break with my family. You're all—" Maggie's voice cracked "—very important to me."

They rode the rest of the way to Red Rock in silence, and when they arrived at the bus stop and got out of the truck, Cruz hugged Maggie.

"Good luck tomorrow, Maggie," he said with emotion. "I mean it."

She smiled, if a bit weakly. "Thank you, Cruz."

Rosita was frantic. "I've called Dallas's house a dozen times, and all I keep getting is his answering machine. Ruben, you have to go out and find him."

"It's Sunday, Rosita. He could be anywhere."

"He's somewhere on the ranch, I know it. Please take a ride and look for him."

"Did you try calling the big house?"

"Yes, and I left a message for Dallas to contact me if he should show up there." Rosita looked at the clock on the wall. "Maggie's already on the bus for Houston. Ruben, time is rushing by. Dallas should know what she's doing, and he won't know anything if we don't find him."

"Rosita, maybe we're sticking our noses into Maggie's business a little too much. And into Dallas's. He might not appreciate what we're trying to do."

"Ruben, he's in love with our Maggie," Rosita said firmly. "And she's got so many screwy ideas in her head about his being a Fortune and her not being good enough for a man like him that she doesn't realize that she's in love with him, too. Should you and I sit by and do nothing, when we know they are perfect for each other? You agreed to help with my plan, and we each must do our part. Right now your part is to go out, find Dallas, and ask him to come and talk to me. Once he's here, I'll do the rest. You won't have to say a word, I promise." She hugged and kissed her husband. "Go, sweetheart. I know you'll find him."

Ruben smiled. "You still know how to twist me around your little finger, don't you?"

"And may I never forget it," Rosita said with a teasing

laugh. She might be a few months past sixty, but she still knew how to be a woman for her man.

Dallas had spent the day outdoors, most of it on horseback checking the water level in creeks and ponds. On his way back to the ranch in late afternoon, he decided to stop by the Perez home and say "hi" to Travis. Maggie might not like him, but her son did. And Dallas liked Travis. He was a wonderful little boy, full of the devil at times and so sincerely sweet and innocent at others.

And he never failed to greet Dallas with a big grin. "Hi, Dallas!" Travis called out when Dallas and Vic rode up.

"Hi, yourself." Dallas dismounted and left Vic to fend for himself. "How're you doing, Trav?"

"I'm doing fine, Dallas. So is Baron."

"Has he gotten you into any more trouble?"

"Nope. He's the best puppy ever."

Dallas laughed and bent down to pet the squirmy little pup. "You know, he's going to grow up to be a pretty good size, Trav."

"That's okay. He'll always be my dog, no matter how big he gets."

"That he will," Dallas agreed.

"Mama's gone away, Dallas."

Dallas froze. "Your mama went away? Where did she go, son?"

Travis shrugged. "For a bus ride...I think."

Dallas's mind raced, and something cold and clammy seemed to be gripping his spine. Slowly he rose. "Is your grandma in the house?"

"Yeah, she's watching me."

Dallas glanced at the house. "Right now?"

Travis giggled. "No, I mean she's *watching* me."

"Oh, you mean she's taking care of you. Trav, I think

I'll go and talk to your grandma. You stay out here, all right?''

"Sure, Dallas.''

"I'll see you again later.''

"Okay.''

Heading for the front porch, Dallas stumbled over nothing and nearly took a fall. He caught himself in time, but as numb as he felt the near tumble didn't surprise him. Where would Maggie go? And how long was she going to be gone? My Lord, had she gone away for good and left her son with her parents? But Rosita had a job. Was she planning to quit working and assume full responsibility for the care of her grandson?

Feeling as though something had ripped a gigantic hole in his gut, Dallas rapped on the door. Rosita opened it.

"Dallas! Did Ruben find you?''

"Is Ruben looking for me?''

"Yes, for a couple of hours now. Oh, do come in.''

Dallas went in and Rosita shut the door. "You didn't see Ruben at all?''

"No. Rosita, Travis said that his mama went away. For a bus ride, he thinks. Where did she go?''

Rosita splayed her hand at the base of her own throat, conveying concern. "She went to Houston, and I wanted you to know. That's why Ruben's out looking for you. Please have a seat. Would you like something to drink?''

"Nothing, thanks. Is Maggie coming back?'' The anxiety he felt over the answer to that question showed on his face.

"This time, yes. Dallas, *please* sit down.'' Rosita sat on the sofa.

Dallas finally sat, opting for a chair. "What do you mean by 'this time'?''

"She has a job interview at a bank tomorrow morning.

f she gets the job, she and Travis will be moving to Houston.''

"I see." Dallas fell back against the chair. Why was he so damn shook up? Hadn't Maggie told him her visit to the ranch was only temporary? He should have believed her. But he could tell from Rosita's agitation that she hadn't believed Maggie, either.

He needed to get the facts straight. "Her interview is not until tomorrow but she went to Houston today?"

"Her appointment is at nine in the morning, and she didn't want to risk being late. Which—" Rosita gave a long, drawn-out sigh "—makes a certain amount of sense. As far as I'm concerned, her good sense stops there. Dallas, how do you feel about her leaving the ranch and moving to Houston?"

"I've been trying to figure that out," Dallas mumbled. Unable to sit still any longer, he got up to pace the floor. "Did she tell you I asked her to marry me?"

Rosita gasped. "No, she did not! Oh, I knew talking to you was the right thing to do. Ruben was worried about us sticking our noses into your business, but goodness, if you told her you loved her and wanted to marry her, how could he possibly have—? Wait a minute. When you proposed to her, what did she say?"

"She said no," replied Dallas, but he was thinking about what Rosita had just said about him having told Maggie he loved her. He knew he'd said no such thing, and he wondered how he could have been so stupid. He *did* love her. Why in the devil hadn't he told her that, instead of reciting all sorts of trumped-up reasons for them to get married?

You didn't say it because you didn't know it then, you damn fool!

He suddenly felt sick to his stomach and more than a

little weak in the knees. Moving back to the chair, he sank down on it.

"She must be planning to stay somewhere in Houston tonight," he said anxiously. "Do you know where she'll be?"

"I have the name and phone number of the hotel written down," Rosita said triumphantly. "It's in the kitchen. I'll go and get it."

The trip between Red Rock and Houston seemed interminable to Maggie. The bus stopped at every little burg along the way, and the chain of interruptions made Maggie so impatient that she got a tension headache. The tension reached far inside her and made her whole body feel like a clenched fist, which puzzled her. Why couldn't she just relax and enjoy the ride? So what if she wasn't on an express bus? The only thing waiting for her in Houston was a hotel room, for goodness' sake.

Staring out the window, absorbing very little of the passing countryside, her thoughts became even more troubled. When it struck her that she was beginning to doubt the wisdom of her decision to work and live in Houston, she caught herself, and immediately took up a mental argument against doubt of any kind. Her decision had not been a hasty one, she reminded herself. In truth, it had been made in Phoenix, before she'd even come to Texas.

But it was made before you met Dallas again. Before you made love with him. Before you fell in love with him.

Was this the way her life was going to be from now on, Maggie wondered grimly, with memories of Dallas constantly needling her?

No! She was not going to let memories destroy her future. She was going to make a good life for herself and Travis in Houston, and she was going to forget Dallas For tune. Forget everything about him: his good looks, his kindness to Travis, his…kisses.

Maggie's heart suddenly felt shattered.

The hotel room was nice, Maggie decided. When checking in, she had explained that she didn't require child care in the morning, as she'd thought when she had made her reservation. The clerk had been pleasant about it, and Maggie had taken her key and walked to her room.

After hanging the dress she'd brought for tomorrow in the closet, Maggie laid down to take a nap until dinner time. After she awoke, she went to the restaurant next door. She wasn't really hungry, but she figured she should eat something, so she ordered a chef's salad. She was in the restaurant about forty minutes, and when she returned to her room she checked the time: it was after eight. She decided to take a shower and get ready for bed. Even if she didn't immediately fall asleep, she thought, she could watch TV until she got sleepy.

It struck her that this was the first time she'd spent a night without Travis since the day he'd been born, and she wished that she'd brought him with her. He was her sidekick, the one and only extension of herself, and she missed him terribly. But she supposed he was better off with her mother, and tomorrow he would not have to stay with a strange sitter. Yes, it's best that he's at the ranch, she told herself while stepping into the tub for her shower.

Ten minutes later she dried off, applied lotion to her skin as she always did after a bath or shower and then pulled on a nightgown. She brushed her teeth and left the bathroom. Turning down the bed, she switched on the television set with the remote control and then clicked through various stations until she landed on one broadcasting a movie.

She stacked the pillows and lay down. After a few

minutes, she reached out to the lamp on the nightstand and turned it off. The changing images on the television screen cast eerie reflections around the room, and Maggie felt a surging loneliness.

Sighing, she forced herself to stare at the TV.

Grim-lipped and tense, Dallas drove like a bat out of hell from the ranch to Houston.

He had the address of the hotel with him, and once in the city it didn't take long to locate it. With his heart in his throat, he parked in the hotel lot and turned off the ignition. Which of those many rooms was Maggie using? And was she registered under Perez or Randall?

Well, there was only one way to find out. He would try both names. Climbing out of the car, Dallas headed for the hotel entrance. At first the front desk clerk was uncooperative. "I'm sorry, sir, but we cannot give out the room numbers of our guests. I could phone Ms. Perez and let you speak to her, however."

Dallas produced a hundred-dollar bill. "I'm a very good friend of hers, Chuck," he said, reading the young man's name tag. "She isn't expecting me, and I'd like to surprise her."

Chuck eyed the bill longingly, then gave Dallas a thorough once-over. Obviously he decided that this tall Texan wasn't dangerous, because he quickly snatched the bill from Dallas's hand and slipped it into his own jacket pocket.

"She's in room 140. That's just around the far corner of the building, ground floor."

"Thank you, Chuck."

Walking toward the room, Dallas shook his head over his own behavior. He'd never bribed anyone before but he guessed that he would do just about anything to see Maggie tonight, to surprise Maggie tonight. And a phone call from the clerk would have ruined everything. Dallas knew Maggie well enough to know that she wasn't above refusing to see him—and he couldn't take that chance.

Nope, tonight he was going to get things straightened out with Maggie. He had a lot to say to her. And he hoped that once everything was out in the open, she would have a lot to say to him.

Reaching the door to room 140, Dallas drew a deep breath and knocked.

Fifteen

The droning of the TV had made Maggie drowsy. She heard the knocking, but since there was no reason for anyone to contact her, she assumed that it was someone knocking on the door of a neighboring room.

But then it happened again, and she nearly jumped out of her skin. Someone was at her door! *Why? Who?* She sat up and nervously stared at the door. Every lock was in place; she was perfectly safe.

Or was she? She stole a quick glance at the clock. It wasn't quite ten—certainly not the middle of the night when fear might be justified.

For the third time the person knocked. Gathering her courage Maggie asked herself if she was a woman, or a mouse. Good heavens, there were people in rooms on both sides of hers. Surely if someone was intent on doing her harm, they wouldn't be knocking—they would be breaking in.

Getting off the bed she tiptoed to the door and peered through the peephole. *Dallas!* Disbelieving her own eyes, she took another look and suddenly felt a rocketing joy. He was here! Was she really asleep and merely dreaming?

When he knocked for a fourth time she knew this was no dream. "Just a minute!" she called, and after switching on some lights and turning off the television set she ran for her robe. It was as short as her nightgown, hitting her about mid-thigh. Since she'd thought she would be alone and had packed only one small suitcase, she had brought a gown and robe that wouldn't take up much space.

As hastily as she got her robe and put it on, it was enough time for Maggie to start thinking. Someone—undoubtedly her mother—must have told Dallas where to find her. Cruz driving her to Red Rock hadn't been Rosita's last-ditch effort. *This* was! Still, it didn't make sense that Dallas would drive all that way to see her tonight when she would be back at the ranch tomorrow afternoon.

Oh, my God, she thought as panic seized her. Something terrible had happened, and Dallas was delivering the news in person instead of doing so over the phone.

The elation she'd felt at first seeing him through the peephole had completely vanished by the time she finally unbolted the door. Her first words were frantically spoken: "What's wrong?"

The sight of Maggie in that short, pink, silky thing addled Dallas's brain. She was so damn beautiful...and sexy...and—and worried? He frowned. "The only thing that I know is wrong is your going off without so much as a hint of your plans," he said gruffly.

She blinked incredulously, even while feeling an enormous relief that he wasn't here to deliver bad news. "I beg your pardon. Since when do I have to report in to you?"

Ignoring her sarcastic tone and her question, Dallas pushed the door open and brushed past her to walk into the room.

"Well, do come in," she drawled. "Whatever you do, don't stand on ceremony." She shut the door.

"I didn't come here to beat around the bush about anything—least of all to stand outside for an hour while you decide whether you should or shouldn't invite me in."

Maggie sniffed disdainfully. "Now why doesn't that surprise me? Since you *always* do exactly as you please, I

should have known you would bully your way into my
room the second I saw you.''

"I'm not here to fight with you.''

"No, you're here because my mother can't seem to mind
her own business.''

"You are her business. All of her children are. I wish
my mother were still alive to stick her nose into my business. Instead of finding fault with everything Rosita does,
you should thank your lucky stars that you still have her.''

"I do not find fault with everything Mama does! But
sometimes she goes too far. She had no right to give you
the name of this hotel.'' Maggie was beginning to feel uncomfortable in her short gown and robe. Dallas's gaze kept
rising and falling as he studied her from head to toe, and
he didn't even have the courtesy to pretend that he wasn't
thrilled with what he was seeing.

"You at least could have phoned ahead so I would be
dressed,'' she said angrily.

"Let's not forget that I've seen you without a stitch,''
Dallas shot back.

"Oh, sure, remind me again what a fool I am,'' she
snapped.

Dallas heaved a weary-sounding sigh. "You're not a
fool. In fact, if there's a fool in this room, it's me. Maggie,
the day I asked you to marry me—''

"No!'' she cried, and covered her ears with her hands.
"I don't want to talk about that.''

Dallas muttered a curse, rushed forward and took her
hands in his. "You don't have to talk, but you are going
to listen.''

"No, I am not going to listen!'' With her eyes blazing,
she glared into his. "Mama put you up to this, and no one,
least of all you, is going to prevent me from going to that
interview in the morning!''

"You are the most stubborn, pigheaded woman I've ever known!"

"Thank you very much. There's just no end to your flattery," she said scornfully. "Now, would you please let go of my hands and just leave? I was almost asleep when you got here, and I would like to go back to bed."

Dallas looked at the bed, then brought his gaze back to her. The simmering heat Maggie saw in his eyes set off warning bells in her head.

"Don't even think it," she said in the most threatening voice she could muster.

"Think what, Maggie?"

The devilishly innocent look on his face jangled those warning bells again. "Don't play dumb, Dallas. You know very well what I meant."

"Did I really? Could you have meant this?" With her own hands, he pulled her forward until her breasts were against his chest. She tried to break away, but then in a fast move he released her hands and wrapped his arms around her to keep her against him. "Damn, you feel good," he whispered into the scented strands of her hair. "This is where you belong, you know."

She fought against her own responsive feelings. "Did Mama also suggest that you seduce me?"

Dallas chuckled softly. "Hardly. You know your mother better than that. No, what Rosita would like is for you and me to get married. I'm sure it's never entered her mind that we might already have made love. And not just once, Maggie—if you've got the guts to remember—but twice."

Maggie's ire rose. He didn't need to keep reminding her of what an idiot she'd been. "If I had as much physical strength as I have guts, you'd have been thrown out of this room two seconds after you got in," she said furiously. "Damn you, let go of me!"

Dallas held on tight. "Do you agree with Rosita that you and I should get married?"

"Oh, for Pete's sake! Will you get off it?"

"There's something I didn't tell you the day I proposed," Dallas said softly. "I love you, Maggie."

She stopped struggling. "Wh-what did you say?" she whispered, before taking a much-needed breath.

"I said 'I love you, Maggie.' It's not a line, either. It's how I really feel. I wish to God it hadn't taken me so long to recognize what was happening to me."

Maggie felt as though every event of her life was bombarding her, coming at her from different directions and mixing inside her brain in a cauldron of mass confusion. If she told Dallas that she loved him, too, would everything even out? Would life suddenly become carefree and wonderful? The plans she had lived with since coming to Texas would fall by the wayside, of course, no longer important or significant—

"Maggie? Can't you say something?" Dallas asked quietly.

She lifted her chin to see his face. "I—I don't know what to say," she stammered.

"I've surprised you."

"Yes."

"Even if I didn't realize it myself, didn't it ever occur to you that I might be in love with you?" he asked gently. When she didn't answer, he knew that he'd done more than surprise her. He'd shaken her to her very foundations.

"I'm sorry, Maggie." She looked so forlorn that he couldn't resist comforting her. Only, instead of a compassionate hug or caress, he found himself kissing her lips. At first he merely took little love nips, whispering soothing words as he did it, but then his feelings for Maggie overwhelmed his good intentions and he settled his mouth on hers in a kiss that made his blood sizzle.

She gave up—simply gave up, accepted her defeat and let him kiss her. But then the blood in her veins began stirring, too, her heart started fluttering and she no longer felt defeated, but rather like an eagle, soaring high above earthly concerns. She did love him so. Why hadn't she been able to tell him?

Dallas knew the exact moment when she stopped fighting herself and started feeling what he did. He gentled his kisses and was thrilled when she responded. He slid the silky robe from her shoulders, and then pressed his lips to the soft skin of her throat. Raising one of her arms, he tenderly kissed the underside of her elbow.

"You're so beautiful, Maggie," he whispered huskily. "So desirable. Your skin is like satin. I want to kiss every part of it, every part of you." For the moment he satisfied his overwhelming hunger by kissing her mouth, and while his tongue toyed with hers, he slipped the straps of her gown down her arms. The flimsy garment fell to the floor.

Her total nudity startled her, and she pushed him away and ran for the bed, where she lay down and covered herself. "Turn out that bright ceiling light," she told him. "The switch is by the door."

She had scared him for a second, but then he knew she was waiting for him, and he quickly extinguished the ceiling light and moved to undress by the bed.

The lamp on the nightstand still burned, and Maggie watched him shed his clothes. She wouldn't let herself think of afterward, or speculate about what they might talk about later. Her mind wasn't made up yet. Maybe she would never be able to tell him she loved him.

But she wasn't lonely now, and he'd actually said that he loved her. If he'd said it the day he'd proposed...? No, she wouldn't think about that, either. It was strange how often she changed her mind about Dallas, but she couldn't seem to eliminate confusion from her system. With Dallas nothing seemed cut-and-dried. They truly connected in only one area: lust for each other's body.

As though proving her theory on that point—if only to herself—she turned back a corner of the blankets in invitation. He was a beautiful man, and she wanted him in her bed. For tonight, at least. Who knew what tomorrow would bring?

Dallas slipped into bed next to her and pulled her into his arms. He suddenly felt very emotional and whispered raggedly, "Maggie...oh, Maggie."

His hot skin against hers raised her own temperature, and she closed her eyes and moaned softly.

Dallas wasn't content to make love under the covers, and he threw them back so he could watch his own hand tracing the contours of Maggie's incredible body. That day when they'd made love in Rosita's kitchen, everything had happened much too fast. Tonight he intended to go slowly, to savor each second himself, and to give Maggie every pleasure.

Maggie lifted her eyelids just a little and saw the ardent expression on Dallas's face as he slowly slid his hand down her side, from just under her arm to her waist and then to the curve of her hip. Her heart skipped a beat. That single caress was more intimate than anything else that had ever occurred between them, and it scared her. Physical intimacy was one thing, but she wasn't sure she could deal with emotional intimacy, and that was what Dallas seemed to be concentrating on tonight.

If he continued to make love to her in this way, she would be lost forever! She would become mindless, she would confess her own feelings, and then she would let him completely take over her life.

She wasn't yet ready to give another man so much power over her. She'd lived Craig's life during her marriage and had vowed never to repeat that mistake. Now, here she was, on the verge of doing the same thing with Dallas.

She couldn't let it happen. She took his hand from her thigh and brought it to her breast. Breathing unsteadily she whispered, "Do it, Dallas. Make love to me."

Her urgency startled Dallas; he'd been mesmerized by his exploration of her body. But a man didn't argue when his lady-love demanded immediate action, and he positioned himself on top of her and thrust his aching manhood into her hot and velvety depths.

"Yes...oh, yes," she whispered hoarsely when he began moving.

He looked at her face and saw what she was feeling. Except that she was feeling it with her eyes closed, and he felt shut out, as though he were merely the mechanical means by which she was gaining such pleasure.

"Open your eyes," he said gruffly. "Let me see what you're thinking. What you're feeling."

"Oh, please, let's just...enjoy."

He remembered then that *she'd* said nothing about love tonight, not a word, and that every time they had made love she had kept her eyes shut. Most of the time, anyway. Occasionally he'd caught a glimpse of her soul, but it had never lasted long enough for him to fully understand Maggie. It struck him as sad that she was still withholding a part of herself, and he wondered if even love was enough to crush such a strong barrier. Then, of course, there was the possibility that she didn't love him at all. Or maybe she only loved him enough to use him to satisfy her natural need for sex.

Joined as they were, it wasn't possible for Dallas to back off and leave her hanging, because he would also be left hanging himself. But his thoughts were no longer tender and loving, and he drove into her fast and hard—almost angrily.

In mere seconds Maggie reached the pinnacle and cried out, and a moment later so did Dallas. Then they both had their eyes closed as they waited for their hearts to slow down and their breathing to return to normal.

To Dallas's surprise, Maggie spoke first. "That was...great."

He lifted his head. "It could have been better."

Her eyes were open now, and the hard light in Dallas's unnerved her. She looked away and said, "Sorry if I didn't satisfy you. You certainly satisfied me."

"But any man could do as well, right?" Dallas rolled away from her.

She propped herself on an elbow and frowned at him. "Are you insinuating that I would sleep with any man who might come on to me?"

"You told me you didn't like me, and you still made love with me. You were mad at me that day in your mother's kitchen, and you still made love with me. Now, tonight, when I told *you* that I'm in love with you, you acted as though I hadn't even hinted at any such thing, and you *still* made love with me. What should I think about all that, Maggie? What would any man think?"

Maggie lay down again on the pillow and stared at the ceiling.

"Can't you give me an answer?" Dallas asked. He rose on an elbow to see her face. "Talk to me. Tell me what you're thinking." After several long moments of silence, he said, "You can't let anyone know you, can you? Why not, Maggie?"

"You know me," she said defensively.

"The hell I do. No one knows you. Not even your parents."

"That's absurd," she scoffed. But even while she was denying it, she knew it was true. She'd erected such a staunch barrier around her inner self during her marriage to Craig that no one—other than Travis—ever really got past it. Dallas had come very close to breaking through her defenses the day he'd proposed marriage. He just might have succeeded if he'd told her then what he had tonight.

Dallas was thinking hard. "Why didn't you let me make love to you the way I wanted to tonight? Were you afraid that I might make you feel something?"

"Oh, you made me feel a lot," she retorted. "Don't ever doubt your sex appeal, or your competence in bed."

"Why does that sound more like an insult than a compliment? Dammit, Maggie, I love you. Doesn't that mean anything to you?"

She took a deep breath. "I suppose it means you love me."

"But you really don't give a damn, do you?"

"Dallas," she said with a sigh, "I'm tired. If you want to stay the night, that's fine—I know it's a long drive back to the ranch and it's getting late. But I have to get some sleep. My interview is at nine in the morning, and I want to get up early so I have plenty of time to get ready for it." She gave him a few moments to reply, then reached out and turned off the lamp. "Good night." Turning her back to him, she closed her eyes.

About five minutes went by. Maggie felt every movement Dallas made, and he seemed restless and dissatisfied. She would never get any sleep with him thrashing around, and she wished he would either lie still, or get up and leave. Then she heard him say quietly, "Maggie, don't go to that interview. Come home with me in the morning. For God's sake, give us a chance. What if you get that job? You'll move to Houston, and we'll never see each other. Maggie, I still want to marry you. You and I and Travis could have so much together. Why can't you see it the way I do?''

I cannot become a Fortune! The truth hit Maggie so hard that she felt faint from it. She'd told Dallas in the line shack that she needed time to figure herself out, and then, later on, she'd decided she had merely said that to put Dallas off. She'd wished many times that he wasn't a Fortune, and she might even have told him so. Her memory was vague on that point, but she knew for certain that she'd talked to her mother about it several times.

Now, for some unknown reason, the truth was as clear as glass. All along, from the day Dallas had rescued Travis right up to the present, she'd been afraid that she could never measure up to the rest of the Fortunes. Yes, she loved Dallas, and after tonight she also believed that he loved her, too. But marriage? And living the Fortune life-style?

She trembled from just the thought of it; the reality of herself in that situation would be much worse. And there was something else to remember, something that would cool the hottest passion: the painting of Sara above Dallas's fireplace. He'd told her that he'd taken it down, but she would bet anything that it was still somewhere in his house.

In *Sara's* house!

So there it was—all of it, she thought. Not only couldn't she visualize herself as a Fortune, but she could never live in Sara's house.

Although tears clogged her throat and made speaking difficult, she managed a few words. ''Sorry, but there's no way I can see it the way you do.''

''And you won't marry me.''

"Good night, Dallas," she said wearily. In the next heartbeat she felt him getting off the bed. From movements and sounds in the dark room, she realized that he was feeling around for his clothes. Sitting up, she switched on the lamp. "You're leaving?"

The look he laid on her was cold as ice. "Yes, I'm leaving. Obviously there's not much point to my hanging around here."

He dressed quickly and walked out without a goodbye.

Sixteen

Maggie was stunned. Numbly she sat there and stared at the door. The silence of the room bore a deathly, almost smothering quality, and the loneliness she'd felt earlier that evening returned to taunt her. Then her numbness turned into unbearable pain, and her mind screamed, *Dallas, don't go! I love you, I love you!*

And then, *My Lord, what have I done?*

She fell across a pillow and began sobbing so hard that her shoulders shook. He'd done everything but get down on his knees and beg her to marry him, and she'd chosen loneliness over living with the only man she would ever love. She deserved to suffer. She deserved the pain that gnawed at raw nerves and caused great gulping sobs. She was a despicable, small-minded woman, and she didn't blame Dallas for walking out.

She couldn't stop thinking terrible thoughts about herself, nor could she stop crying. She felt as though her entire body was filled with tears, and that she would cry until there was nothing left of her but a dried-up sack of skin. She cried until her eyes were red and swollen, and when her nose began to run, she got off the bed and went into the bathroom for some tissues.

But blowing her nose and wiping her eyes did nothing to stop the flow, and she took a handful of tissues and went back to bed, stopping only long enough on the way to pick up her robe from the floor and put it on. Then she crawled into bed and continued to sob.

Her own brain condemned her. What kind of fool was she? The greatest guy she'd ever known wanted to marry her—or he *had* wanted to marry her. Dallas would never propose again, and why should he? How many times could a man forgive a kick in the teeth? She'd treated him shabbily, disdainfully and sometimes cruelly, again and again, and he'd kept coming back.

But this time she knew in her soul that it was over between them. Tonight Dallas had washed his hands of her, and it was her doing. She'd caused her own misery, and she knew it wasn't going to end simply because she had finally faced facts. She had sentenced herself to a lifetime of loneliness, all because she hadn't been able to see herself as a member of the Fortune family, and because of Dallas's house.

How ludicrous that seemed now. A house was merely a building, and any woman with the slightest imagination could make a home hers. Why had she been so leery of moving into the house Dallas had shared with Sara? That poor dead woman was no threat.

Every thought delivered more pain and another onslaught of tears. Maggie cried for so long that she was hoarse, and still it went on. Her next thought was maybe the worst one of all: she hadn't only deprived herself of a wonderful husband, she had deprived Travis of a wonderful father!

She was still weeping passionately when she heard a knock on the door and a voice quietly calling, "Maggie?"

Leaping off the bed, she ran to the door and yanked it open. She nearly knocked Dallas over when she threw herself at him. "You came back...you came back," she sobbed.

"Something told me I should." Dallas walked her into

the room and shut the door. "You've been crying. You're crying now." He put his arms around her, and she sobbed into his shirt.

"You...came back," was all she could say in between the heaving sobs shaking her body.

He took her chin and looked at her face. Her hair was disheveled and her eyes and nose were red and swollen. "My God, Maggie, how long have you been crying?"

"Since—since you left." Her voice was so hoarse that it didn't even sound like hers, but she had things to say, so many things, and she rushed into them. "Dallas, I love you. I've loved you for a long time, maybe from the first. I have so much to apologize for that I don't know where to begin, but if you'll listen—"

"I'll listen, honey," he said gently. "But first let's get you settled down." He led her into the bathroom, and he bathed her feverish face with cool water. "There, doesn't that feel better?"

"Yes, thank you," she whispered, though she still couldn't keep the tears at bay. "Dallas, I've been such a terrible fool."

"You're talking about the woman I love," he said with a tender kiss to her forehead. "So be kind." Then he smiled at her. "The restaurant next door is still open. Why don't I run over and get us some coffee. Or maybe you'd rather have cocoa or tea."

"Hot tea sounds good. No sweetener, no lemon, no milk. Just plain tea."

"I'll be back in two shakes." His gaze held hers. "Don't be too hard on yourself while I'm gone." He hugged her for a lovely long moment, then left.

Maggie glanced at herself in the mirror over the sink counter; she had never looked worse. It didn't matter. On her way out of the bathroom, she leaned her forehead against the frame of the door, closed her eyes and whispered, "Thank you, God."

While Dallas and Maggie were talking the night away in that hotel room in Houston, evil was at work in Maria Cassidy's trailer near the town of Leather Bucket. It was the six-month anniversary of baby Bryan's kidnapping, and Maria thought it was an appropriate date for a first contact with the Fortunes regarding the child. Her letter would, at the very least, shake them up, and she liked the idea of shaking the Fortunes so much that she couldn't stop smiling malevolently.

Newspapers and magazines were strewn over the furniture and floor of Maria's small living room. She had planned everything very carefully, down to the smallest detail. She wore surgical gloves so there would be no fingerprints on the letter and envelope, and she had purchased the necessary items to accomplish her scheme in four different stores, so her trail would be difficult to follow. Everything she was using was a common product, available in most stores. And even the smartest investigator would soon learn that there was nothing unusual in the physical qualities of the letter.

She had taken other precautions. Her heavy dark hair was wrapped in a turban; there would be no hairs on the letter for an investigator to send to the FBI laboratory. Clean, untouched paper from the package she'd purchased covered the small table at which she worked; there would be no telltale fibers to investigate.

This could not be a handwritten letter—someone, probably her mother, would recognize the writing as hers, even if she disguised it—and she had gone through the scattered newspapers and magazines and cut out words and letters to make up the message, which she was now gluing to a sheet of paper. It was shaping up nicely, and Maria was exceptionally proud of her own cleverness. Investigators would never be able to link this letter to her; she was certain of it.

There, she thought, *all done.* Sitting back, she read the assembled message:

Bryan is safe and well cared for. We will contact you again with instructions for ransom money.

She smiled gleefully over the "we" in the message. That had been a particularly clever idea, because it indicated that more than one person was holding Bryan.

Her smile faded then. The most dangerous part of her plan was delivering the letter without being seen, and it was now two a.m.—time to get to it. Cautiously sliding the sheet of paper with its glued-on, mismatched letters into a manila envelope, she secured it with the attached string. She would not lick the envelope flap to seal it, because even a residue of moisture could identify her. Or so she believed. She'd seen enough movies in which people were trapped by their own DNA—it was not going to happen to her.

Although she would have liked to shed the gloves, she would be touching the envelope again later, and she was not going to take any chances. To make sure the envelope picked up nothing from her car, she slid it into a plastic food-storage bag. It was now ready for transportation.

Turning out the lights in the trailer, she waited a few minutes in the dark, then gingerly opened the door and peered outside. It was a still night; not even a small breeze rustled the dry grasses and ill-tended bushes and trees around the trailer. Her own heartbeat was the only sound, and she saw not one light or any other sign that someone might be out and about.

Carrying the plastic bag containing the envelope, she quietly hurried to her car and laid it on the floor just behind the driver's seat. Returning to the trailer, she turned on one small light and looked at the sleeping baby. Taking him with her went against her grain, but so did leaving him alone in the middle of the night. Anything could happen. He could wake up and put up such a howl that someone might hear him and knock on her door to ask if anything was wrong. That wasn't likely to happen because her trailer was isolated from the others in this dilapidated little trailer court, but she still couldn't rule it out.

There were other dangers to consider, as well—a fire, for one. Maria winced over that thought. Her rented trailer was old as the hills, and she really didn't trust its worn-out electrical system. If she lost baby Bryan because of a fire, she would never collect a dime from the Fortunes.

But the final reason she couldn't leave him alone at night was that he was an endearing, adorable little boy, and though she had tried very hard to keep herself distanced emotionally from Bryan she hadn't quite succeeded. While caring for the baby, she had also come to *care* for him. She wished she didn't, but it was something she couldn't seem to control.

Gently lifting him from the crib, she placed him in his car seat. Tucking a blanket around him, she picked up her purse, turned off the light and quietly left the trailer. After securing the car seat, she slid behind the wheel of her car and started the engine. She drove away without headlights, and only turned them on when she was on the highway.

Breathing more freely now that she was away from the court, she went over everything she'd done tonight, making sure she hadn't overlooked something that would lead investigators to her door. Satisfied that she'd done everything right, she passed the rest of the drive in an enjoyable fantasy of the Fortunes reading her letter and going wild.

She would hear about it from her mother, of course, and she would act astonished and outraged, but in actuality she would give almost anything to be a fly on the wall when the letter was discovered.

"They're going to go crazy," she said out loud with a rather demented giggle. Oh, yes, she would love being there when her letter was passed among the family.

Approaching a grove of trees—her intended parking place—Maria's levity vanished. She pulled the car into the trees and turned off the ignition. Her heart had started pounding, and she took several deep breaths to calm herself. Glancing back at baby Bryan, she could tell he was still sound asleep. Even if he woke up and cried, the car was too far from the ranch for anyone to hear him.

Wriggling around, she reached behind her seat for the plastic bag. She had furtively studied the path she would be walking during previous visits to the ranch, and she knew where the ground was hard and where it was soft. She would stick to the hard ground and leave no footprints. The Fortunes and even their investigators would think that a ghost had delivered the letter.

Smiling again, Maria got out of the car and silently closed the door. She walked cautiously but quickly, and was fully prepared for the dogs that came bounding out of the darkness to bark at and sniff her. From her jacket pocket she produced a handful of wieners; the dogs happily began eating the unexpected treat and forgot her. She began walking again and was soon very close to the big house.

She had only one unknown to deal with: Was anyone on night guard? Lily had mentioned night guards since the robbery, and Maria hunkered down behind a bush to look everything over. If someone was walking guard duty, he wasn't anywhere near the house. She waited five minutes, ten minutes, and when twenty minutes had gone by and she still hadn't seen anyone, she decided it was safe to proceed. Surely a guard would have circled the house by now. She crept from her hiding place.

The yard lights around the big house were her biggest hurdle, but she had that figured out too. Dodging the circles of light, she stayed in the dark spots and made her way to the house. Hastily she took the envelope from the plastic bag and shoved it under the front door. It was a tight squeeze because of the door's weather-stripping, but she managed to push it through.

Then she ran, retracing her route to perfection in spite of her speed. Winded when she finally reached her car, she hurriedly climbed in, started the engine and drove away.

Elation dizzied her. She'd done it! And without a hitch.

Leaving Houston and heading for the ranch the next day, Maggie realized that she had never been happier or more lighthearted. The changes within her were astounding. For the first time in her life, she felt truly and completely linked with a man, almost a part of him. She knew now that she could talk to Dallas about any subject on earth, and her spirit soared because of that simple fact.

"Love has many facets, doesn't it?" she murmured.

"I'd say so," he agreed, taking his eyes from the road long enough to send her one of his great smiles.

"It's really a very complex emotion," she added.

"That's because it's more than one emotion, sweetheart."

"Yes, I suppose it is," she said thoughtfully. "It's liking a man and admiring him, respecting him and wanting to share your life with him. And, of course, it certainly has to include physical attraction.''

"*Lots* of physical attraction, Maggie.''

She smiled serenely. "I think we proved our mutual attraction last night, don't you?'' Between their bouts of conversation they had made love, again and again. Oh, yes, they had definitely proved the chemistry between them.

"We did that in the line shack, the first time we made love,'' Dallas said huskily, sounding as though he would like to do so again.

She couldn't help teasing him a bit. "Dallas Fortune, you're insatiable. Did you know that about yourself?''

"Not like I know it with you.''

Maggie's heart seemed to swell with love. They had already discussed the fact that sex had never before been so good for either of them. Maggie had confessed that she'd never really enjoyed sex with her husband, and Dallas had surprised her by saying, "Maggie, you know I loved Sara. I'll never try to kid you about that, but I can't kid myself, either. I want you more than I've ever wanted any woman, and that's the God's truth.''

Dallas chuckled raggedly. "You've got my wheels spinning, sweetheart. We'd better talk about something else or I'm going to start looking for a motel. How about us making some decisions about our wedding? What do you want—a big wedding with all the trimmings or something simple? It's your call, sweetheart.''

Maggie deliberated a few moments. "Well, considering all that's going on in your family—baby Bryan's kidnapping and your father's troubling divorce, in particular—maybe we should keep it simple. Also Christmas is this coming Saturday, and I haven't done one speck of shopping. Have you?''

"My mind's been on other things, I'm afraid—namely you, sweetheart."

She smiled at him. "I'm pleased to have been such a distraction."

Dallas laughed. "That you were, darlin', that you were." He drove for a minute, then suddenly pulled off the freeway, taking the next off-ramp.

"What're you doing?" Maggie asked.

"We're going Christmas shopping," he announced, and sent her a grin. "Is that okay with you?"

She clapped her hands together and laughed. "Yes!"

Late that afternoon they were once again heading for the ranch. The trunk and back seat of Dallas's car were overflowing with Christmas gifts, and both he and Maggie were happily exhausted.

"Okay," he said. "Now that we've got our shopping done, we can talk about our wedding. I believe you said you would prefer keeping it simple?"

"I think simple would be best, don't you?"

"I think you're one terrific lady, that's what I think. Yes, I agree with you. A splashy wedding right now probably wouldn't be well received. And I don't intend to put it off, Maggie, not for any reason. I want us to be married as soon as we can arrange it."

"Family only, then?"

"Absolutely. Family only."

Maggie couldn't help laughing. "Mama is going to flip out when we drive up and tell her we're getting married."

"No, I don't think she will. I think Rosita has always known this would happen."

"Well, I have to admit that she does have premonitions," Maggie said. "And a lot of them actually come to pass. So maybe she won't be surprised at all." Dallas had pulled into a side road and parked the car. "We're almost home. Why are we stopping here?" Maggie asked.

"So I can kiss you. Come here, gorgeous wench."

Laughing gaily, she slid over and into his arms. She had phoned the bank and canceled her interview, and she was going to marry this fabulous man. Life could not be sweeter than it was at this moment, and she kissed Dallas with all the love in her heart.

"Wow," he said softly when they came up for air. "You make my blood boil, Maggie. How am I going to wait to make love to you again until we're married?"

"How am I?" she whispered.

He disentangled their bodies and backed up the car to turn it around. "That's the best argument I can think of for not delaying our wedding," he said with a look of utter yearning in his eyes—as though they hadn't made love for most of last night.

Maggie felt exactly the same way. They'd gone through a lot to reach this point, but now they both knew that they loved each other too much to live in separate houses, to sleep in separate beds. "It won't be for long," she said with a quiet sigh.

"Damn right it won't," Dallas growled. They were on the road again. "Listen, tomorrow we'll drive to Leather Bucket and get the legalities out of the way. But the actual ceremony could be a problem because of Christmas. Do you have any ideas about that?"

"I suppose it should be put off until after Christmas," Maggie murmured.

"That would mean waiting at least a week."

"Even a week is short notice, Dallas. You do want your whole family there, don't you?"

"If they can make it, yes. But there are so many Fortunes, honey, that they probably wouldn't all be there if they had three months' notice. It's not something I'm going to worry about, and I don't want you worrying about it, either.''

Maggie frowned. ''Mama might worry about it. She loves you all, you know.''

''Yes, I do know. But we have to settle on and then stick to one certain date, Maggie. If we let other things get in the way, we might not be married for months.''

''You're right, darling. It's going to be our wedding, and you and I will set the date. So, what do you think? One day next week?''

''Tuesday,'' he said firmly. ''A nice simple ceremony on Tuesday.''

Maggie sighed contentedly. ''You're wonderful. Thank you.''

When Dallas and Maggie pulled into the Perez driveway, Travis ran full tilt from the house, yelling, ''Mama! Mama, you're home!''

Rosita stepped out onto the porch and watched as her daughter got out of the car and hugged her son. Then Dallas picked up Travis and hugged him. The three of them made a lovely picture, Rosita decided, a lovely *family* picture. She smiled knowingly.

After a half-hour of breathlessly explaining their plans to a beaming Rosita, Dallas asked Maggie to go to the big house with him so they could tell his father the news together.

''Yes, yes, you must do that,'' Rosita exclaimed.

Travis looked shyly at Dallas. ''Are you really gonna be my daddy?''

''Yes, son, I am.'' Dallas squatted to be on a level with the little boy. ''How do you feel about that?''

Travis squirmed a little. ''Do I get to call you Daddy?''

Dallas felt an emotional stinging in his eyes. "Yes, Trav, you get to call me Daddy."

Maggie suddenly had to bite her lip; her eyes, too, were burning with unshed tears. Even Rosita dabbed at her eyes with the hem of her apron, but it was she who cleared her throat and stopped them all from breaking down completely. "You two run along and talk to Ryan," she said.

Maggie cleared her own throat. "Do I look all right, Mama? Should I change clothes...or something?"

"You look beautiful, Maggie. And happy. Very, very happy."

"We won't be gone long, Trav," Dallas said to the boy, and after Maggie kissed her son's cheek, they left the house and got into Dallas's car again.

"Your mother didn't say a word about our hurry-up wedding date," Dallas said as he started the engine. "Let's hope Dad feels the same way about it."

The drive took only a few minutes, and Maggie admitted to some nervousness over talking to Ryan Fortune as his future daughter-in-law. But Dallas held her hand for the walk to the house, which bolstered her confidence immensely. Whatever took place inside that fabulous house, Dallas would be at her side.

What she could never have imagined when they walked in was the sound of someone weeping. Dallas sent her a frowning, questioning look. "Something's wrong," he told her, shaking Maggie's resolve to remain confident.

"It's coming from the library," Dallas said uneasily, and led her to the incredibly beautiful room.

Claudia and Matthew Fortune were seated on a blue velveteen settee, and it was Claudia who was weeping. Matthew was attempting to comfort his wife, although he, too, looked distraught. Standing at the fireplace and wearing a scowling, enraged expression was Ryan. No one else was in the room.

Dallas and Maggie stopped at the doorway. "Dad?" Dallas said. "What's going on?"

"Dallas, you're back. Good. I'll tell you what's going on. The kidnappers were here in the night, and they left a message. Slid it right under the front door, if you can believe it. The original is in the hands of the FBI, but I have a copy." Ryan walked over to a table and picked up a sheet of paper. "Here, read it for yourself."

While Dallas read, Ryan roared. "They were *here*, dammit, invading our home again! While we slept and the men hired to guard this house at night were God knows where, they were here! What bloody damn nerve! What does a man have to do these days to safeguard his family?"

Dallas handed the paper to Maggie. "Go ahead and read it," he told her. "You're part of this family now, or you soon will be. Claudia, Matthew, I can't tell you how sorry I am about Bryan, and yes, Dad, whoever delivered this message should be crucified. But I came here to tell you something, and I still have to say it."

"No, don't," Maggie whispered. "Not at a time like this, Dallas."

Dallas drew a breath. Maggie was right. They could wait to deliver their news until the family settled down.

But Ryan had figured out a few things for himself, and he did his best to calm down. "You came here to tell me something that's very important to you and Maggie, son. I insist on hearing it." He looked at Maggie's stricken face and said gently, "It's all right, Maggie. Please let Dallas speak." She bit her lip for a moment, then nodded.

Dallas cleared his throat. "Thank you, Dad. Maggie and I were planning to get married next Tuesday. Considering what just took place, maybe we should delay the ceremony.''

No one said a word for several long moments, and then Claudia said softly, ''I can't deny that we're all very upset, Dallas.'' She rose from the settee and walked over to hug him, then Maggie. ''But it would be terribly unfair of us to ruin your plans when we have no reason to hope that things will be different in the near future. I think you should go ahead with your wedding, and I even have a suggestion. Have either of you considered marrying on Christmas Day? It would be a very special wedding.''

''Yes, it would,'' Maggie said huskily, ''but—''

Claudia interrupted her. ''Please don't put off your wedding, Maggie. I'm sorry you had to witness my sorrow. You came here to bring good news and were greeted with bad news—''

''Claudia, if it were my child in trouble, I would be grieving too,'' Maggie interrupted with an emotional catch in her voice.

''That's right, you have a son,'' Ryan said. ''How old is he now?''

''Travis is five,'' Dallas said. ''And I'm going to legally adopt him, Dad. He's going to be my son and your grandson.''

Ryan tried very hard to smile, though it was obvious his heart was still broken over losing Bryan to an unscrupulous kidnapper. ''That's wonderful news, Dallas. A man can't have too many grandchildren. Maggie, what about that Christmas wedding? Do you think Rosita and Ruben would approve?''

''Yes,'' she said in a near whisper. ''I'm sure they would.''

''Then it's settled,'' Ryan declared. ''Dallas, are you going to invite anyone other than family?''

"No. Maggie and I had already decided it was going to be a family-only affair."

Claudia took Maggie's hand. "Maggie, don't hesitate to call upon me if there's anything I can do to help with the preparations."

Maggie was so close to tears for this kindly woman's heartache that she could barely speak. "Thank you, Claudia." She turned to Dallas. "I'm going to walk home. Please stay with your family. They need you very much right now."

"I'll drive you home and come back," Dallas said.

"No, please, it's only a short walk. Call me later. Ryan, Claudia, Matthew, I appreciate your kindness on what has to be a terrible day for you. Call me if there's anything I can do. Goodbye."

Dallas walked her to the front door, put his arms around her and held her close. Maggie could no longer contain her emotions. "I feel so bad for them," she whispered tremulously.

"Everyone does, Maggie."

"Maybe...maybe we *should* postpone the wedding."

"They don't want us to do that, Maggie. I would do anything to ease their pain, but the only thing that will ever heal their wounds is getting their son back. Unless you change your mind about me, Maggie, we are getting married on Christmas." His mouth tipped in a self-deprecating manner. "You didn't realize that marrying me also meant marrying into a passel of problems, did you?"

"Of course I did," she said, and raised on tiptoe to kiss his lips. "And I'll never change my mind about you. I love you now and forever. I just wish I hadn't been such an idiot for so long." Smiling sadly, she backed away and opened the door. "Call when you can. You know where to find me."

Seventeen

Ironically, the kidnapper's letter left the Fortune home the same way it had arrived—in a plastic bag. The only fingerprints found on both the envelope and letter in the FBI lab were Ryan's, because he'd risen unusually early Monday morning and, while restlessly wandering the house, had spotted the manila envelope sticking out from under the front door. Naturally he had opened it.

Early reports from the lab were not encouraging. The paper, envelope and glue were common items, available for purchase in countless stores throughout the country. There were no hairs or fibers to examine. Minute dust particles did seem to indicate that the package had been prepared in southeast Texas, but that clue was so broad that it was barely pertinent.

Ryan fired the night guards, who had literally fallen asleep on the job, and hired new men to watch the house. But his trust in hired guards had been badly damaged, and he himself began patrolling the grounds after dark at various intervals. He wasn't sleeping well anyway, so every time he woke up at night he would go outside and take a walk around the house.

Ryan was suffering some sleepless nights, and he was beginning to wonder if things would ever return to normal. His divorce proceedings seemed to be at a standstill. Parker Malone was a brilliant attorney and a fighter, and he and his staff were doing everything legally permissible to move it along. But Sophia's lawyers were every bit as tough as Parker, and they had the additional incentive of acquiring perceivable wealth. Obviously they were determined to get their share of the huge settlement Sophia had demanded.

The sordid battle sickened Ryan, and sometimes he wondered if he shouldn't just give Sophia half of everything and get her out of his life, once and for all. But whenever those moments of weakness struck, so did stubbornness. Fortunes had never been quitters, and he could not let himself be the first Fortune to be taken for a ride by an unscrupulous woman. As head of the family, he had to remain strong to the bitter end.

Regardless of seemingly unsolvable problems to contend with, life had to go on. Dallas and Maggie's upcoming wedding was a note of normalcy that Ryan welcomed. And there was something uniquely wonderful about it being a Christmas wedding. Decorations were going up, turning the ranch into a Christmas fairyland.

The sight of twinkling Christmas lights seemed to soothe Ryan's frazzled nerves. For one day, at least, he and the family could perhaps put aside the pain of the kidnapping and the divorce, and enjoy themselves. He ardently hoped so.

It was a period of roller-coaster emotions for Maggie. As happy as she was in her own life, she couldn't forget Claudia's unhappiness. Picturing herself in Claudia's situation, and Matthew's too, of course, never failed to lower Maggie's spirits, and it bothered her so much that she brought up the subject with Dallas on Tuesday, when he picked her up for the drive to Leather Bucket to take care of the "legalities," as he'd described them.

"I couldn't bear it if someone kidnapped Travis," she told Dallas.

He understood where Maggie was coming from, but he couldn't let her start their life together afraid that she had immediately put her son in danger by marrying a Fortune.

"Maggie, we can't live in fear," he said gently. "And the very worst thing we could do is make Travis afraid of every stranger that comes along. Bryan's kidnapping was a terrible thing, but we are going to have to let Travis lead a normal life. He's an active, naturally friendly little boy, and destroying those qualities by making him afraid of his own shadow would be a crime in itself. And you and I must also lead a normal life."

"Can we?"

"Yes, Maggie, we can."

"Are you as confident of that as you sound?" she asked. "At the hotel the other night I bared my soul to you, Dallas. I told you how hard I fought against letting myself love you, and I explained why it was so difficult for me to see you and me as a couple. We grew up on the same ranch, but nothing else about our lives was even remotely similar."

"Yes, we discussed all that," Dallas agreed.

"I think that what I'm getting at now is this—what is normal to you is not the same as what's normal to me. I think I—I'm afraid again, Dallas. I had a lot of fears before our engagement, and then when I thought I'd lost you forever and had to finally face my own feelings, something happened and I forgot to be afraid of anything. But now…I just don't know. Your family is so…complicated."

Dallas heaved a sigh. "And there's no way that I know of to change that, Maggie. The Fortunes have always been complex people. Their lives have been complex, *are* complex, and they wouldn't have it any other way. Except for me and a few others, Maggie. You have to know by now that I'm really a very ordinary guy. I don't give a hoot about big business or living anywhere but at the ranch.''

"You're a multimillionaire," she whispered, then cried, "Oh, Dallas, I've tried so hard not to think of your wealth—not to worry about it—but it's everywhere I look. How am I going to make the adjustment from Maggie Perez to Maggie Fortune?''

"One day at a time, sweetheart, starting with our wedding day. And I'll tell you something else, Maggie. Travis is going to grow up like any other ranch kid—just like you did, just like I did—and he's going to be safe in our care. You're an incredibly good mother, and I'm going to be the same kind of father.''

She drew in a long breath. "I have to stop worrying, don't I?"

"Yes, my love, you do. We're going to be happy, Maggie. I guarantee it.''

She smiled at him lovingly. "You're very convincing.''

"Good, because I don't hand out guarantees to just anyone," he said, and sent her a smile of utter adoration. "I love you, Maggie.''

"I love you, Dallas.''

Lily's daughter Hannah owned a boutique in San Antonio that specialized in all aspects of the perfect wedding, and Lily, with Maggie's permission, enlisted Hannah's aid in planning the Christmas wedding. With so little time to do much of anything, Maggie was impressed with Hannah's ideas.

Hannah suggested a red, white and green color scheme, then asked, "Do you have your dress yet, Maggie? The color of your dress should set the standard for flowers, napkins, etcetera.''

Maggie thought of the beautiful silk dress that her mother had bought for her. "It's the color of old ivory."

"I can work with that just fine," Hannah said confidently.

And so the wedding preparations went on, seemingly flowing around Maggie with only an occasional question about her personal preference on one thing or another. When she and Dallas had decided on a family-only wedding, she hadn't realized what a Fortune family affair consisted of. She was startled by talk of a caterer and a live band. Then there was more shopping to do: Rosita needed a new dress, and Travis needed a suit. Dallas had insisted that Travis be part of the wedding party, and the little boy would stand by his new daddy's side during the ceremony.

Maggie truly appreciated Dallas's thoughtfulness toward Travis, but the rest of it was pretty confusing. Obviously her adjustment from Maggie Perez to Maggie Fortune had already begun. At times she still worried about it—how could she not? She was accustomed to watching every penny, and now more money was being spent on her wedding than she could have earned in three years.

And it was an extremely hectic time. She hardly saw Dallas after Tuesday. He was busy, she was busy. She took her mother and son shopping, and she spent every dollar of her hoarded money for some more new clothes for herself. Dallas had mentioned their going away for a honeymoon week or so after the wedding, and her current wardrobe was so pitifully limited. With all her money gone, it occurred to her that the only thing she was bringing to her marriage was herself. And Travis, of course.

By Friday—Christmas Eve—her sisters had arrived with their families for the big doings, and the Perez home was a madhouse. It was great seeing her sisters, but their kids were everywhere, running in and out of the house, and by bedtime Maggie was so keyed up she couldn't even help decide on the sleeping arrangements. Rosita handled that with her usual efficiency, and Maggie and Travis were to sleep on the sofa that night. Frieda and her family were going to stay with Cruz and Savannah. Anita and Carmen and their husbands would use Rosita's second and third bedrooms, and all the children would use sleeping bags and sleep on the floor in the kitchen.

It was all fine with Maggie, and she made up the sofa bed for her and Travis, and snuggled down with him. Only she was still on edge, and she knew why, too. She hadn't seen Dallas even once today, and, in fact, she had barely spoken three words to him in days. Her own wedding plans were getting her down, she realized dismally, and she needed, almost desperately, a dose of Dallas's reassurance that everything was going to turn out just fine.

When the kids finally stopped giggling in the kitchen about Santa Claus, and Travis was sleeping, Maggie got up, pulled on her robe—the only garment she had with her in the living room, other than the nightgown she already had on—stuck her feet in her slippers and quietly left the house.

The night air was cold, and she walked fast to keep warm. She was glad to see a lighted window in Dallas's house, but she would have knocked on his door even without an indication that he was still awake.

It took a minute, but he finally opened it. "Maggie!" Taking her hand he pulled her inside. "You're wearing a robe! Is something wrong?"

"It's a long story," she told him. "Let me sum it up by saying that I simply needed to see you."

He put his arms around her and rocked her gently. "You're letting all the hoopla get to you, aren't you? Honey, didn't you know this would happen?"

"No, I honestly didn't. Perez family affairs are obviously very different from Fortune family affairs. Dallas, why didn't we just go somewhere and get married by ourselves? We would have avoided all of this fuss and bother."

"We couldn't do that because both of our families would have been very hurt, Maggie. Picture your mother's disappointment if we had eloped. We can deal with it, honey. By tomorrow night it will all be over. Think of it that way." Leaning back from her he gave her a sensuously wicked grin. "Now that you're here, let me show you my etchings."

"They're in your bedroom, of course," Maggie said wryly.

"Where else would a man keep his etchings?" Chuckling, Dallas brought her to his bedroom.

During the next two hours she got all the reassurance she'd needed so badly, and by the time she finally slipped back into her parents' home and into bed with her son, there wasn't the smallest sign of edginess anywhere in her system.

Yawning contentedly, she fell asleep.

Everyone crowded into Ryan's beautifully decorated library for the ceremony. When Maggie made her appearance on her father's arm, she was astonished to see so many people. Apparently most of the Fortunes had shown up for Dallas's wedding, and along with her own family, the library was a sea of expectant faces.

Then she saw Dallas, Travis and the minister waiting for her, and she smiled as her father led her over to them.

Dallas had never seen a more beautiful, more radiant bride, and he had to swallow hard to get rid of the emotional lump in his throat. He laid his hand on Travis's shoulder, and Maggie saw the gesture and became very emotional herself.

Then she was standing next to Dallas, and the minister began speaking. The ceremony took no more than ten minutes, and Maggie received her first kiss from her husband. It was, she was certain, the loveliest wedding ever.

Turning, she and Dallas faced the crowd. People began coming forward, and they were both hugged and kissed until it became funny and everyone was laughing.

Finally the party began in earnest, and gradually, as people ate and drank and came over to talk to her, Maggie was able to put names with Fortune faces: Zane, Logan, Holden, Eden—people Maggie hadn't seen in years. And they were so nice to her, welcoming her into the family. These people weren't snobs, they never had been. But she sure couldn't say that about herself. Why on earth had she believed so fervently that she wouldn't fit in?

Dallas mingled awhile, then returned to her side. He put his arms around her and kissed her. Though he smiled lovingly, his eyes probed hers. "Are we happy yet, Maggie?"

"Yes, my darling, we're very happy. Oh, Dallas, what can I say? I almost lost you, and I'll never forget that."

"We almost lost each other. I won't forget it, either." He smiled then. "Hey, where should we go for our honeymoon?"

"Surprise me, darling."

"I thought you didn't like surprises."

"Did I say that? Well, I'm a changed woman, and you're the fella who done it to me."

"I'm also the fella that would like to do it to you again right now."

They were still laughing when Rosita walked up. "What a lovely wedding this is!" she exclaimed. "Dallas, I am so glad that so many Fortunes came for the occasion."

"Yes, well, they've always liked a good party, and it is Christmas," he said with a chuckle. Spotting his father, he excused himself. "I'm going to have a few words with Dad," he told Maggie.

"Of course, darling," she murmured, then felt her mother staring at her. "What, Mama? Do I have dirt on my face?"

"Don't be silly. I have something to tell you. Do you remember when I told you of my dream about Logan Fortune?"

"Yes, I remember. Why?"

"Well, do you also recall my predicting trouble for Logan?"

Maggie nodded. "*Is* Logan in some kind of trouble?"

"He could be. I just heard that he only recently discovered that he has a child—a little girl named Amanda Sue."

"Really. And who's the mother?"

"This is sad, but apparently she died quite suddenly." Rosita became thoughtful. "I wonder what he will do about Amanda Sue."

"I would hope that he would assume responsibility and take care of her," Maggie said bluntly.

"Yes, but he is a bachelor, you know, and caring for a sixteen-month-old child would certainly change his life-style."

"Tough toenails," Maggie said. "If he knows Amanda Sue is his child, he should take her into his home and be a good daddy to her."

"Well, we'll just have to wait and see what he does." Rosita smiled rather smugly. "Just don't forget that I predicted it, Maggie."

Maggie laughed. "No, Mama, I won't forget."

Rosita strolled off, and for the first time in hours Maggie found herself alone. With a furtive glance around to make sure no one was watching, she darted behind a huge fern and heaved a relieved sigh. The Christmas wedding was wonderful, but she needed a break from kisses, hugs and gushing enthusiasm. She was not accustomed to being the center of attention, and she was rather pleased with her temporary hiding place—

Dallas peeked around the fern. "There you are!" He crowded into the small area with her. "I'm about ready to blow this joint. How about you?"

"May we? I mean, is it all right if we leave first?"

"Honey, nobody expects the bride and groom to hang around for long. They all know what we really want to be doing. Let's escape by the back door and go to my house. Travis is in good hands with your mother, and besides, every woman here adores him and the men think he's a fine little guy."

"I'm so proud of him, Dallas."

"I am, too. He stood with us during the ceremony like a little man."

"Dallas, I've been thinking about our honeymoon. I know I told you to surprise me, but...well, the idea of being away from Travis with a kidnapper on the loose is just too unnerving. Would you mind terribly if we postponed the honeymoon until the kidnapper is caught?"

"That could take a while," Dallas said slowly. But he realized that as convincing as he'd been when he'd told her that Travis would be safe, she was still concerned. And could he blame her?

"I know that, darling. But everyone is so busy. I know Mama and Savannah and others have said they would watch Travis, but you know how he wanders. He needs almost constant supervision, and I wouldn't relax for a second worrying about him."

"Sweetheart, if you feel that strongly about it, then we won't go anywhere right now."

Maggie smiled adoringly. "Thank you. You're a wonderful man."

"And you're a terrific lady. Now, this wonderful man wants your beautiful, sexy body. Are you with me?"

"Forever and always, my love, forever and always."

Holding hands and giggling like two kids, they ran through the house and out the back door.

In the library, Rosita smiled to herself. They thought they'd made a clean getaway, but she'd seen them. Oh, yes, she'd seen them go off to be alone. Positive that bringing Dallas and Maggie together was her crowning achievement, Rosita's bosom swelled with pride and self-satisfaction.

Life was good right now, she thought happily. Oh, my, yes, life was *very* good.

* * * * *

Here's a preview of next month's

*Will a roguish Fortune CEO surrender his
playboy ways and play house with his
oh-so-tempting personal assistant,
and his newfound daughter, in*

CORPORATE DADDY

by Arlene James

Emily Applegate, like everyone else in the building, heard the screams even before the elevator doors opened. She lifted her head, absently smoothed the heavy, sandy brown bun on the back of her head, and listened. The cries obviously belonged to a child—a very angry, desperate child. She couldn't imagine who would have brought a child into the office, but she would shortly know. They all would. Office doors were opening. People were stepping out into the hallway.

She stayed at her desk, gold-framed reading spectacles perched on the end of her nose, and watched the stir through the glass wall of her office, thinking that her boss, Logan Fortune, had picked a good day to be out on personal business. He'd left a cryptic message on her voice-mail some time last night, informing her of his change of plans. She'd been shuffling appointments and standing in at meetings all day, and desperately needed about two hours to catch up on her weekly report.

Thoughts of the weekly report had been supplanted by curiosity, however, when the wails had first reached her. What caught her attention now, though, were the looks on people's faces as the wailing drew nearer. They were stunned, all of them—stunned speechless, apparently. And suddenly she knew why, as Logan Fortune himself stepped into view, a squalling bundle of auburn curls and flailing arms and legs caught against his chest.

Emily stood, chin dropping, in a complete state of shock, as Logan turned, maneuvering briefcase, child and—wonder of wonders—diaper bag to push through the glass door. He stumbled into the room, yanking free the diaper bag as the door closed against it. Inside the closed room, the sound was deafening—shrill enough to split eardrums if not shatter glass. Logan looked at her as if she was the one making it, then he juggled the child in her direction.

"For pity's sake, Applegate, take her!"

Emily scrambled forward. "Mr. Fortune, what—"

He shoved the child at her, threw her almost. Emily caught the wailing bundle and clasped her tight. Suddenly she was looking down into an astonishing pair of bright blue eyes rimmed with thick, red-brown lashes and sparkling with diamond-bright tears. Emily drew back, taking in the angelic face and tousled curls. The little one shuddered on a sob, and Emily's heart turned over.

"Well, hello there," she said softly. "What's wrong, sweetheart?"

"Ba-ba-ba-ba," the little one cried, bottom lip quivering. "Ba-ba-bobble."

Emily looked at Logan Fortune. "What's wrong with her?"

Logan lifted his chin, stretching his well-muscled, six-foot frame. "She hates me, that's what's wrong with her," he grumbled, plunking the diaper bag on top of her desk.

The baby suddenly lunged for the bag, crying, "Baba-ba! Babable!"

Emily spied the top of a bottle protruding from an end section of the bag. "I think she wants a drink."

The little one shook her head wildly. "No!" She reached again, opening and closing her little hand pleadingly. "Ba-a-ba-ob-ba!"

Emily suddenly understood. For a child this age, a drink

must be something taken from a tippy cup—a bottle was nourishment. "She's hungry. She wants her bottle."

Logan looked as though he'd been dragged through a keyhole backward. His strong, aristocratically sculpted features were haggard, his full mouth turned down at the corners, his dark brown hair rumpled rather than waving back sleekly from his high forehead. He wrenched open the diaper bag and started tearing through it with broad, long-fingered hands.

"It's right there on the end," Emily pointed out.

He turned the bag on its end and plucked the pink bottle from its pocket. The baby reached for it, making a sound somewhere between a relieved laugh and an accusing sob. He jerked off the nipple cover and thrust it at her.

"You should check it first," Emily advised, as the child snatched it out of his hand. "The milk could be spoiled."

"Mother filled it before we left the ranch," Logan muttered, "and with the outside temperature in the fifties, it isn't likely to have spoiled yet. I just didn't know where Mother had put it."

The baby had already guided the nipple to her mouth and now put her head back, nursing strenuously. "Let's get your sweater off, little lady," Emily crooned, carefully slipping free one arm and then another while the child nursed industriously, passing the bottle back and forth from hand to hand.

Logan leaned a hip against the desk, folding his arms. "She's been screaming for the last half hour," he said. "I tried the pacifier, but she spit it at me."

"Wouldn't you spit out rubber if you wanted milk?" Emily teased, lifting her chin as the baby reached for her glasses with one hand while holding the bottle with the other.

Logan sighed resignedly. "I just don't know how to read

her. She's like an alien life form! How am I supposed to deal with that?''

Emily tossed the sweater onto the desk and shifted the little one in her arms, sweeping a well-practiced censorious glance over curious faces beyond the glass. People quickly shifted away, moving back into their offices. Emily looked at the man whose personal assistant she had been for the past two years. ''Want to tell me what's going on here?''

He straightened and took a deep breath. ''Emily Applegate,'' he said wearily, making it a formal introduction, ''I'd like you to meet Amanda Sue Fortune. My daughter.''

SPECIAL EDITION

Stories of love and life, these powerful
novels are tales that you can identify with—
romances with "something special" added
in!

Fall in love with the stories of authors such
as **Nora Roberts, Diana Palmer, Ginna Gray**
and many more of your special favorites—as
well as wonderful new voices!

Special Edition brings you
entertainment for the heart!

SSE-GEN

Do you want...

Dangerously handsome heroes

Evocative, everlasting love stories

Sizzling and tantalizing sensuality

Incredibly sexy miniseries like **MAN OF THE MONTH**

Red-hot romance

Enticing entertainment that can't be beat!

You'll find all of this, and much *more* each and every month in **SILHOUETTE DESIRE**. Don't miss these unforgettable love stories by some of romance's hottest authors. Silhouette Desire—where your fantasies will always come true....

INTIMATE MOMENTS®

Silhouette®

If you've got the time...
We've got the
INTIMATE MOMENTS

Passion. Suspense. Desire. Drama. Enter a world that's larger than life, where men and women overcome life's greatest odds for the ultimate prize: love. Nonstop excitement is closer than you think...in Silhouette Intimate Moments!

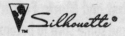

Silhouette®

Silhouette ROMANCE™

What's a single dad to do when he needs a wife by next Thursday?

Who's a confirmed bachelor to call when he finds a baby on his doorstep?

How does a plain Jane in love with her gorgeous boss get him to notice her?

From classic love stories to romantic comedies to emotional heart tuggers, **Silhouette Romance** offers six irresistible novels every month by some of your favorite authors! Such as…beloved bestsellers **Diana Palmer, Annette Broadrick, Suzanne Carey, Elizabeth August** and **Marie Ferrarella,** to name just a few—and some sure to become favorites!

Fabulous Fathers…Bundles of Joy…Miniseries… Months of blushing brides and convenient weddings… Holiday celebrations… You'll find all this and much more in **Silhouette Romance**—always emotional, always enjoyable, always about love!